MURDER

ON THE

LAKE OF FIRE

Dedicated to my BSM.

CHAPTER 1

BRITT HADN'T BEEN able to even look at her skates since the embarrassment of her last competition, and now as they dangled from her shoulders, she faced the frozen lake like it was a pervy ass-pincher about to get slapped. Knowing someone had drugged her didn't soothe the humiliation of that night and didn't make returning to the ice any easier.

"I can do this," she chanted while her shins cut through the crouching morning fog and her boots crunched a path onto the snow. As she unburdened her shoulder at the lake's bank, the blades clinked against each other like engaged sabers, shocking the silence to attention. She changed her footwear and stepped onto the frozen water, prepared for battle.

Britt plowed through the thin layer of snow atop the ice and warmed up with minor moves of little friction that evolved into grander displays of gifted athleticism. From a Y-spiral she leapt into a butterfly jump and followed it with a double Axel. When she landed, she spotted something protruding from the ice in her path. *Branch!* She shuffled her feet and averted a tumble, but the back of her blades scraped each other, which caused a slight spark.

Composure regained, Britt twisted into a purposeful spin. As she drew in her arms to increase her speed, her visible breath encircled her head like the arms of the Milky Way. She couldn't focus on the white and grey world that whirled around her, but she noticed that the sun had risen and was now warming her face. The sun, however, was still in its place, hiding behind the snow-covered pines.

Fire surrounded her petite frame and spread across the lake. Britt tried to scream, but the smoke she gasped in gagged her throat.

She continued spinning, unable to stop, as the blaze engulfed her body. In a fiery vortex, Britt plunged through the melting ice.

With the confidence of a man who loved his job, Emory Rome entered the Knoxville Consolidated Facility of the Tennessee Bureau of Investigation. Dressed in a battleship-grey suit, the twenty-three-year-old special agent glided past rows of desks in the auditorium-sized office, nodding and half-smiling at the occasional co-worker who made eye contact with him. Without stopping at his own desk, he continued to the back of the room until he stood in front of a desk that was askew from the others, just outside the door to the only private office.

The fiftyish woman tapping on her computer keyboard smiled with genuine sweetness when she saw the handsome man and greeted him with her usual, "Mornin' Emory."

Emory matched her smile. "Good morning, Fran."

"I have something for you." She handed him a large thermos. "Sassafras tea. It'll help you sleep."

"You shouldn't have gone to the trouble—"

Fran looked like she was swatting at an invisible fly as she brushed off his concern. "Lord, it's no trouble."

"Well, thank you. I appreciate it." Emory locked his brown

eyes on the closed door. "I got a message she wanted to see me first thing."

"Wayne's already in there."

He held up the thermos. "Can I leave this here until I come back out?"

"Of course."

Emory placed it on Fran's desk and took a deep breath. He rapped on the door a couple of times before entering the office and closing it behind him. Seated at her desk, Eve Bachman glanced at him without breaking from her conversation with Wayne. Like a tic that spasms once a day, her eyes darted to the red digital clock on her desk. Emory was never late, but she checked the time whenever she saw him. He didn't know why.

Bachman was the special agent in charge of this TBI division, and she left no doubt to those in her purview that she was, in fact, in charge. Humorless and direct, she had two tones to her voice – informative and invective. When she paused for breath, Emory greeted them both, removed the wool satchel strapped to his shoulder and took a seat next to his partner. "...You must be at the courthouse at 1 p.m.

"I'll do it, but it's a total waste of a work day," Wayne Buckwald grumbled. He had been partnered with Emory when the younger agent started more than a year ago, and while their working relationship clicked for the most part, they were not friends and did not socialize together. Any personal conversations they had on the job revolved around Wayne's life only, as Emory was a master of deflection.

Wayne's response evoked clenched lips from Bachman before she redirected the conversation. "Both of you take a look at these."

Wayne reached his stubby fingers across the desk for the photos she produced from a file, and he handed each to his partner after he viewed them. Emory tried to conceal a wince when he saw the first one – burned human remains on a bed of snow at the edge of a lake. The blackened parts of the skin glistened with a sickening sheen formed when the body was pulled from the lake and the clinging water froze before it could evaporate. Another picture looked to be a yearbook photo, and it revealed just how beautiful the victim had been.

Bachman explained, "These photos were taken in a little mountain town sixty miles southeast of here called Barter Ridge."

Emory perked up at the town's name. *Did she say Barter Ridge?* Aloud he asked, "ID?"

"Her name's Britt Algarotti. She was a figure skater shooting for the Olympics. According to her father, she left the house at five-thirty in the morning to practice her routine at the lake before school. The local sheriff fished her out yesterday evening. Their prevailing theory is that someone attacked her when she arrived yesterday, burned her and dumped her in the lake. No known motive."

With his dark brown hair now dipping over his eyes, Emory looked up from the photos. "Could be sexual assault."

Wayne proposed with a smirk, "Maybe someone Nancy Kerriganed her."

"What's that?" Emory asked.

"Not what. Who. Nancy Kerrigan. That skater who was clubbed in the knee by her rival so she wouldn't be able to perform." He looked at them both, but neither responded. His attempt at humor was lost on his youthful partner and stoic boss.

Examining the photos, Emory pointed to one of the lake. "It's not frozen over."

Wayne scoffed at his observation. "Of course not. The killer wouldn't have been able to dump her body in the lake if it was covered with ice."

"Why would she go to the lake if it weren't frozen over? She's not a water skier."

"She could've been killed somewhere else and taken there."

Emory turned his attention to Bachman. "Any tracks in the snow?"

"Plenty. The sheriff had half a dozen people all over the area before anyone thought to preserve the crime scene."

Wayne snorted. "As much as I'd love to help clean up their mess, couldn't someone else handle this one? We just closed the Danner case yesterday and haven't even finished our report, and now I have to prepare for a court date."

"I'm with Wayne on this." *I can't believe I just said that.*

Bachman interrupted their protests to say in her most invective tone, "Well, Emory, the sheriff asked for you by name."

Wayne joined Bachman in glaring at Emory, whose face turned bright red.

CHAPTER 2

DURING THE NINETY-MINUTE drive to Barter Ridge, Emory kept the conversation focused on Wayne – asking about everything from his daughter's school grades to the renovations on their house, but listening to none of the answers. In Bachman's office, he had said he didn't know the reason behind the sheriff's request and left it at that.

A few miles from Barter Ridge, the dispirited shades of hibernating flora gave way to landscapes brightened by fallen snow – the result, Emory figured, of the same storm front that had dropped an inch of rain on Knoxville two days earlier. To his relief, the roads had already been cleared, along with many of the driveways. With each mile added to the odometer, his grip on the steering wheel tightened, as did his breathing.

He hated Barter Ridge, and he hoped all the emotions regurgitating inside him wouldn't cloud his thinking. He needed to solve this case in a day or two and get the hell out again. After all, it was one murder in a small town. How many suspects could there be? He brushed a hand against his jacket pocket to ensure he had indeed brought his pill bottle and relaxed when he felt the bulge on his chest.

Almost as soon as Emory's white crossover passed a sign welcoming visitors to town, they arrived at the short driveway to the sheriff's station, which was nothing more than a double-wide trailer on a foundation of cinder blocks. Instead of turning into the driveway, Emory pulled the car to the side of the road. He looked at Wayne as if he were dropping him off at home.

"Aren't you getting out?" Wayne lifted his eyebrows at his partner, his hand on the door handle.

Emory shook his head once. "We'd make better time if we split up."

"What's the rush?"

"I don't like the cold. I'll interview the parents while you talk to the sheriff."

Wayne snarled at the change in plans, pulled his body from the passenger seat and slammed the door shut. He stamped toward the station but slipped on the slushy driveway.

Once out of sight of the sheriff's station, Emory pulled over to the side of the road long enough to take a pill and wash it down with a gulp from his bottled water.

A town of eight thousand people, Barter Ridge offered a secluded retreat for non-fussy tourists and the occasional black bear. The town poured from the eponymous ridge connecting two Smoky Mountains, as if it had spilled over from the valley on the other side. Its least elevated border was outlined by a tributary of the Little Tennessee River, where Crescent Lake used to be.

If there were a rich section of Barter Ridge, the Algarotti family would've had the right side of the tracks all to themselves. The only local residence that could be deemed a mansion, their twenty-one-room house was fronted by six Doric columns, and it offered an unrivaled view of the town, as well as a peek at the valley beyond the ridge.

Emory parked in front of the house, beside a red sports coupe. As he turned off the ignition, he saw a tall man exit the front door and hurry off the porch. With a brown messenger bag draped from his shoulder, the man wore black jeans and a blue, slim-fit pea coat with the hood resting between his shoulder blades.

The man – who was about the same age as Emory, give or take a year – walked around the front of the red car and dipped his head to make eye contact with the special agent. Raising his eyebrows into his thick, wavy brown hair, the stranger offered a smirk that made Emory's eyes ping-pong about before settling on him again. The man nodded and continued to the coupe, plopping himself into the driver seat.

Emory kept his eyes forward as he pulled on his parking brake. *Why hasn't he started his car yet?* He cranked his head to the right so he could peer through his passenger window at the other driver. The man seemed to sense it because he shot his eyes toward Emory and flashed a cocky smile.

Emory's eyes retreated to the windshield once more. He clenched the door handle and waited until the coupe's engine purred to life. *Finally!* Emory emerged from his car. As he walked in front of the coupe, he could feel the stranger's eyes on him, but he refused to look back.

Emory ascended the seven steps to a front porch furnished with a wrought-iron dinette set and a veranda sofa glider, behind which was parked a blue bicycle. Once he stood before the green door, he pressed the button at its side, eliciting an elaborate tolling of bells within the house. Half a minute later, a woman dressed in a maid's uniform with a grey face and no muscle or fat to keep the skin from gnarling over her bones, answered the door. Her red eyes rolled up to him as she asked in a meek voice, "Could I help you?"

"Emory Rome from the TBI. I'm here to talk to the parents of Britt Algarotti."

"Mr. Algarotti isn't home."

"And his wife?"

The maid opened the door wider. "Come inside."

Emory glanced over his shoulder to see the red car had not yet moved. *What's he waiting for?* He walked into the foyer, and the maid closed the door behind him.

"She's in the parlor," the maid informed him. She waved toward a doorway to the left of the stairs and led him there.

They had yet to reach the room when a woman's voice from inside beckoned, "Margaret, where's my protein drink?" The maid quickened her pace.

When Emory entered the parlor, he was struck by a shock of long platinum hair against the wood-toned room, bathed in amber lighting. The thirty-something, athletic and attractive – thanks to experienced makeup application – woman lounged on an antique fainting couch, reading something on her computer tablet.

Every piece of furniture looked to be antique except for a leather-padded bar in one corner. Hung at random spots along the paneled walls were a few family pictures featuring the blonde woman with whom Emory assumed to be Mr. Algarotti, Britt and her little brother. A rather macabre painting of the foursome in a hunting lodge watched over the room from above the fireplace, and it looked like a colorized version of a mid-nineteenth century photograph with serious expressions focused on the artist. A single frame hanging above a roll-top desk was covered with a black cloth. Emory assumed it to be a portrait of Britt.

"I'm sorry," the maid replied. "I had to answer the door." She hurried to the bar to mix one scoop of protein powder from a ceramic bucket, ice, a little water from a reusable glass bottle and a shot of Tennessee honey whiskey into a blender.

The blonde looked up from her tablet. "Who the hell are you?"

Emory had never been comfortable shouting, but the sound of the blender gave him no choice. "Emory Rome!" he yelled as he handed her a business card. "I'm a special agent with the TBI!"

"Do you have a badge?" she asked, as if perturbed at having to tell him how to do his job. Emory showed it to her, and she barely glanced at it before yelling at Margaret, "It's blended enough!"

Margaret turned off the blender, poured its contents into a crystal goblet and stabbed it with a pink straw.

"I'm here to talk to you about your daughter." Emory pulled out his phone to type notes of the conversation.

She sneered. "I thought you were a detective." Margaret placed her drink on a ceramic coaster atop the nearby Pembroke table before leaving the room. "Do I look old enough to be her mama?"

"You're not Mrs. Algarotti?"

She siphoned a generous amount of the protein drink through the straw. "Just call me Pristine, and for god's sake, have a seat and stop hovering over me. I feel like I'm taking a quiz."

"My apologies." Emory sat on the nearest available option – a burgundy-upholstered, giltwood settee. The illogical positioning of the ill-padded piece forced him to crane his neck to the left to face her.

"I'm the second Mrs. Algarotti." Pristine's face hardened, but her eyes belied fragility. "A ranking they never let me forget."

Emory noted the information on his phone. "Okay. Christine—"

"No!" She slammed the goblet onto the coaster so hard that Emory was surprised neither broke. "Pris-tine, as in 'pure.' I hate when people do that. It's not a difficult name."

Emory masked a snarl with a polite half-smile. "My apologies. Where is your husband?"

"He was going crazy sitting around the house, so he went in to the office."

"He's working the day after his daughter's death?"

In between sips, she told him, "He's a multitasker. He can work and grieve. He's done it before." Watching Emory type on his phone, her face twisted in anger. "Are you actually texting while I'm talking to you?"

"I'm taking notes." He nodded toward the family portrait. "And your so…stepson?"

"Now him, I wouldn't mind you calling my son. Ian's a great kid. He's probably upstairs studying, if you need to talk to him." She glanced at the wall clock. "Actually, he should be down in a few minutes."

"Your maid, is she a live-in?"

"She lives in the little servant's house out back."

"Anyone else live here or stay here recently?"

Pristine glared at him. "This isn't a shelter, detective."

"Special agent," Emory corrected, growing flustered at her attitude. "I'm simply trying to get a handle on everyone with access to the victim's home."

"You think she was murdered here?"

"I didn't say that." Emory was unwilling to share too much information about the case with a potential suspect, so he redirected. "When did you last see Britt?"

"Night before last. I passed her on the stairs as she was going to bed."

"Did you talk?"

"Just the usual. I said, 'Good night,' and she told me to fuck off."

"Do you know who would want to harm her?" Emory asked, refraining from adding, *besides you.*

"I never pried in her life. Do you have kids?"

Uncertain why she would even ask that, he told her, "We should stick to relevant matters. Was Britt dating anyone?"

"I just told you I don't pry in her life," she growled. "Will you be asking me any questions you can't get answered from someone else? My maid knew her better than I did. She could stand in for me."

Emory could feel his face redden, and although he tried

maintaining his composure, his voice rose when he told her, "I didn't know your daughter—"

"Stepdaughter."

"Stepdaughter." Emory took a breath to calm himself. "Stepdaughter. That's why I need to ask some basic questions to get a feel for what her life was like. Now how would you characterize your relationship with Britt?"

She laughed. "I'm her stepmother. How do you think she felt about me?" Drink in hand, Pristine walked to the covered frame and removed the black cloth. It wasn't a portrait of Britt after all. "This is Meredith, the first Mrs. Algarotti. They buried her two years ago. Cancer." She raised her glass to the portrait in a venomous toast.

Emory could see she was grieving too, even if it weren't over the girl who had just died. "I understand. The kids resented you."

"Not Ian. Maybe because he was younger when I met Victor. He sees me as… maybe not a mother, but at least someone who cares about him. Like an aunt maybe."

"How does Mr. Algarotti see you?"

"What a strange question." Pristine pointed the index finger of her goblet-clutching hand at him. "Oh, I see what you're asking. Victor loves me, detective. And before you ask, I love him, too. I wouldn't marry a man I didn't love, I don't care how much money he has."

Emory surmised he'd get no more useful information from her, so he asked her a final question. "Where does Mr. Algarotti work?"

Pristine rolled her eyes. "Margaret!" She stomped toward the door, arriving there just as her maid appeared. She pointed with her thumb to Emory and told her, "Answer his questions." With that, she left the room, and clopped up the stairs.

"Yes?" Margaret asked.

Emory met the maid in the doorway. "I just need to know where Mr. Algarotti works."

Past the maid, he saw a boy engulfed in a large parka descend the stairs and head toward the front door.

"At the water bottling factory," the maid answered, and she pointed her withered index finger. "It's about three miles further down the road."

Emory thanked her for her time and excused himself. Once he reached the front porch, he saw the Algarotti boy rolling his bike from behind the sofa glider. "Treacherous conditions for biking, don't you think?"

The blond boy, somewhere around the age of thirteen, turned around to display a puzzled look. "Huh? I can handle it."

Emory put his hand forward. "My name's Emory Rome. I'm with the Tennessee Bureau of Investigation."

"I'm Ian." The boy shook his hand and looked up at him with tear-glistened eyes. "Are you going to find out what happened to my sister?"

Emory gave him a smile of assurance. "I promise you I'm going to do my best. You two were close, weren't you?" Ian nodded. "Can I ask you something? Do you know anyone who maybe didn't like your sister?"

Ian shook his head and shrugged. "Everyone loved her. She did have some haters, mostly online. Trolls who would say bad things about her skating. She always said that kind of talk just made her want to succeed even more. I think she might've even kept some comments for motivation. You want me to get her laptop for you?"

"Oh no, that's okay. I'll ask your dad for permission to look at it if I need to. Thank you anyway."

Ian shrugged and rolled the bike down the steps.

Emory followed him down and noticed the red sports coupe was gone. As he approached his car, he saw a note under the windshield wiper. Emory pulled it out and saw it had a ten-digit number and the words, "You're going to need this."

CHAPTER 3

AHEAD ON HIS right Emory spotted an expansive single-story building with three silo-type structures. It abutted a mountain that continued to rise another fifteen-hundred feet above the roof of the building. Behind the building, he could make out a barbed-wire fence enclosing a natural spring that gushed from beneath two large boulders and cascaded down the mountain. He turned onto the ascending driveway and noticed the name on the monument sign – Algarotti Smoky Mountain Springs.

Emory parked his car and plodded up the straight pathway to the front door. He entered the lobby, which had a few seats, plants and a standalone display with brochures about the company and each type of water it distributed – spring, flavored, carbonated and distilled. There was no receptionist desk or anyone to greet visitors, so he assumed the factory didn't get many.

Emory followed a directional sign for the administrative offices to a long corridor. Just past a bathroom for each sex, he came to a windowless room. Adjacent to the room's lone desk sat a table featuring neatly aligned rows of Algarotti Smoky Mountain Springs bottled water, a glass-door refrigerator chilling bottles of flavored water and a sign inviting visitors to take one. The desk was positioned to the right of the entrance to a smaller hallway that ended at a door. Seated at the desk was someone familiar.

"Hello," Emory said to the man he had seen leaving the Algarotti house earlier.

The man closed the desk drawer he was rifling through and lifted a stolid face that softened when he saw Emory. "Hi again," he replied with a flawless smile framed by mischievous lips. His pea coat was now unbuttoned, exposing a tight blue sweater molded over square pecs. He leaned back in the chair, interlocked his fingers over his chest and peered at Emory with eyes as sparkling green as the Southern Lights. "Are you following me?"

The stranger's question and his assuredness knocked Emory's demeanor off balance. "No," he answered with more volume than intended. "No, I'm here to see Victor Algarotti."

"So am I." The man erected himself without using his hands and walked to the front of the desk to stand before Emory. Both six-foot-two, their eyes locked – an alignment that rattled Emory. "Jeff Woodard," the man said as he extended his hand.

Emory shook his hand and told him his name. "What do you mean, you want to see him too? Is Victor not here?"

Before Jeff could explain, another man exited the nearby bathroom and approached them. A work badge hanging from his right collar informed them that his name was Scot Trousdale. In his late twenties or early thirties, Scot stood about five inches shorter than the other two men, but the wide back and thick shoulders pushing against the seams of his dress shirt gave him an imposing presence nonetheless. The curls of his dark brown hair twisted around cauliflower ears and an attractive face misshaped by more than a couple of punches. *A fighter. Wrestling or MMA.* Scot's dull eyes looked at them from behind rimless glasses that slid down the wide bridge of his nose. "Gentlemen. Which one of you is Mr. Woodard?" he asked in a voice lighter than his looks would suggest.

"That would be me," responded Jeff with a slight wave.

Scot pulled some papers from the printer at his desk, stapled them and handed them to Jeff. "To save time, Mr. Algarotti dictated all the information you'll need to start your investigation. Oh wait." He retrieved a picture of Britt from his top drawer and gave it to Jeff. "Here's a picture."

"Excuse me." Emory glared at Jeff. "Who are you?"

Jeff smirked at him. "We met earlier."

"I know we met earlier. Why are you receiving information about my victim?"

Jeff flashed his right palm. "Let's not get possessive. I'm a private investigator—"

Scot looked over his glasses at Emory. "And who are you?"

"I'm Emory Rome from the TBI."

Jeff taunted him by asking, "Do you have a badge?"

"Of course I do." Emory retrieved his badge and showed it to both of them, eliciting a smile from Jeff.

Scot stared at Emory for a moment. "Have we met before?"

Emory answered, "I don't believe so," although he questioned if they had run into each other when he lived in Barter Ridge as a kid.

Scot seemed to register a sudden glimmer of realization, but if he did, he kept it to himself. "Hang on one second." He went to his computer to print another copy of the document he had given Jeff. "Mr. Algarotti had me compile all the information you might need." He stapled the papers and handed them to Emory. "Mr. Algarotti asked that no time be wasted before getting started."

Emory glanced at the top page. "How thorough."

"I don't have another picture, though," Scot told him. "Maybe you two could share it."

Jeff snapped a picture of the photo with his phone. "I'll text it to you. What's your number?" After a silent second, he added, "It's only fair. You already have mine."

So it was his number. Emory shook his head. "I have my own picture." He turned back to Scot to ask, "Where's Victor's office?"

"As I said, he asked that you – I guess both of you now – not waste time."

"I need to talk to him," insisted Emory.

"That won't be necessary," Scot countered. "Everything he would tell you is in the document I just gave you."

Emory's stern face matched the tone of his voice when he said, "It wasn't a request."

Without turning his head, Scot pointed his ink pen over his shoulder to the hallway behind him. "End of the hall."

Emory walked past the desk, his footsteps echoed by Jeff's. "Where are you going?" he asked the PI.

"I want to talk to him too."

"I need to talk to him alone. This is a murder investigation." Emory continued walking until Jeff grabbed his arm.

"This isn't my first murder case."

Emory had a growing disdain for private investigators. In his experiences with them since becoming a special agent, they often muddied the waters so he couldn't see the bottom-dwelling truth until the effects of their interference dissipated. With very rare exceptions, however, he had always maintained his composure in his dealings with them – or anyone else for that matter – regardless of how much he didn't like who he was talking to or how combative they were. Right now, though – probably because of Jeff Woodard's earlier taunts or his ever-oozing cockiness – Emory had a great desire to belt him in the mouth. He refrained. "Really? What others have you worked on? Who were the victims?"

Jeff counted on his fingers. "Lara Crawford, Zelda Princeton, Jill Valentino—"

"Why do all of your victims sound like video game characters? Look, I have no unsolved mysteries under my belt. I'm not going to let an amateur muddle up one of my investigations."

"Muddle? Who says that outside a Christmas song? I got

news for you. It's our investigation, and I'm not going to muddle up anything."

"What were you doing at his desk when I arrived?"

"It's called investigating." Jeff pointed toward Scot's desk. "Dilbert there could be our killer."

Emory continued to Victor's closed office, telling Jeff, "Don't follow me."

An oversized cherry desk served as the focal point of Victor Algarotti's office, which was drowning in a dreary atmosphere of brown and black tones – wood furniture, black vinyl upholstery and walls the color of desiccated hemlock. Behind the desk, a large window offered a view of Barter Ridge, and to the right of it was a closet door.

Standing beside his desk with his back toward the door, Victor Algarotti hung up his office phone. Once he turned around, his teary eyes did not seem at all pleased to see Emory standing in his doorway. "My assistant tells me that the information we've provided you is somehow insufficient."

As Emory shut the door, he noticed a second and much smaller desk in an adjacent corner. He held up the document Scot had given him. "Black ink on white paper. No color."

Towering and immaculate, Victor rounded his desk to sit at his chair. "I don't know how much color I can provide."

Emory sat at one of the two chairs facing the front of the desk, and as he did, he caught the lavender scent of Victor's wake. *Expensive cologne.* "I realize this is difficult for you, and I'm so sorry for your loss…"

Victor's eyes darted from Emory to the door.

"Sorry I'm late," Jeff said as he entered the room. He took a seat next to Emory and smiled at him. "I was on the phone tying up some loose ends in a murder case I closed last week. I won't bore you with the amazing details."

"Are you the PI?" Victor asked.

"At your service, and thank you for the opportunity. You'll be glad you called me."

Emory whipped his eyes back to Victor. "Mr. Algarotti, could I ask why you hired a private investigator?"

"I'm not about to let my daughter's killer get away because a backwoods sheriff lacks the skills to catch him. I'm surprised he had the good sense to call the TBI for help."

Emory was annoyed by his answer, but he didn't vocalize it. "Now that the TBI *is* here—"

Jeff interrupted with, "Hey, I'm right here. Stop trying to get me fired! The TBI doesn't have a lock on deductive reasoning in this state. I'll solve this case before you—"

Emory scoffed at the notion. "I'd like to see that."

"That's not a bad idea," said Victor.

Emory and Jeff asked in unison, "What?"

"Competition delivers results. I'll give one hundred thousand dollars to whoever brings my daughter's killer to justice – death or jail."

Emory shook his head. "I'm a government agent. I can't accept a reward."

"Fine, but you obviously don't care for this guy." Victor pointed to Jeff. "Find who did this, and keep him from getting the reward."

Jeff placed his business card onto Victor's desk. "The name of my agency so you can write it correctly on the reward check."

Emory told Victor, "I can't have this *PI* interfering with my investigation—"

Jeff smirked at Emory. "Well, you'll have to muddle through somehow."

"Gentlemen!" Victor boomed, punctuated with a fist on his desk. "In five minutes I'm going to start planning my daughter's... funeral." His voice cracked on the last word as his eyes began to tear up. "You have until then to ask me questions."

Emory spoke first. "My apologies. When did you last see your daughter?"

Victor pointed at the papers in Emory's lap. "That's in the information you were given."

"I'd like to hear it from you, in your own words."

"Yesterday morning. Before she left for the lake."

"When did you notice she was missing?" asked Emory.

"Dinner. She kept to a strict schedule when she was in training. Up early every morning to practice – at the rink during the warm months, but she always preferred to be outdoors whenever she could. She didn't take up any extracurricular activities at school so she could be home right after, have dinner by 6 p.m. and be in bed by nine. She had taken some time off after her last competition, and yesterday was to be her first day back in training. When she didn't come downstairs to dinner, I realized that she hadn't even come home. Then I called her best friend, Tati, and she said she hadn't seen her and had been texting her without any response. I drove past the lake and found her car in the driveway, but she wasn't there. That's when I called the sheriff. As I waited for him, I walked around the lake…" Victor turned away from them and wiped his eyes. "I saw the end of her scarf sticking to a sheet of ice floating on the water." Tears fell from his cheeks to the lapels of his raven-colored suit. "As I got closer, I saw the rest of the scarf in the water, around her neck. I couldn't even tell for certain that it was her neck. She was…burned. Who would do that to someone?"

Emory spoke through a lump in his throat. "I promise you we will find whoever did this."

In a gentle tone, Jeff said, "We will."

Emory frowned at the PI. "I meant *we*, the TBI."

Jeff ignored him. "Victor, did she practice alone?"

Victor wiped his eyes. "Since I fired her coach."

Emory was about to ask the reason the coach was fired, but Jeff spoke first. "Which lake is this?"

"We call it Cicada Lake, but it's more of a pond really. It's on a few acres we own a couple of miles from the house, down Black Bear Lane."

Jeff asked, "Can anyone access it?"

Victor nodded. "An old stone wall lines the property, just two feet high in most places."

"Did Britt have a boyfriend?" asked Emory.

"School and skating expended her time."

"Does your daughter have any enemies?" Jeff asked.

"Who has enemies at seventeen, for Christ's sake! She's a beautiful girl." Victor looked at his watch. "Your time is up, gentlemen."

In silence, the two investigators left Victor's office. Once in the hallway, Jeff told Emory, "I have a proposition for you."

"What do you want?" Emory asked, being more polite than curious.

"Don't worry. I'm not going to interfere with your investigation. Okay?"

"Okay."

"But it's a two-way street. You don't interfere with my investigation either."

Emory hesitated before answering. "Fine. Why do I feel a contingency's on the way?"

"Listen, I really need this money, and since you can't collect it, I want to offer you a mutually beneficial deal." When Emory said nothing, Jeff explained, "If I solve it first, I'll let you take credit."

Emory crossed his arms. "What do you get out of that?"

"I'll let you take credit officially – in whatever paperwork you have to file. That way, no matter what, you'll look good to your superiors. What I want in return is for Victor to be told the truth so that I can collect the reward."

Emory tried not to show his amusement at the notion. "And if I solve it before you?"

"Same thing. You take official credit, but Victor is told that I'm the one who cracked the case. Agreed?" Jeff put out his hand and turned on his killer smile.

Emory knew there was no chance in hell of a PI solving the case first, so he saw no harm in a truce since it would ensure the PI stayed out of his way. He nodded, half-smiling in return. "Agreed." He shook his hand to seal the deal.

The two started walking again, but Jeff's pace quickened so he could be the first out the front door. Emory hastened his stride to match, but when he reached Scot's desk, the assistant called out to him. "Agent Emory, could I speak to you?"

Perturbed at having to stop, Emory told him, "Rome."

"What?"

"Never mind. What is it?"

"I wanted to tell you something before you leave – something I couldn't put in the document. It might be helpful in your investigation."

"What is it?" Emory asked, but his tone was saying, "Spit it out!"

"Britt was never going to make it to the Olympics."

"Why do you say that?"

Scot crinkled his nose. "I've seen her skate."

CHAPTER 4

EMORY DROVE DOWN Black Bear Lane, along the stone wall that bordered the property around Cicada Lake. The metal pole fence that kept people from driving down the property's narrow, gravel road remained unlocked and open. As he turned off the main road, he saw Wayne standing with the sheriff near the lake, their breath rising in the cold air as they spoke. Emory parked behind the sheriff's truck and stepped out just as Jeff drove up behind him.

While he waited for Jeff, he pulled the strap of his satchel over his shoulder and retrieved gloves from his jacket pocket to cover his numbing fingers. "What are you doing here?"

"Same as you. Investigating the case. How'd you beat me here anyway? My map app lost the signal."

"My partner's going to have a fit when he sees you. He's not as understanding as I am."

Jeff chuckled. "Is that what you've been? I had another word for it all together. Look, I give you my word, I will not in any way hinder your investigation." He held up his right hand. "I swear it. Just please let me do mine too. I really need this job."

With Wayne following, the sheriff hurried up the gentle slope toward the parked cars. "Emory!" A fit fifty, he gave Emory a powerful hug. "It's so good to see you, Son."

Wayne stopped a few feet away. "The sheriff is your father?"

"Lula Mae's going to be over the moon when she sees you." The sheriff released his hold but kept his grin.

"It's great to see you too." Blushing, Emory changed the subject. "Can you point out exactly where the body was found?"

Dressed in black galoshes, a green utility uniform with a seven-pointed-star badge and a campaign hat, Sheriff Rome started back toward the lake. "I'll show you."

"Whoa." Wayne threw his palm to Jeff's chest. "Are you a deputy?"

"He's not one of mine. I thought he was one of yours."

Wayne growled, "Get out of here! This is a restricted area."

Jeff grimaced at him. "Restricted to who?"

"To authorized personnel. It's a crime scene."

Jeff pushed his hand away. "I am authorized. I'm a private investigator hired by the victim's father to find her killer."

"Wayne!" Emory yelled. He glanced at Jeff and tried not to notice how the sunlight reflecting from the snow made his green eyes shine even brighter. "Jeff, you can watch as we investigate."

"Why the hell are you defending him?" Wayne asked. "You don't like dicks any more than I do."

Trying to ignore Jeff's laughter, Emory could feel his face flush again. "I'm not defending him, but we all want the same thing. Rather than fighting and blocking each other, let's expend our energy on working together to bring Britt's killer to justice as quickly as possible."

"Okay then," Sheriff Rome said. "Let's go."

They walked in pairs from the gravel road toward the lake. As his galoshes squeaked through the slushy path trampled in the snow, the sheriff asked about his son's well-being. Meanwhile, Wayne barked a list of "don'ts" at the PI, in essence telling him to stay quiet and not touch anything, and he ended with a question. "Understand?"

Reaching the water's edge, Jeff turned a blank face to him. "I'm sorry. I wasn't listening."

Wayne gritted his teeth. "Asshole."

Emory snapped photos of the ground, counting at least six different sets of shoeprints in the two inches of snow. Although none seemed distinctive enough for identification at this point, he could distinguish prints from four pairs of larger shoes, likely male, and two smaller sets of prints. He told himself one of the small pairs must have been the victim's, and he had a hunch about who was responsible for the other. "Is Sharon Marcel still on your team?"

"She's my lead deputy now," the sheriff answered. "She's married and has a kid."

Hands on his hips, Jeff scanned the scenery. "What a beautiful spot for a murder." The others looked at him as if he had just sworn in church. "If you're given a choice about where you're going to die, wouldn't you choose somewhere like this?"

Sheriff Rome nodded. "There's always something special about the first snowfall of the season. Just seems to come later and later each year. Cuts into tourist season. Sure grateful for it, though."

Emory examined the condition of the lake. Two thirds of it was covered with a thick layer of ice, but on the third of the lake nearest them, broken sheets of ice floated on the water's surface.

Sheriff Rome pointed to an uncovered section of the lake about twelve feet away. "We pulled her out from right about there. I got here after her dad spotted her." The sheriff shook his head and looked as his boots. "God a'mighty, not a sight anyone should see, much less when it's someone you love. Victor was just bawling." He again faced the water. "I had to call one of my deputies to bring a raft so we could get her. I asked Victor to go home so he wouldn't have to see, but he refused. She was so badly burned, I think he was looking for something recognizable to make sure it really was her."

"Did you take pictures before moving the body?" Wayne asked.

The sheriff jerked his head back. "Heavens no! That's corpse desecration."

Wayne's mouth opened seconds before he spoke. "That's documenting—"

Sheriff Rome pointed at the ground. "We follow the letter of the law in this town."

Emory could tell Wayne wanted to argue about the sheriff's misconception of the law, so he grabbed his partner's arm and signaled him with a slight shake of the head. Wayne sighed and walked away.

Emory asked his father, "What did you do with the body?"

"The deputies took her up to the road and loaded her into the ambulance when it came."

"I had the body transferred to Knoxville for an autopsy," Wayne told Emory, who nodded his approval.

The sheriff continued, "I tell you, if it wasn't for that scarf sticking to the ice, we might not have found her – not right away. I don't think what was left of her would've floated."

Wayne scratched his scalp inside the U-shaped row of hair lingering just above his ears. "Someone must've had a boat of some kind to dump her that far in."

"Why go to all that trouble?" asked Emory. "If someone wanted to dump her in the deep part, why not walk on the frozen section over there and throw her in?"

Jeff nodded. "A better question – why isn't the lake frozen all the way across?"

Emory gave him an approving glance before turning his attention to the pieces of ice floating nearby. Some were still covered with snow, and under the snow on one piece, he spotted a thin black layer. "What is that?" Squatting, he stretched out the full length of his arm to retrieve the ice. With a gloved hand, he skimmed away the snow above the black layer. "There's some kind of powdery substance on the ice. It looks like it was here before that snowfall you mentioned, Dad."

Jeff knelt beside him and pointed at the ice. "May I?"

Emory shook his head. "It could be evidence."

"Fine. Then can you pick some up so I can get a closer look?"

Emory frowned and hesitated before pinching some of the powder, holding it up to for both of them to inspect.

"What is it?" asked Jeff.

Wayne laughed at the question. "It's called dirt, Einstein."

Detecting a faint odor, Jeff brought his nose closer to Emory's fingers. "It smells like...garlic."

Emory sniffed it too. "You're right." Removing his right glove, he scooped up some snow and held it above the ice so the snow melted onto the powder. The mystery substance started to dissolve. "Dad, do you have a light?"

Sheriff Rome pulled a tiny cardboard box from his pocket. "Will matches work?"

Emory tossed the remaining snow and reached for the box. "Sure."

Wayne crossed his arms. "You do realize you don't cook mud pies?"

Emory ignored the remark, as he often did with words from Wayne. He stood, as did Jeff, before he lit a match and threw it at the wet powder. The air popped into flames before the match even hit the ice. Wayne and Sheriff Rome both jumped back. As the fire melted more ice, the flames spread to the rest of the powder on the sheet.

Jeff sneered at Wayne. "Some dirt."

Emory nodded at the flaming ice. "There's our murder weapon. It's calcium carbide."

Wayne furrowed his brow at his partner. "How in the hell would you know that?"

Sheriff Rome answered for him. "Emory was supposed to be a doctor."

"Actually, I always wanted to be in law enforcement, but I went against my better instincts. Double-majored in biology and chemistry."

"Now your mama and me never made you do that."

"I know you didn't, Dad." Emory forced a smile for his father's benefit.

"What else don't I know about you, partner?"

Emory nodded toward the lake. "Can we get back to the case?"

Jeff crouched beside the dwindling flame. "Britt Algarotti wasn't dumped here."

The sheriff took off his hat and waved from one side to the other. "Someone threw this stuff on the ice as she skated?"

Emory shook his head. "It was under the snow, and she came here the morning after the snow fell. Calcium carbide can lie inert on ice. It reacts with water to form acetylene gas. Highly flammable."

"I see where you're going," Jeff said. "I remember this from physics class. Ice skaters skate on water, not ice."

Emory looked at Jeff as if he had read his mind. "The skater's weight on the blade pinpoints so much pressure on the ice—"

Jeff finished his sentence. "That it turns the ice beneath the blade into a thin layer of water."

"Exactly. The water dissolved the calcium carbide, releasing the acetylene gas."

Wayne shook his head. "You'd still need a match or something to ignite it, so the killer must've been here when it happened."

Emory held up an index finger. "Unless he knew Britt herself would ignite it."

"Why would she do that?" asked Sheriff Rome.

Emory responded, "One little spark from the blades scraping each other—"

Jeff finished his thought, "Fire."

Wayne frowned at them both. "Have you two rehearsed this?"

Emory told his partner, "We should bag some of the powder for evidence."

Wayne produced a baggie from his pocket and walked between Emory and Jeff, grazing their shoulders. "I'll get it." He pulled another sheet of floating ice to the bank and scraped some of the powder from it.

Emory noticed his father's wide grin. "What?"

"I made the right call," Sheriff Rome answered. "I don't think there's any way in the world I would've seen that on the ice."

Wayne sealed the baggie of calcium carbide and told them all, "We hold this information close to the vest."

The sheriff asked, "What do you mean?"

Emory explained, "We try to keep some information that only the killer would know from public knowledge. It could be a key to a conviction."

Wayne glared at Jeff. "You understand that, amateur? Not a word about this to anyone."

"I heard you the first time," responded Jeff. "No need to reiterate."

Wayne told Emory, "That's why we shouldn't have people outside law enforcement at a crime scene."

"I can keep a secret." Jeff turned his attention to the encroaching mist sifting through the distant trees. "It's getting late, and I have a last stop to make before heading back to Knoxville."

"Your office is in Knoxville?" asked Emory.

"You didn't think I lived here, did you? Nice to meet you, sir." Jeff shook hands with the sheriff and smiled once more at Emory before leaving.

"We should probably be heading back too," Emory told Wayne.

"Agreed." His partner started toward Emory's car.

The sheriff frowned at his son. "So soon? Why don't you have dinner with us and spend the night?"

"I can't. I'm Wayne's ride, and I don't trust him enough to drive my car."

Still in hearing range, Wayne yelled back, "Hey, I'm a great driver, granny!"

"I drive the speed limit!" Emory responded.

Sheriff Rome asked, "You'll be back tomorrow?" When Emory nodded, he said, "Well, make him drive his own car so you can stay."

"Okay, maybe—"

Sheriff Rome placed his hands on Emory's shoulders. "Son, I know how you feel about this town, but don't take it out on us. We miss you."

"I'm not. Seriously. It's just finding the time." Emory grabbed the strap of his wool satchel like it was a rip cord he couldn't wait to pull. "Hey, how about after this is over, y'all come to Knoxville and spend the weekend?"

Sheriff Rome released him and clicked his tongue in the corner of his mouth. "Well, you know Lula Mae doesn't like to travel."

CHAPTER 5

As EMORY DROVE back to Knoxville, Wayne called the medical examiner's office from the passenger seat. Once he hung up, he informed his partner, "She'll have a report on Britt Algarotti for us at ten o'clock tomorrow."

As trees blurred past his periphery, Emory grimaced at the news. "Crap. That means we'll be late getting back here."

"So? Why are you so anxious to finish with this case? I don't think you're going to have any news cameras waiting for you at the end of this one."

Wayne's dig referenced a big drug bust the two oversaw four months earlier – the largest ever in the southeast. At the time, he was very vocal with his opinion that the press coverage focused too much on his younger partner, although an instigative special agent had pointed out that Wayne's arm was visible in the doorway behind Emory in a now-famous newspaper photo.

"I'm not anxious. No more than with any other case. I just want to solve it and move on to the next." Emory didn't give his partner time to retort before changing the subject. "So what did you find out today?"

Wayne thumbed through a small notepad with tattered edges to debrief Emory. "The sheriff...Your dad must be the town historian. He can tell you the story on anyone, and he knows all these details. He filled me in on all the scoop about the Algarottis. The father, Victor Algarotti, might seem to be rich, but he's not."

Emory tilted up his right ear. "What do you mean?"

"His first wife, Meredith, was the one with family money. Victor dropped out of college to serve in the Navy, and then he came back to Barter Ridge. He was working as a projectionist at the town's theatre when he knocked up Meredith. I wonder if he did her up in the booth while a movie was playing." Wayne made an obscene gesture with his hands and laughed alone. "Anyway, they got married, and her dad gave him a job at the water bottling factory. Victor started at the very bottom, emptying trash cans, filing paperwork – stuff like that – and he had to work his way up. By the time Meredith's dad died nine years ago, Victor was the vice president, and he took over running the company. It used to be called Barter Ridge Water—"

Emory slapped the steering wheel. "I remember that! And there was a big fuss when the name changed."

"Well, even though he renamed it after himself, the company was actually inherited by Meredith alone."

"So she owned it, but Victor ran it," Emory restated, and Wayne nodded. "Didn't Victor inherit it when she died?"

"You would think, but Meredith's dad insisted on Victor signing a pre-nup before he would allow them to marry. Then Meredith left nearly everything to the kids, cutting her own husband out of the company and the house – giving him some token money."

"Why would she do that?"

"The sheriff didn't know for sure, but he said there were rumors Victor had been unfaithful, especially since he married his current wife a year later."

"So let me guess. The inheritance was entrusted to Victor until the kids turned eighteen."

"Eighteen," Wayne said at the same time as Emory. "Britt would've turned eighteen in three months, at which time, she would've taken possession of half the estate. Her father would continue to be entrusted with her brother's half until he turned eighteen."

"Now that she's gone?"

"Victor is in control of everything until the son turns eighteen. Now if the son..." Wayne rifled through his notes. "What's the name?"

"Ian."

"If Ian happens to die before his eighteenth birthday, Victor keeps everything."

"Not just Victor," Emory pointed out. "His current wife would share in that fortune – a wife Britt apparently hated."

"Do you think Victor could've killed his own daughter?"

"Parents have killed their children for lesser motives, but then why hire a private investigator?"

Wayne huffed. "Yeah. He hired him, but to do what?"

"What do you mean?"

"Was it really to solve the case or for misdirection – maybe to throw suspicion on someone else?"

Emory didn't say it, but Wayne had brought up a good point. Maybe the handsome PI had more to gain than the reward.

"So what was all that with your dad saying that taking pictures of a murder victim is corpse desecration?"

Emory sighed before delving into the explanation. "You have to understand that my dad hasn't had any formal legal training. He was first elected sheriff when he was twenty-nine, and before that, he was a ranger at Smoky Mountains National Park. That's how he and my mom met. Over the years, he's established a lot of procedures based on his kind of home-spun understanding of the law. He doesn't back down from his beliefs, so it's best not to argue with him."

"Okay then," Wayne said with a whatever smile. "Apart from that, I have to say I really like the guy. He's quite the character and a hero to boot. I saw the Tennessee Medal of Honor hanging in his office. A deputy told me it was the only one ever given for heroism while not on active military duty. Of course, I guess you already know that."

"I remember it."

"What was it for? The deputy didn't know, and the sheriff wouldn't talk about it."

Emory didn't like to talk about it either. "It's a long story."

Wayne frowned at him. "I guess it runs in the family. By the way, I thought you were from Nashville."

Emory kept his eyes on the road. "I went to college there."

"Why didn't you tell me you grew up in Barter Ridge?"

Emory glanced away from the road to face him. "You never asked where I was from."

After dropping off Wayne at the office, Emory returned to his apartment, warmed a cup of sassafras tea in the microwave and sat on the couch for a quick self-debrief. He transferred the day's notes and pictures into a file on his work laptop and bulleted some tasks for the following day. When he was satisfied with his documentation, he typed "Britt Algarotti" into a search engine, and several links to videos of ice-skating competitions popped up.

With the last words of Scot Trousdale, Victor Algarotti's assistant, repeating in his head, he clicked on one posted two months earlier to see how she skated. About one minute into the routine, Emory mumbled, "She's really good." The video ended with the audience united in applause. "I don't get it. What was he talking about?"

He clicked on a video from a competition in Nashville three weeks ago, titled, "Britt Algarotti, Ass Skater." This video was much different than the previous one. Britt seemed distracted and, true to the title, she spent more time on her ass than her ice skates. After forty seconds, she gave up and skidded off the ice, where her coach offered her a consoling hug.

Emory cupped his mouth with his hand. "What happened?"

CHAPTER 6

FIVE THICK CANDLES gripped in an iron chandelier above the claw-foot bathtub illuminated the bathroom. Blue wax traced paths onto the candles' sides and dripped into the full tub below. As the wax hardened at the water's touch, it blanketed the surface with a thin skin, broken only by the exposed head and knees of the body lying inside.

Thick, dark brown hair wicked water into droplets that trickled over the closed eyes and smooth, pale skin. The water formed a brief pool in the sunken cheeks before coursing over the angular jawline and dribbling onto the wax choked around the body's neck.

A cell phone alarm pelted the silence, eliciting a gasp from Emory Rome. His lean, muscular body convulsed, breaking the water's waxy surface. He lurched out of the tub onto the plush tan rug, almost hitting his head on the chandelier. Grabbing his phone from the toilet cover, he turned off the alarm and looked at the time. *Almost four hours. That's better.* He had never been one to sleep more than five or six hours, but a recent bout of inexplicable insomnia made even that duration seem like a luxury. Fran's sassafras tea that he drank the night before was soothing, even though he hated the taste, but if it invited sleep, it did so at a whisper that went unheard. After two fidgeting hours in bed, he tried the bath and aromatherapy candles, which he estimated put him to sleep after half an hour.

Dipping his hand into the water, he pulled the drain plug, and with his wet fingers, he pinched the wick of each candle in the chandelier to extinguish the flames. He peeled off the wax that had leeched onto his body and flung it into the wastebasket before giving himself several quick pats with a towel. He examined his face in the mirror. His eyebrows ascended in a seductive curl before dipping just a touch, like the corners of his full, masculine lips. *No bags under the eyes.*

As he exited the bathroom and stepped onto the hardwood floor of his one-bedroom apartment, the sudden chill to his soles shivered his body but numbed as he continued walking naked through the living room to his dust-free desk. He pushed aside his TBI badge to retrieve the remote control and turn on a satellite dance music station. His fingers grazed a half-folded newspaper from four months earlier that had, above the fold, a color photo of Emory escorting a man in handcuffs from a brick building and a headline announcing, "Massive drug bust!" with a subhead stating, "Southeast meth & MDMA supplier shut down." He stared at the article that chronicled the epic ending to an investigation that had consumed much of his first year as a special agent. He thought again about framing it, but he wondered if doing so would monumentalize the first in a career of great achievements or a summit he would never again reach.

Emory looked away from the newspaper and remembered when he started working at the TBI right out of college. One of his professor's favorite phrases had become his life's mantra: "Focus on what you want or live a life blurred by indecision." He made the decision to sequester his personal life in favor of the career that he loved even more. It was a choice he had never regretted, except during moments of weakness – moments that came more often with insomnia.

Retreating to his bedroom, he opened the closet and scanned suits varying in shades from charcoal to black, and he whispered his selection, "Battleship." Moments later, he returned to the living room wearing a black field jacket over his grey suit. He grabbed the wool satchel hanging from his desk chair, his badge and a prescription bottle – popping a pill into his mouth before placing the bottle inside his jacket pocket.

As he picked up his phone from the bathroom, he heard the ping of a text message dropping. He didn't recognize the number from the text's sender, but the message read, "Meet me in my office at eight. I need to ask you something," followed by an address. Another text sent seconds later read, "BTW, it's Jeff Woodard."

"How'd he get my number?"

Before leaving his apartment, Emory texted Wayne to let him know he was following a lead and would meet him at the medical examiner's office at 10 a.m.

Once in his car, he followed his phone's directions to Knoxville's Old City – an area formerly called The Bowery, which served as the red-light district during the first half of the last century. Now remade into a trendy neighborhood, Old City was the site of Jeff Woodard's detective agency. He parked in front of a two-story, brown-brick building with connecting walls to similar buildings on either side.

Exiting the vehicle, he saw a blue sedan parked across the street. The car was unremarkable, but the unusual appearance of the driver caught his attention. He was wearing a white ski mask that concealed his face, except for his eyes. The eyeholes were perfect circles instead of ovals, but the mask's most striking feature was the chaotic red stitching where the mouth would be and beyond – like a hideously deformed wide grin. The driver seemed to be staring at him.

It's not that cold. Why the mask? Crap! Is he about to rob a place? Emory scanned the street to his left and right but saw nothing that would suggest a typical target – no bank, no convenience store and no gas station. When he glanced back at the other side of the street, the ski-mask man and the blue sedan were gone. He shrugged it off and returned his attention to his destination.

The second floor of the building had four narrow, white-paned windows, while the street-level floor had two large green-framed windows with an arched doorway between them. The lower windows were all covered from the inside with brown drapes, and the one to the left of the door had a painted sign that read, "Mourning Dove Investigations."

Emory turned the brass knob of the front door and entered a reception area that looked more like a library from a twisted gothic novel. The walls were almost hidden behind full bookshelves, and the only apparent door was the one he had just come through. Lantern light fixtures illuminated a harpsichord, four antique chairs and a desk of repurposed wood, behind which sat a beautiful young woman with flawless ebony skin and short, curly black hair.

As he approached the desk, he had to sidestep a smooth tree trunk that was anchored into the floor with one of its main branches extending to a small flap-covered opening above a bookshelf. A name plate on the desk read, "Virginia Kennon."

"Hello. I'm here to see Jeff Woodard."

Virginia kept her eyes on her laptop as she typed. "Emory?"

Emory noticed a Buddha statue atop a rosewood altar table at her side. "Yes."

Virginia looked up and gave him a coy smile. "He was right about you."

"What do you mean?"

She didn't answer but nodded to the chairs. "If you care to wait, he'll be here soon."

Emory meandered toward the chairs, checking out the books on the shelves. They were filled with complete sets of mystery novel series, many of which appeared to be first-edition hardcovers. He saw everything from Agatha Christie's sleuths and Sherlock Holmes to Nancy Drew and The Three Investigators. When he did make it to a chair, he saw on the nearby lamp table a stuffed bobcat, staring at him with black eyes and tufted ears perked in a pose of curiosity. Emory reached out to touch its tan and brown-spotted fur and was shocked when its large padded paw gave his hand a playful swat.

"Holy sh…" he screamed as he jumped from the chair.

Virginia laughed at him as if she never tired of the scare the bobcat elicited from first-time visitors. "That's Bobbie. Don't worry. She won't bite."

"I didn't think it was real." He extended his hand to pet her, but before he could make contact, the front door opened.

Jeff entered wearing his pea coat and jeans, and carrying two steaming paper cups of coffee. "Here you go, Virginia." As the cup tapped her desktop, he followed her gaze and noticed the visitor. With a wide grin, the PI hurried across the room and shook Emory's hand. "You're here," he announced as if it were a pleasant surprise.

"Why did you want to see me?" asked Emory, startled by his own abruptness.

Jeff motioned for him to follow. "Let's talk in my office. Virginia, are you ready for us?"

She sipped her coffee as her eyes returned to the laptop. "Couple of minutes."

Jeff walked up to one of the bookshelves and without even looking, he pulled on the only non-mystery book on the shelf – John Knowles' *A Separate Peace*. The shelf swung open, revealing

Jeff's office on the other side. As soon as the door opened, Bobbie darted through it and leapt onto his desk.

Emory couldn't keep from scanning the room as he stepped inside. No matter where he looked, something caught his eye. It was similar to the reception area but with fewer shelves, more hanging art, a single window and an exquisite map of the world painted onto the floor. A tree trunk identical to the one in the other room stood in the corner closest to Jeff's desk, including a branch ending at a flap-covered opening near the top of the wall.

Hanging his coat on a wooden rack stand, Jeff took a seat behind his desk and petted Bobbie.

Emory nodded toward the feline. "You know, bobcats are illegal to own in Tennessee."

"Not if you get it from a licensed breeder. I have the documentation to support it, so stand down, Agent Rome." Jeff patted the bobcat on the backside. "Go home, Bobbie."

The bobcat jumped from the desk to the tree trunk and, although twice the size of a housecat, climbed it with grace and speed to the flap-covered opening, disappearing on the other side.

"Where did she go?"

Jeff pointed up. "I live upstairs."

Emory spread out his arms. "You have an impressive office."

A glittering smile cut across Jeff's face. "Thanks. Sometimes you have to create your own mystery."

"I have a mystery for you." Emory sat at one of the two tracery cathedral chairs that faced Jeff's desk. "How did you get my number?"

"From your business card."

"I didn't give you—"

"You intrigue me, Emory Rome."

"Me?" Emory could feel his face flush. "Why do you say that?"

"I can tell you've got something inside you that your muted demeanor and dull, grey suits aren't going to keep pent up forever."

Before Emory could respond, Virginia entered. "I'm in, and I have some leads for you to check out." Carrying the laptop under her arm, she walked over to Jeff's side of the desk and opened it.

Jeff glanced at the computer and at Emory. "We're about to share information with you in good faith because I need some help from you."

Emory eyed him with cautious intrigue. "What sort of help?"

Jeff waved off the question. "We'll get to that later. Go ahead, Virginia."

The young woman nodded to the screen, the back of the computer facing Emory. "Britt had a boyfriend, Dan Claymon—"

Jeff interrupted her. "Victor said she didn't have a boyfriend."

"He lied. Well, sort of. The two were all ODA up until a week ago."

Emory tapped on the desk. "ODA?"

Jeff rolled his eyes up from the screen. "Online displays of affection."

Virginia continued, "At that point, their exchanges became hostile over—"

"Wait a second." Emory raised his right hand as if calling for a timeout. "How are you getting access to information like that?"

Jeff pointed at the laptop. "Through Britt Algarotti's computer."

"Her comp…Where did you get that?"

"Her brother gave it to me."

Exasperated, Emory stood and pointed at the laptop. "You obtained this illegally."

Virginia backed away from the desk. "Perhaps I should let you two settle this." She left the room, closing the door behind her.

Jeff glared at Emory with obvious annoyance. "Did you not hear me? Her brother *gave* it to me."

"He's thirteen. He doesn't have the authority. Anything gleaned from it now would be unusable."

"Well I don't plan on *gleaning* anything from it. I'm just

getting some information about her life, so I can solve the case and collect my check."

"But that's wrong."

"I'm not going to keep it."

Emory threw up his hands. "That's not the issue."

Jeff walked around the desk to stand before the TBI special agent. "No, the issue is that you and I are in the same game, but I have a different playbook." He pointed at Emory's chest, and the tip of his finger tapped his sternum. "I don't have to follow yours."

"The right thing to do—"

"The boundary between right and wrong isn't stationary. It moves according to circumstance."

"No, it doesn't. What's right is right, and what's wrong is wrong!"

Jeff brandished his right hand. "If I slapped you right now because you're getting annoying, that would be wrong." He lowered his hand. "If you had just fainted, and I slapped you to wake you up, you'd be thanking me."

Emory scowled at him. "I've never fainted."

Jeff let loose a little laugh. "Now who's missing the point? You can't tell me you've never bent the law, not even a little."

"I follow the rules."

"Why? What have the rules ever done for you?"

Jeff was standing so close now, Emory could see the rhythm of his heart in the veins of his muscular neck. "Listen, I'm going to pretend I didn't see this." He motioned toward the laptop. "Don't look at it anymore, and give it back to that kid. I'm outta here."

Emory turned to leave, but Jeff stopped him. "You're forgetting I needed to ask something of you."

Emory faced him again, his arms crossed. "What is it, Jeff?"

"Are you hungry?"

CHAPTER 7

JEFF TOOK EMORY to Dolly's Café, a trendy Dolly Parton-themed restaurant with an exterior made to look like a shanty. Inside the restaurant, country music memorabilia adorned the walls, and the waitresses dressed up like Dolly Parton, complete with wigs and enhancements. The host, costumed as Porter Wagner, showed them to a booth for two.

Before Emory took a seat, he excused himself to wash his hands. Upon his return to the booth, Jeff presented a stoic glance. "I didn't know what you wanted to drink, so I ordered you clam juice."

Emory snarled his lip in disgust, prompting a laugh from Jeff. "I'm just kidding. I ordered coffee for you, but I don't know if you'd prefer sweet tea."

"No, I don't like tea, although I have forced down some sassafras tea that a friend at work made for me."

Jeff cocked his head and grinned at him. "I can't stand it either. Not very Southern of us."

As Emory took off his jacket to place on the seat, a bottle of pills fell from the pocket and bounced on the floor. Jeff retrieved it and, after reading the label, gave Emory an I-caught-you look. "For panic attacks?"

Emory snatched the bottle from his hand. "That's private."

"They let you become an agent, knowing you're prone to fits?"

Emory's face reddened as he returned the bottle to his pocket. He snarled through gritted teeth, "I don't have fits."

Jeff raised his hands in a sign for Emory to calm down. "Okay, I believe you. Take a chill pill, man."

Emory grabbed his jacket and shoved his ass out of the booth. "All right, I'm outta here."

Jeff grabbed his arm. "I'm sorry. I was just teasing. Come on, sit down." The PI took a big whiff of the air. "Just smell that bacon. They have a great breakfast here."

Emory threw his jacket onto the seat and hesitated before sliding back into the booth. "You have to swear to me that you won't say a word about this to anyone. Swear."

"I swear, I won't say anything to anyone." Jeff held up his right hand as if taking an oath. "So what would happen if they found out? Would they fire you?"

"I might be confined to a desk," Emory answered with obvious distaste for the prospect.

"Ooh. No more high-profile drug busts for you."

"You know about that?"

"I Googled you last night. Congratulations on that, by the way. Very impressive."

"Thanks, but why am I here?"

"Because I thought you looked horny..." Emory's eyebrows perked up, and Jeff's tongue jumped to correct itself. "Hungry! I swear I meant to say hungry. Plus, I thought we could just talk. You and me – no distractions."

"I can't share any information I have about the case."

"Not about work. As a matter of fact, for the next hour, no talking about work." Jeff rested his left arm on the top of the booth seat. "I'll start. Are you seeing anyone?"

"Wh…What?" Emory looked around to see who was within listening range.

"You heard me."

Emory placed his forearms on the table and slid his head and chest closer to Jeff so he could respond in a whisper. "I can't. Not with my job."

The PI laughed. "What are you talking about? You're not in a monastery."

"I want to have a long, successful career—"

"So you don't want someone to share that with?"

"Of course I do!" Emory said with more intensity than he intended. He again looked around to see if anyone was listening.

"Why do you keep doing that? Are you embarrassed to be seen with me?"

"I'm embarrassed to be talking about this in public." He pushed back from the table. "Enough spotlight on me."

A short waitress under an exaggerated wig of hairspray-hardened platinum hair ambled toward them as if she were balancing a basket full of grain on her head. "Are you fellas ready to order?"

The two men said that they were and placed their orders. Once the waitress left, Emory tried to think of something to say. "I liked your receptionist. She seems nice."

Jeff shook his head. "She's not my receptionist. She's my business partner. I handle the investigative footwork, and Virginia takes care of research and the office. She's also my best friend – has been since we were kids, even though she was two grades ahead of me. After high school, she served six years in the Marines, in intelligence. We formed the agency almost two years ago, after she got out and I finished college."

"Which college did you go to?"

"UT," Jeff answered, referring to the University of Tennessee in Knoxville. "What about you?"

"Vanderbilt."

Jeff grimaced at the mention of the cross-state rival. "Ooh, Vandy?"

"What's wrong with that?"

"They're a bunch of rich snobs—"

"I was there on a scholarship."

"Didn't you feel out of place?"

"When do I not?"

Jeff gave him a knowing smile. "So you were going to be a doctor?"

Emory nodded. "I'm not being boastful, but I've always excelled in chemistry classes. Defined chemical structures, interactions with calculable results – there's a beauty to their predictability."

Jeff threw open his arms. "But chaos is so much more exciting."

"Okay, now I'm embarrassed to be seen with you."

"Sorry." The PI drew in his arms and lowered his voice. "Why the switch to law enforcement?"

"Partly to follow in my father's footsteps. And I just hate to see people get away with shit. Figured I could do something about it. What about you?"

"What about me?"

"Your major."

"Oh." Jeff glanced at the approaching waitress. "Criminology."

"I didn't know UT had a criminology major."

"They do," Jeff assured him as the waitress placed their food on the table.

"When are you going to tell me why I'm here?"

Jeff waited for the waitress to leave. "Now, I guess." He took a deep breath and let it wisp from his mouth before speaking. "I'm on the government's no-fly list."

Emory didn't know what he was expecting Jeff to say, but he for sure wouldn't have guessed this. "Why?"

"I don't know. The week after I graduated college, I had my bags packed for my dream vacation to Australia. I always wanted to travel the world, and I thought I'd start with the furthest point. I was so excited when I arrived at the airport, but after I tried to get my boarding pass, the airline rep said they couldn't issue me one because I was on the list. Of course, I laughed. I thought it was a weird joke. I mean I'd never done anything even remotely terroristy. When I understood that she wasn't kidding, I contacted every agency I could think of to ask why I was on the list, and all I got was a string of contradictory non-answers." Jeff sipped his coffee. "Since then, I've tried to find answers on my own, and I finally hired a lawyer, who's been having no luck whatsoever." He sighed. "I'm an adventurer stuck in an adventureless land. After I realized I was going to be in Tennessee for a while, I put the money meant for the trip, and a good chunk from my parents, toward starting my own detective agency."

"You want me to see what I can find out?"

Jeff nodded. "You're on the inside. Maybe you can get to the bottom of what's going on."

Emory thought in silence for a moment. "Okay. I'll see what I can do."

The killer smile returned to Jeff's handsome face, and the two men started eating.

CHAPTER 8

HAVING LOST ALL track of time during his brunch with Jeff, Emory was twenty minutes late when he pulled into the parking lot at the Regional Forensic Center. Spotting Wayne returning to his car, he pulled up beside him and lowered his passenger-side window. "Sorry I'm late."

Wayne dropped his car keys into his pocket. "You didn't miss much. As best the ME can tell, burning is the cause of death. Unfortunately, it wasn't done postmortem. The lab verified that the powder we found on the ice is calcium carbide and the likely cause of the fire, and they were able to peel Britt's cell phone from her clothes. They're working on retrieving info from it, but between the fire and the water, I doubt we'll get anything. Someone must've really hated her to murder her like that."

"Or maybe it was just a convenient way to kill her and not be at the scene of the crime when it happened. Do you have the copy of Victor's document I gave you?"

"Somewhere." Wayne opened the door to rest his battered briefcase on the passenger seat. He rifled through the disordered stack of papers held within and pulled out the coffee-stained document. "Here it is."

"He included information on Britt's best friend in there somewhere."

Wayne pointed to the paper. "Her name is Tatiana Burrett. Tatiana. Isn't that a fairy or something in a Shakespeare book?"

Emory raised his eyebrows, more in admiration than derision. "Titania."

"Don't look at me like that. I had mandatory reading when I was in school too, Mr. Know-It-All."

"I say we go talk to her and find out who Britt really was."

"Sounds like a plan. She's probably in school right now."

Emory waved him inside. "I'll drive."

"Didn't your dad want you to spend the night?"

"I'm not doing that," Emory snapped, offering no elaboration.

Wayne slipped into the passenger seat, moving the briefcase to his lap. "Okay. If you want to disappoint your dad."

Emory started to drive again. "I also think we should talk to the coach today."

Wayne sneered at him. "Does that mean we're splitting up again?"

"We can go together to both."

"I feel so honored. It'll be better this way. You're no good with kids."

"Why do you say that?"

"How many kids do you have?"

Emory pulled out of the parking lot, wondering, *Why does everyone keep asking me that?*

Emory and Wayne followed a petite, fiftyish woman down a crowded high school hallway. The slamming locker doors, cliquey chatter and squeak of shoes on over-waxed hardwood floors took

Emory back to his own tortured days roaming these halls – a memory he now tried to shudder from his mind.

"She should be finished with photography class and is probably at her locker now," the woman said before coming to a stop. She pointed to a curly-haired teenage girl with soft features, wearing a brown sweater and faded jeans. "There she is."

Emory nodded to the woman. "Thank you, Principal…" He couldn't remember her last name, but it didn't matter since she was already making her way back to her office.

Wayne and Emory approached the girl as she hung a large camera in her locker and closed the door. Wayne spoke up first. "Tatiana?"

The girl jumped and turned around. "Yes?"

Wayne flashed his badge and introduced them both to her. "We want to talk to you about Britt Algarotti."

A tear rolled down her pale freckled face. "Okay."

"How close were you and Britt?" Wayne asked.

"Very. We've been best friends since kindergarten."

"Tatiana, did you—" Emory began before she interrupted.

"You can call me Tati."

"Tati, do you know anyone who would want to hurt Britt?"

"No." Tati waved her arm at the students in view. "I mean, not enough to hurt her like *that*. Britt was our town's biggest celebrity."

"Because of her skating?" asked Emory.

Tati nodded. "And she's from the richest family. A lot of the students here have parents who work at the water factory. Everyone wanted to be her friend, but Britt was very selective about who she'd let in. She knew people would just cozy up to her because of, well, who she was. Britt could see through that, most of the time."

Emory watched the students who walked past them, most displaying suspicious glances toward the two strangers talking to Tati. "I would think a lot of the ones who didn't make the cut would be jealous of her, maybe even hate her."

Tati shook her head. "No. I mean, jealous yeah, but hate her?"

Wayne asked, "Was anything going on between Britt and her coach?"

"Going on?" Tati's eyes shrunk from wide to squinty. "Eww, gross. He's an old man."

Wayne's face snarled at the remark. "Are you sure you would know?"

"Yes. Dan Claymon is her boyfriend."

Emory acted as if he hadn't already been told about the boyfriend by Virginia, but in his head, he was high-fiving Tati for giving them this piece of information in a legal manner instead – since the first time was through the dubious hacking of Britt's laptop by the PIs.

"I mean he was. They broke up about a week ago."

"Did her dad know that she had a boyfriend?" asked Emory.

Tati looked at him as if the answer were obvious. "Yeah. Britt wasn't one to sneak around. She couldn't keep a secret to save her life."

Wayne asked, "You know where we can find Dan?"

Tati pointed to a young man walking away from them down a perpendicular hallway. "He's right there."

"Hey Dan!" Wayne yelled out, prompting at least half the students in the hall to turn his way.

Dan Claymon looked at the two men walking toward him and took off running.

CHAPTER 9

WAYNE SIGHED AS Britt's ex-boyfriend ran down the hall, bumping students left and right. "Ah shit." Emory gave pursuit, followed by his slower partner. Dan Claymon ran into several students – collisions that did little to slow him. The fleeing teenager then slammed the panic bar of a glass side door, which popped open to the outside. As soon as his feet stamped the snow-covered ground, his momentum diminished. Emory pounded the closing door a second later and hurled himself at Dan's back, sending the teenager face-down into the snow.

"I didn't do it, man! I didn't do it!" yelled Dan, snow sputtering from his mouth.

"Then why'd you run?" Holding Dan's wrists behind his back, Emory placed handcuffs on him and helped him up.

Catching up to them, Wayne bent forward and rested his palms on his knees to catch his breath. He pointed to the impact Dan's body made in the snow. "Nice snow angel."

Emory turned Dan around to face him, and the teenager told him, "Man, you're fast."

Emory couldn't stop a little laugh from escaping. "You said you didn't do it. What exactly didn't you do?"

"Kill Britt," Dan responded.

"If you didn't do it, why did you run?" Wayne asked.

Dan shook his head. "People have been asking me if I did it. I thought one of them called the cops on me. I don't know. I panicked. I don't want to go to jail."

Emory noticed the bruise around the teenager's right eye. "How'd you get the shiner?"

Dan hesitated. "Someone was joking about Britt."

"Emory?" Sheriff Rome trudged across the school grounds toward them. "What's going on here?"

Emory responded with a question of his own. "What are you doing here?"

The sheriff pointed with his thumb. "I was next door getting gas, and one of the teachers called the station about a man chasing a student."

Wayne scowled at the sheriff's answer. "What? There were two men chasing him. They didn't see me?"

Emory told his father, "This is Dan Claymon, Britt Algarotti's ex-boyfriend. We wanted to question him, and he took off running."

Sheriff Rome frowned at his son. "You couldn't have waited until after school to question him instead of making a scene?" He nodded toward the glass door and the students watching from the other side. "Uncuff him."

"But—" Emory began.

The sheriff turned Dan around so that his back faced Emory. "Take the cuffs off."

Red-faced, Emory complied.

The sheriff placed a hand on the teenager's back. "I'll take him to the station and call his parents, and you can ask them if it's okay to speak with him." He told Dan, "Come on," and he led him to his car.

Wayne looked at Emory. "We don't need his parents' permission to question him."

"I know."

"You know, you really need to tell him when he's wrong about these things."

Emory shrugged. "I can't. He's my father."

Barter Ridge was the seat of one of Tennessee's least populous counties, and the sheriff's station reflected the necessary frugality of its residents. When Emory opened the front door to the double-wide trailer that served as the station, the corners of his mouth creaked upward for a millisecond. He found mild comfort in the changelessness of it all. He hadn't been here since college, but it still looked and smelled the same – like old carpet, burnt coffee and gun oil.

Wayne followed him inside, and Emory nodded to one of the two wooden benches on either side of the front door. "Why don't you wait here. I'll just be a minute." His partner complied without argument.

Emory walked past deputies talking on the phones at two of the four desks, and he gave a two-fingered salute to the one he knew. His eyes meandered around the deputy room – from the interrogation room to the hallway that led to the holding room, break room, bathroom and supply closet – before they came to rest on the glass door to his father's office.

He could see that the office was empty, but he entered anyway. Affixed to one wall was a small, locked armory, but apart from that, the rest of the wall space was covered by framed pictures, certificates and newspaper articles. Next to the Tennessee Medal of Honor Wayne had mentioned seeing yesterday hung the full article about Emory and Wayne's big drug bust from four months ago. *Wayne failed to mention seeing this.* Emory smiled at his father's obvious pride in him.

"You can't be in here."

Startled by the voice, Emory saw that the deputy he had yet to meet was now off the phone and standing in the doorway with his right hand glued to the knob. Blonde with a farm-boy face, he had a thin but sturdy body, just under six-feet tall.

Emory read his gold name badge and gave him a courteous smile. "Deputy Harris, I'm looking for Sheriff Rome."

"The sheriff is in the interrogation room and can't be disturbed."

Emory figured his father, as angry as he was, wanted to talk to Dan Claymon alone, so he didn't bother asking to join him in the interrogation room. "Okay. I'll just wait."

"You need to wait out here."

Emory stretched his lips into an awkward frown. He walked out of the office, and the deputy shut the door behind him. Joining Wayne on the bench, Emory watched the deputy return to his desk. "Dad will be with us in a few minutes." His partner grunted before crossing his arms and closing his eyes.

Emory took the opportunity to flip through crime scene pictures on his cell phone. Before he reached the third picture, the front door opened, and Scot Trousdale entered with a five-gallon bottle of Algarotti water riding on his left shoulder. *What's he doing here?*

When Scot noticed Emory, he pushed up his glasses and greeted him. "Agent Emory."

"You make deliveries too?"

"No, but sometimes I'll take care of the sheriff's station myself so I can clean the cooler and make sure everything's working properly – as a courtesy for our local law enforcement. It's on my way home, so it's not any trouble."

Scot pulled his phone out of his pocket and read something

on it. Since Emory didn't hear any notification, he assumed the phone was on vibrate. "Unfortunately, I'll have to come back to service it. I have to run."

Emory nodded. "See you later."

Scot walked to the hallway entrance and unloaded the bottle onto the floor next to the water cooler and an empty bottle before leaving.

Once Scot exited, Wayne asked, "Who's that?"

"Victor Algarotti's assistant."

"He's a secretary?" Wayne snickered. "He doesn't look like a sissy."

Annoyed by his partner's statement, Emory popped out of his seat. "I need some water."

"I could use some myself."

Emory didn't wait for him, but the older man caught up to him at the water cooler. He pulled a cup from the dispenser and filled it.

Wayne followed suit and pointed to the hallway past the cooler. "What's down there?"

Emory glanced at Deputy Harris, whose eyes were focused on his computer. "I'll show you." Three steps later, they were out of view of the deputies and approaching a white door with a square shatterproof window. Emory looked inside to see a room empty except for a commode in one corner and a folded blanket, some pillows and a six-foot mat on the floor.

Wayne peeked inside. "What's this room?"

"It's the holding room."

"Holding room?" Wayne laughed as if Emory weren't serious. "You mean this is the jail?"

"That's it." Emory walked a little further down the hall to a small, unlocked cabinet built into the wall. "Dad doesn't think that they need to spend money on a jail." He opened the cabinet and pulled out a key on a souvenir keychain from the Great

Smoky Mountains National Park and returned to Wayne. "People are only here for a night or two before being released or sent to Knox County."

"But anyone could knock this door down with a swift kick."

"Not really." Emory unlocked the door so Wayne could see inside. "He had the wall and door reinforced, and there's a double-key deadbolt." He pointed at the lock and at the twelve-by-eight-inch window in the opposing wall. "The window's way too tiny for anyone to squeeze out, so the only way in or out is with the key."

They could hear a door squeak open. "I think that's the interrogation room. Dad must be finished with Dan." Emory relocked the holding room and returned the key. The two agents hurried back to the deputy room in time to see the sheriff holding open the front door as Dan Claymon left the building. Wayne and Emory exchanged confused glances. "Dad, we wanted to talk to him."

The sheriff shook his head. "After the way you two embarrassed him today, I didn't think that would be a good idea."

Wayne's eyebrows reached for his former hairline. "That's not your call to make, all due respect."

Emory grabbed Wayne's arm. "Dad, what did you find out from him?"

"We just talked but not about the case. He did offer up that he only ran because he panicked."

"Jesus!" Wayne chopped the air like a preacher giving a hellfire sermon. "We already knew that was his excuse."

The sheriff brandished a look of disapproval. "He got ahold of his mom, and she didn't give permission for us to talk to him about Britt's murder."

Wayne threw up his hands. "So that's it?"

"Until you have more to go on. Look here, Dan's a decent kid. He's had a few problems with us, but nothing too serious."

"Could I see what you have on him?" Wayne asked.

Sheriff Rome hesitated. "Sure. I guess I can let you see his file."

Emory seized the opportunity to dump his partner for a while. "Wayne, while you're doing that, I'm going to talk to Britt's skating coach."

"You told me we're not splitting up today."

"I'll be back in a half an hour, max."

"Fine," Wayne responded, although his tone suggested he was anything but.

CHAPTER 10

JEFF WOODARD FOLLOWED his phone's directions to Rick Roberts' house, which was less than five miles from the lake where Britt Algarotti had died. The neighborhood consisted of small ranch-style homes and occasional trailers. Maybe half of the homes had fenced-in backyards, and the house of Britt's former coach was one of them. Jeff parked on the road next to an embankment of black snow and proceeded up the shoveled walkway to the front door. Four breaths after knocking, a man in a V-neck T-shirt and jeans answered the door. His full black hair and fit body gave him the look of someone in his forties, but Jeff figured he was closer to mid-fifties.

"Mr. Roberts?"

"Yes."

"I'm Jeff Woodard. I'm investigating—"

Rick sighed. "Oh, thank god you're here. From the reaction I got on the phone, I didn't think the sheriff would be sending anyone out."

Jeff almost corrected Rick's assumption that he was with the sheriff's department, but he figured the misplaced authority would make the man more forthcoming with information than if he knew he were there on behalf of the man who had fired him. "We're always happy when people want to help us out with a murder investigation."

"Good!" Rick's ruddy cheeks tensed. "I want that murdering bitch put in jail for what she's done!"

Could he know who killed Britt? Jeff asked himself. "Who do you mean?"

"My damn soon-to-be ex-wife," Rick growled.

"You think your ex murdered Britt?"

"Britt?" Rick wiped the anger from his tone. "No, I'm so sorry. I thought you were here about my dog. Please, come on in out of the cold."

Jeff stepped inside to see an utter mess of a living room – clothes strewn over the couch, several pairs of old gym shoes kicked off in random spots on the floor and mail sticking to dirty plates on the coffee table. Under his breath, Jeff muttered, "Nice decorator. Rorschach?"

"Can we talk in the kitchen? I was just getting some tea." Rick started walking, as if presuming the answer before Jeff vocalized it. "I'm sorry for my confusion. I'm a little out of it from everything that's happened. I couldn't even go to work today."

The kitchen was in better shape, with only a few dishes in the sink and clutter-free counters, except for a glass with ice in it. *I must've interrupted his yearly cleaning.* Jeff's eyes moved to the oven mitts resting on the grease-spattered stovetop.

Rick opened the refrigerator and retrieved a full pitcher of tea. "Would you like some?"

"No, thank you. I don't drink tea."

"I have some water in here too. Grape-flavored. That's all Britt would drink."

Jeff saw something crawl out of one of the oven mitts. *Roach!* "Uh, I'm fine."

Rick closed the door and filled his glass. "I tell you, I'm still in shock over Britt. Do you have any idea who would've done this?"

"We're following a few leads." Jeff checked the floor and the tops of his shoes. *Don't want to take home any hitchhikers. I need to get out of here.* "Rick, tell me why Victor fired you."

Rick took a gulp of his tea and shook his head. "I trained that girl for six years – looked out for her when we'd travel to competitions. I took my responsibilities seriously." His lips quivered before he took another gulp of tea. "Three weeks ago, we were at a competition in Nashville, and right before she went on the ice, I noticed she was acting funny."

"What do you mean?"

"She was kind of giggly, which she never is except maybe after a competition. When she started to skate, I knew something was definitely wrong. It was like she was drunk." Rick dropped his shoulders and sighed. "She couldn't even complete her routine, which she knew backwards and forwards, literally. We left the rink right away – didn't even wait for her results – and I took her straight to the hospital. When the bloodwork came back, they said she tested positive for MMA—"

"MDMA?"

Rick darted the air with his index finger. "That's it. And they had another name for it."

"Ecstasy. Had she used that before?"

"No, and she didn't do it then either. We figured someone spiked her water, but we already threw the bottle away, so we couldn't find out for sure."

Jeff squinted and raised a questioning hand. "Why would someone do that at a skating rink?"

Rick huffed at the question. "Competition. It had to be someone who didn't want her to win."

"So Victor fired you for that?"

Rick drank some more tea and nodded. "I was supposed to look out for her. Victor blamed me for not watching her closely enough and said I couldn't be trusted anymore."

"I'm sorry."

"Me too. I loved her like a daughter."

"Do you think any of these competitors would've gone further than spiking her drink?

Rick scowled at him. "You mean...kill her?"

"Yes."

"Competition is fierce, Deputy Woodard, but it's not deadly. Of course, some people think that whole family's just cursed – Fate's way of equalizing the advantaged."

Jeff was seeking a more grounded explanation. "Is it possible one of the other girls you train drugged her?"

Rick looked confused. "I don't train anyone else."

Now Jeff was confused. "You mentioned work earlier."

"Ah. Victor insisted that my focus be on Britt alone as far as skating was concerned, but he didn't pay me enough to make anywhere near a decent living. I had to keep my teaching job. Fortunately, the school is understanding when I have to go...had to go on the road with Britt." Rick looked to the floor and shook his head. "What the hell is going on? First Britt dies, and then I came home this morning to find my dog killed."

Jeff's next question was interrupted by a knock at the front door.

"I'll be right back." Rick left to answer the door, and a moment later, he returned to the kitchen with Emory following him.

Jeff greeted him with a purposeful smile. "Emory."

"Jeff? I swear, you're like a reverse shadow."

Rick looked from Emory to Jeff. "Are you two partners?"

"No," they responded in sync.

"I'm with the TBI. He's a—"

Jeff jumped in before Emory could blow his cover. "The sheriff's department is working in conjunction with the TBI and the family to bring Britt's killer to justice. No need to retread. I'll fill Special Agent Rome in later on what we've discussed so far. Now, you were talking about your dog." While Rick wasn't looking, Jeff mouthed, "Be cool," to Emory.

"Anyway, as I was saying, since I got fired, I picked up a night shift at the convenience store on Highway 33. It's a bit of a drive, but I need the money until I get another skater. When I got home this morning, I called to Lex because he didn't greet me at the door like he normally does. I almost didn't go looking for him since I only had a few minutes to get ready for school, but I just had a sense of dread. I went out to the backyard and found him near the gate."

Jeff tapped Emory on the arm and pointed out the doggy door in the kitchen door, leading to the backyard.

"Someone shot him…in the head. I know my wife is behind it. If she didn't do it, she put her new boyfriend up to it. Either way, she's guilty. She never did like…" Rick started crying. "Who could do that to a dog?"

Jeff patted his back. "I'm so sorry."

To Jeff's surprise, Rick hugged him and held the embrace as he continued recounting the details of that morning. "I just piled some snow on him to keep him fresh until I could think of what to do."

Rick stopped talking to let a burp erupt from his throat, prompting Jeff to turn his face away and mouth, "Can you believe he just did that on me?" to Emory.

Emory's eyes were instead focused on a faint wisp of smoke rising over Jeff's head.

Rick finally released Jeff. "I don't feel so good." He clutched his stomach with both hands and burped again, spitting out an undeniable cloud of smoke. He started screaming as flames erupted from his stomach and ate their way up his body!

Jeff yelled, "Oh my god!"

"Get him on the floor!" Emory ordered.

Rick's upper body was now engulfed in flames, but he was still standing – screaming and writhing.

Jeff grabbed the oven mitts from the stove and pushed Rick to the floor. He tried to roll the burning man to put out the fire, but he could no longer get close enough to touch him.

Emory turned on the faucet and shot water from the sprayer onto the flames.

Their efforts were too late.

Rick was no longer moving, no longer screaming.

As the flames subsided, Rick's legs remained unfazed. From the belt up, however, was nothing but a charred, tortured torso with blackened arms frozen in a defensive pose in front of the still-smoking skull.

Emory clenched his fists. "What the hell just happened here?!"

Jeff shook his head. "Spontaneous human combustion?"

CHAPTER 11

WHILE EMORY TALKED to his dad on the phone, Jeff vomited in the kitchen sink. The room reeked of the sickly scent of burned rotting meat and hair. Jeff splashed his face with water and dried it with a paper towel. "God, that smell," he exclaimed with wretched vehemence.

Emory hung up his phone. "They're on the way. Are you okay?"

Jeff threw the wet towel into the sink. "I'm fine. I've just never smelled burning flesh before. Shaking his head in disbelief, he pointed at Rick Roberts' body. "That right there is without a doubt the freakiest shit I have ever seen in my life!"

"I agree."

"Why aren't you freaking out about this?"

Emory squatted to take another look at the charred torso. "What exactly do you want me to do?"

Jeff shrugged. "I guess what you're doing." He squatted beside him and covered his nose with his forearm.

Emory pointed to just above Rick's melted belt. "I first saw the fire there. It just exploded out of his stomach like in *Alien*."

"Yeah, at the stomach. Do you think it's something he ate?"

They both turned to the glass of ice tea on the counter. Emory rose and pointed his palms to opposite sides of the room. "I need to get a sample of everything in this kitchen."

"I'll help you."

"No, I have to maintain chain of custody. You're not authorized to handle evidence."

Jeff's eyes sprung wide open, and he pointed an accusing finger at a small slash of red on Emory's jawline. "Oh my god, I think you got some Rick on you."

"What?" Emory touched it and realized it wasn't tissue from the victim. "It's just a cut. I probably got it when I tackled Britt's ex-boyfriend at the high school earlier."

"You tackled him?"

"He was running."

"From what?"

Fearing he was just fishing for information, Emory decided not to elaborate further. He held his hands over Rick's body. "Let's stick to the situation at hand."

"Fine."

"I need to take pictures of the body before my dad gets here."

"Why's that?"

"Long story." Emory started snapping photos with his phone. He then flapped his jacket to get some air to his body. "Man, it's hot in here."

Jeff gasped. "You're not going to flame up on me, are you?"

"Don't even kid about that. Listen, when Wayne gets here—"

"The dog," Jeff blurted out as if he were the first to answer an unasked question.

"What about it?" Emory asked before realizing the direction Jeff was heading with the statement. "Someone shot the dog to break in here and poisoned something Rick ate or drank."

Jeff pointed at the kitchen door. "Wouldn't really have to break in. Whoever it was probably crawled through that doggy door."

Emory inspected the door. "It would have to be someone kind of small."

"No it wouldn't. Your spatial recognition is off." Jeff removed his coat and handed it to Emory to hold.

"What are you doing?"

"Showing you I can fit through there."

"No!" Emory pushed the coat back into Jeff's arms. "This is a crime scene. There could be fingerprints on it. Don't touch anything!"

"You're right. Sorry."

Waving his hand in front of his face, Wayne shuffled into the kitchen. "Good god! That smell." He stopped waving and pulled the flap of his coat up to his nose.

Sheriff Rome entered with two deputies following behind. His eyes dropped to Rick's body. "Oh dear lord. That poor soul. First Britt, and now her coach is dead too."

"Both burned," added Wayne.

The sheriff nodded. "I don't suppose there's any chance of this being a coincidence."

"I don't think so, Dad."

Jeff told Emory, "It looks like you have everything under control here. I'll be off."

"I'm glad you were here. I don't think anyone would've believed me if I had been alone with him when this happened." After Jeff left, Emory told the deputies, "We need samples of everything edible in the house. Also, there's a dead dog in the backyard that we'll need to examine. He was shot, so find that bullet. And let's dust everything for fingerprints, including the doggy door."

Sheriff Rome said, "I'll call Judge Harper to get a search warrant." After making a phone call, the sheriff asked a deputy to pick up the warrant. "Emory, what happened here?"

Emory recounted every detail from the moment he walked into Rick's house to the last wisp of smoke curling up from his dead body. Afterwards, they all theorized about Rick's death until the deputy returned with the warrant, at which point, the evidence-gathering began. The sheriff and deputies took care of the bodies, while Emory and Wayne walked around the house for any clues about Rick's life that might explain his death.

Emory knew that key clues often hide like a walking stick in a cedar tree. You couldn't always see them at first glance, so he had gotten into the habit of photographing everything related to a crime scene, even cursory items. At the moment, Emory was snapping pictures on his phone of everything in the bedroom, whether they seemed important or not. Inside the walk-in closet, he found a shelf cluttered with trophies and medals – all won by Rick when he was a young ice skater – and he wondered why he didn't have them on display. When he came out of the closet, he saw Wayne poking around the bedroom. "I meant to ask, did you find anything in Dan Claymon's records?"

Wayne shrugged as he began opening drawers in the dresser. "Nothing major. Some vandalism."

Sheriff Rome popped his head in the door. "We found the bullet."

Emory peered up from his phone. "That's excellent."

"Everything is being loaded into my deputy's SUV, and then he'll head to Knoxville. Are you guys finished?"

Wayne approached the door. "I think that's it."

"All right then." The sheriff jerked his head to the left in a signal for them to leave. "I posted some crime tape on the back door, and I need to do the same with the front."

"Emory, aren't you coming?" Wayne asked.

Noticing several framed pictures on the dust-covered dresser top, Emory snapped some quick photos. "Coming."

The three exited the house, and as the sheriff taped the door, Wayne looked to the sky. "It's getting late. We should call it a day."

"You're coming over tonight, right?" asked Sheriff Rome.

Emory sighed and shook his head. "I can't tonight."

The sheriff frowned at his son. "You said you would."

"I wasn't definite. Besides, I didn't bring a change of clothes."

"You got a bunch of clothes in your room. We haven't thrown anything out."

Wayne took his partner aside. "Emory, give me your keys. I'll drive home tonight and see you in the morning."

"I need to go home."

"No, you don't." Wayne put a hand on his shoulder. "Stay with your dad. You should hear him talk about you. He misses you."

"Fine." Emory handed him the keys.

CHAPTER 12

A S EMORY EXITED Sheriff Rome's truck, he could see
the sun starting to set over the peak that locals called
Crown-of-Thorns Mountain. Although not as evident
under its current shroud of snow, the ring of trees just below the
bare mountaintop were all dead. Some blamed acid rain, while
others had more superstitious explanations. Whatever the cause,
the twisted remains of the naked trunks and their large branches
gave the mountain its tortured name.

Emory scanned his father's two-acre property, bordered by a
wooden split-rail fence and abutting deep woods on two sides. It
looked the same as it did the last time he had come home – right
after he graduated college. A sudden movement caught his eye.
A white French bulldog bolted from the side of the yellow-brick
house, hopping over the snow-covered ground and straight into
his arms. "Sophie!" he exclaimed as the excited dog licked his face.
He looked at his dad. "She remembers me."

"Of course, she does." The sheriff placed a hand on Emory's
shoulder. "Now let's see if Lula Mae does."

Emory released Sophie, who led them to the front door
and barked at it. A short woman with grey shoulder-length hair

answered it. "Well, come in," she said to the dog before noticing her husband and son. "You're here!"

Emory greeted her with a big smile. "Hi Mom."

With a jaw-splitting smile, Lula Mae wrapped her arms around the middle of his torso. "You've grown."

Emory laughed. "No, I haven't."

Sheriff Rome walked past her through the door. "Lula Mae, I told you you're shrinking."

She gave him a playful slap on the back. "Nick, I am not." She clutched Emory's arm to escort him inside. "Dinner's almost ready."

Inside the house, Emory could smell the country-fried chicken and sweet potato cakes without even looking at the crackling cast-iron skillets on the stove. The aroma of Southern cooking, coupled with the warmth of a two-log fire on the living room hearth, created a gentle coziness. Almost two years had passed since Emory last stepped on the creaking hardwood floor, but every picture on the wood-paneled walls, every trinket on the cedar shelves and every piece of overstuffed furniture remained in place where he remembered it – as if the house itself were a fixed point in time and protected from its influence.

Once Lula Mae saw Emory in the kitchen's bright light, she grimaced at his appearance. "Ooh, you need to change those clothes. What is that?"

Emory looked down to see stains on everything he was wearing – some black and some crimson. "Oh my god." He realized the stains came from Rick Roberts' remains.

The sheriff told him, "Oh yeah, you need to get out of those. I didn't want to say anything, but you stink to High Heaven."

"You should've said something."

Lula Mae helped him out of his jacket. "I can wash them for you."

"No, they need to be dry-cleaned. Do you have a garbage bag I could put them in for now?"

"Of course." She handed him one from the pantry.

Emory excused himself and went to his former bedroom. He hung his shoulder holster on the bedpost and removed his clothes, placing them in the bag before tying it. He sniffed his shoulder and realized his skin stunk. After a hot shower, he returned to the room and put on tattered jeans and a high school T-shirt he found in his old chest-of-drawers before joining his parents in the kitchen.

The dinner of artery-clogging courses ended with the best banana pudding in all of East Tennessee. Afterwards, he offered to help clean, but Lula Mae shooed him out of the kitchen. His father retreated to the bathroom and wouldn't be seen again for half an hour, so Emory decided he'd take the opportunity for some fresh mountain air. He returned to his bedroom to throw on some old hiking boots and grab a denim jacket with faux-fur lining – and after a moment's hesitation, put his shoulder holster back on.

Exiting the back door, Emory walked through the snow to a section of the fence near the woods. He leaned his forearms against the top plank and soaked in the surrounding quietness. Listening to his gentle breaths, he looked for the darkness between the trees, where he had often found comfort when he was younger. Tonight, however, the thick Smoky Mountain mist grated through the trees, obstructing his view as it dispersed the moonlight.

Emory removed his phone from his pocket and began scrolling through the pictures he had taken since the beginning of the case. He checked the photos from Britt's murder scene, zooming in on some and giving others a passing glance. He flipped through those taken at Rick Roberts' house and stopped on one that was taken in the bedroom. Something about it bothered him, but he still didn't know why.

Emory heard a scrunching sound coming from the woods, like boots plodding through snow. He drew the pistol from his holster and crouched behind a fence post. He aimed it at the woods and scanned for any movement.

"Don't shoot," a voice said from behind him. He turned to see his dad walking toward him from the house. "I'm only armed with a pipe." He held up his half-bent billiard pipe for Emory to see and flashed him a grin.

Emory turned off the lights and reholstered his weapon. "I'm sorry, Dad. I thought I heard something in the woods."

"Just me." The sheriff took a box of matches from his pocket and lit the tobacco in the pipe as he walked. Once he reached Emory, he rested his forearms on top of the fence and pointed with the lip of the pipe. "The woods and the mist play tricks with sounds."

Emory mimicked his father's stance. "I guess you're right."

"I got a lantern in the house, if you want. You can go check and make sure nothing's there."

"You know I don't like the woods."

"I'm just kidding you. You about ready for bed?"

"I'm not much of a sleeper."

"Oh yeah." The sheriff sucked on the smoldering tobacco. "You were always the last one to bed and the first to rise. So what are you doing out here?"

"Just going over the case in my head."

The sheriff laughed. "You can't turn that head of yours off, can you? Even as a teenager, you were always carrying the weight of the world on your shoulders."

Emory tilted his head. "I definitely hear something. You don't hear that?"

A faint scream canoed its way over the mist. "I do now." The sheriff listened a few seconds more and nodded. "Yeah, that's the Pentecostal church. In the woods over there." He pointed with his pipe.

"It sounds like someone dying."

The sheriff exhaled a breath of smoke that swirled into the mist and drowned in its tiny droplets. "They're speaking in tongues. Sparked quite a stir about a year ago when the church popped up. People here didn't want snake handlers in their backyard. I imagine that's why they chose a property in the woods, away from prying eyes."

"Church on a Thursday?"

"I heard they go just about every night." The sheriff laughed. "Aren't you glad we're Church of Christ?"

Emory smiled and looked down, seeking to avoid a discussion on his religious evolution.

Sheriff Rome didn't seem to notice. "Speaking of that, your ma was wondering if you were planning to stick around over the weekend and maybe go to church with us on Sunday."

Emory's mind flashed back to the Church of Christ congregation they attended when he was a teenager. It had always seemed like a place of punishment and not a place one attends free of choice. He shook his head.

"I know. You have work to do, even on Sunday."

Taking a deep whiff of the smoke, Emory smiled. "I always liked the smell of your pipe."

The sheriff glared at his son. "Don't you even think about starting."

"I'm not."

"Well good. By the way, I wanted to thank you for this. Having you here tonight makes us realize even more how much we miss seeing you."

"It's not like we don't Skype."

"Once a month, maybe. If that. It's no substitute for seeing you in the flesh."

Emory fell silent as he looked to the ground. He listened to his father puff the pipe a couple of times before speaking again. "This town holds such bad memories for me."

The sheriff put a hand on his shoulder. "I know."

"When I'm here…All I can think about is everything that happened. Granny. The woods. My father. Eight years ago, you saved my life. Then you brought me into your home."

Sheriff Rome dropped his hand. "You know we've always thought of you as ours – blood or not."

Emory nodded. "I know."

"What?" Once several silent seconds had passed, the sheriff asked with more force, "What is it?"

Emory couldn't look at him. "I would never want you to regret that decision."

"What would ever give you a thought like that? I know God wanted me to find you, and now you're doing what he meant for you to do. You're helping good people and bringing bad ones to justice. How could we not be proud of you?"

Emory wanted to say more, but fear tightened his lips.

CHAPTER 13

J EFF STOOD IN front of the microwave in his apartment above the detective agency, waiting for the bowl of split-pea soup to finish heating. He felt his bobcat rubbing against his calves. "Be patient. Yours is coming." He stepped back to listen for the sound of running water in the bathroom. "It's probably full enough."

Jeff retrieved a plastic pitcher and a large net from a shelf beside an eighty-gallon aquarium with several five-pound catfish swimming inside. Dunking the net into the water, he caught one, transferred it into the pitcher and rushed to the bathroom with the cat hot on his heels. Once inside, he turned off the faucet and dumped the fish into the half-filled bathtub.

Bobbie leapt into the tub and swatted the water to catch her dinner. Within thirty seconds, she had the wriggling fish in her mouth. The bobcat jumped from the tub, and after a quick shake to eject water from her fur, she settled onto the bathroom floor to eat.

The microwave alarm chimed, but as Jeff walked by the kitchen window, something else caught his attention. He looked down at the street, which was lit with antique street lamps and muted light from the closed shops that lined the block. Parked across the street was a blue sedan, and leaning against it was a man with crossed arms who appeared to be staring at him. The man was wearing a white ski mask with a horrible red smile stitched into it. "Weird."

Jeff found his camera in his messenger bag, but when he returned to the window, the man also had a camera with a large zoom lens aimed right at him. Jeff dropped it onto the counter and ran to the door.

When the man saw him exit the agency's front door, he jumped into his car and sped away.

Jeff locked the office and ran to his car. The tires spun on the pavement as he slammed his sports car into gear. He could see the blue car's tail lights turning left up ahead. He raced to the corner and banked it with the tires skidding. One hundred yards in front of him, the blue car was now stopped on the road.

"What the hell is he doing? Is he waiting for me to catch up to him?"

Jeff was about to slow down when the blue car took off again. He again floored the accelerator to try getting close enough to at least read the license plate.

POP! POP! POP! POP! he heard in rapid succession, followed by scraping metal. The terrible screeching noise made his left shoulder shrug up to his ear.

The front of his car locked, and the back end swung forward, sending the car into a shrill spin. When it came to rest, Jeff was facing the direction from which he had come.

He jumped out of the car to examine the shredded remains of his tires and the contorted metal wheels that held them. Walking back to where he encountered the problem, he found tatters of the tires with a couple of amateur spike strips made of long nails driven through pipes.

"Bastard!"

CHAPTER 14

THE NEXT MORNING, Emory awoke to the staccato purr of Sophie's snoring. He peered over his chest to see that the French bulldog had curled up under his left arm sometime during his four-hour sleep. He petted her gently, and her eyes popped open, although her body refused to move. "You ready to get up?" The dog looked up at him as if trying to understand. "Come on, let's get up." He rolled out of bed, leaving Sophie to stretch before jumping to the floor.

Sophie ran ahead as he emerged from the bedroom, and he followed her to the back door. Letting the dog out to take care of her business, Emory shivered as the morning air hit his warm face. It was still dark outside, but at any moment the sun's rays would start piercing the darkness from over the mountains.

Decked out in her park ranger uniform, Lula Mae walked up behind him. "Good morning."

"Good morning."

"Did you sleep okay?"

Emory lied. "Great."

"There's cereal in the pantry. Will I see you when I get back?"

Emory shook his head. "My partner's picking me up soon, and we'll be heading back to Knoxville tonight."

His words swept the sweet smile from Lula Mae's face. "Aren't you still working on your case?"

"Yes, but the investigation involves some office work too."

"Well, if you don't feel like driving back one night or just need a place to get away."

"I know." Emory gave her a hug.

She kissed his cheek. "Take care of yourself." She opened the door, allowing Sophie to scurry back inside, and left for her post in the Great Smoky Mountains National Park.

Heading back to the bedroom, Emory passed his father, who was dressed in his uniform. "Son, I'm heading to work. You about ready to go?"

Emory looked down at the clothes he had worn to bed and laughed. "No, but that's okay. I don't need a ride. Wayne will be here soon."

"Well, come by if you need anything, and keep me up to speed on how the case is going." When Emory said he would, the sheriff left.

After showering, Emory rummaged through his old bedroom's closet and drawers to find some fresh clothes that he thought would be least embarrassing to wear for work. Since he never owned a suit or tie before joining the TBI, he had to settle for a dark-blue flannel shirt and a pair of khakis.

He grabbed the denim jacket he had worn the night before and the garbage bag with his dirty clothes, and he waited in the living room for Wayne to arrive. As soon as he sat on the couch, the French bulldog jumped onto his lap. He asked her, "So what do you think, Sophie? Is it possible that the murders of Britt and Rick are not related?" He paused for a response and received a lick on the chin. "I agree. It would be too much of a coincidence. But what was gained by killing them both?"

The sound of his phone ringing inside his pocket interrupted his one-sided conversation. He scooted Sophie off his lap so he could reach it. Seeing the caller was Wayne, he skipped "Hello" to ask, "Are you having a problem finding the place?"

"I'm still in Knoxville," Wayne answered, prompting slumped shoulders from Emory.

"Why are you there?"

"I'm going to meet the medical examiner about Rick Roberts." Emory clutched the hair at the back of his head. "I'd like to be part of that."

"No problem. I'll conference you in."

"What time do you think you'll be here?"

Wayne hesitated so long, Emory thought the call had dropped. "I'm not going to be able to come today."

"What? Why not?"

"I forgot I have to be in court this afternoon."

Emory popped off the couch. "You can't leave me here!"

"It's just one more night. Enjoy the time with your family, for Christ's sake. It's just one day. I'll be down in the morning." Wayne paused again. "Wait, tomorrow's Saturday."

"I don't care what day it is."

"If you're that desperate to leave, can't you just borrow your dad's car?"

"No."

"Besides, staying here will also give me a chance to interview Rick Roberts' ex-wife. She lives in Knoxville now."

"What am I supposed to do today?"

"Work the case with your dad. Look, I gotta go. I'll call you from the ME's."

Emory shoved his phone back into his pocket and looked at Sophie. "Don't ever let anyone else drive your car."

He heard someone pulling into the driveway. From the front window, he saw Scot Trousdale, Victor Algarotti's assistant, getting out of a white compact. Emory rushed to the front door to answer it before he had a chance to knock. "Scot, what are you doing here?"

Scot greeted him with a smile. "Agent Emory. You said if I thought of anything."

Emory tried to hide his annoyance. "I was expecting a call. How did you know where my parents live?"

"It's a small town. People here are only too willing to share information, as long as it's not about themselves."

Emory could tell he wanted an invitation inside, but he wasn't about to let any potential suspect in a case enter his home, or his former home. "Why aren't you at work?"

"Victor closed shop today for the funeral."

"You're not attending?"

Scot pushed his glasses up the bridge of his nose. "I sent flowers."

"What did you want to tell me?"

"Is it true that Victor is offering a reward for finding Britt's killer?"

"He mentioned it."

"If I give you information that is helpful—"

"You'd have to discuss that with Victor."

"I came to you because I'd trust you over Pristine's friend to cut me in."

"I can't accept any reward…" Emory stopped when he caught the important part of Scot's last statement. "Who's Pristine's friend?"

"That investigator, Jeff Woodard. When Victor said he wanted me to hire one, she's the one who told me to call him. I got the impression they're friends."

Jeff is friends with Victor Algarotti's wife?! Emory's eyebrows jumped, before he forced them back into place to try concealing his surprise. "What's the information you wanted to share?"

"Have you checked out Britt's ex-boyfriend?"

"We're checking out everybody."

"Were you aware that he threatened Victor with a knife the day before Britt died?"

No longer annoyed at the unexpected visit, Emory stepped out of the doorway toward Scot. After all, the man had surprised him with not one but two important pieces of information. "No, I wasn't."

Scot acted like he was sharing a juicy piece of gossip as he related the story. "Dan showed up at the factory ranting about how Victor had ruined his life. I tried to stop him, but he got past me and confronted Victor in his office. By the time I got there, I saw Dan brandishing a knife and blaming him for Britt breaking up with him. I don't know if you know this, but Victor was a boxer in the Navy. He grabbed Dan's wrist – the one with the knife – and knocked him down with one punch." Scot laughed. "It was pretty sweet."

That explains the black eye. Scot was about to say more when the special agent's phone rang. He saw that it was Wayne placing a video call. "I have to take this. If you think of anything else, give me a call."

"Oh, I will."

"And Scot. Thank you for the information."

Scot grinned and walked away.

Emory went back inside and closed the door behind him before he answered the phone. "Hi Wayne." He looked out the window to make sure Scot was leaving. He was.

"I'm here with Cathy now." Wayne held his phone so that Cathy Shaw appeared onscreen.

A blonde woman with a sweet but vulpine face waved. "Hi Emory!"

Emory waved back as he walked to the kitchen to place the phone on the table and take a seat. "Hi Cathy. How are you doing?"

"I'd be better if you two would stop sending me all this work."

Emory told her, "We hope to make that one the last."

Wayne stationed his phone on a counter so Emory could see

Rick's charred remains sprawled out on one table and the dead German shepherd on another.

Cathy began her report. "Okay guys, as much as I wanted it to be true, the cause of death was not spontaneous human combustion." She held up a vial that was one-quarter filled with a blackish granular substance. "Here's your culprit. Potassium permanganate." She handed it to Wayne for a closer look. "Potassium permanganate reacts exothermically with hydrochloric acid, which is a primary component of stomach acid."

"Exothermically?" Wayne asked, handing the vial back to her.

"Gives off heat. With the large amount he ingested, enough heat to ignite the surrounding tissue. After it started, the body fat kept it going."

Wayne grunted. "Is this potassium whatever available to anyone?"

"Easily ordered online."

Emory asked, "Cathy, do you know how it was administered?"

"I analyzed everything I received." She paused for effect. "It was in the tea." She pulled a glass of brownish liquid from a refrigerator. "Here's a glass of sweet tea I brought from home." She placed it on the counter and emptied the vial of potassium permanganate into it. As she stirred, the tea took on a purple hue.

Emory asked, "Wouldn't he have tasted something in his drink?"

Cathy shook her head. "It has a sweet taste, so his tea might've been a little sweeter."

"So someone came over and dropped this shit in his tea?" Wayne asked before eyeballing Emory on the phone. "Didn't you say that PI was there before you? He could've easily spiked Rick's tea."

"I don't believe that," Emory responded – although the news Scot delivered earlier gave him a moment's pause.

"Why not? You just met the guy. You don't know him or what he's capable of."

"I was there when Rick started to light up, and I saw Jeff's reaction. He was as surprised as I was." Emory turned his attention back to the ME. "Cathy, the tea Rick drank wasn't purple."

Cathy grinned and punctuated the air with her index finger up. "I was wondering if someone was going to ask me about that. I also found tartrazine in the tea."

"What's that?" Emory asked.

"Yellow food coloring." Cathy produced a small bottle of the liquid from her lab coat pocket. She dripped some into the purple water and stirred, and the color changed back to a light brown.

"Well, look at that," said Wayne with the lilt of wonderment to his voice.

Emory pushed his back against the chair. "This took some planning. What about the dog?"

Cathy nodded and walked over to the dog's body. "The bullet that killed him came from a .32 caliber revolver."

Wayne bemoaned, "Why is it never a rare gun?"

"Unfortunately, he wasn't able to get a bite in before he was shot. There was nothing in his teeth."

"I don't get it," said Wayne. "The killer had a gun. Why not just shoot Rick? Why go to all this trouble? It doesn't make sense."

Emory proposed, "Maybe the killer just didn't want to be there when it happened."

Cathy chimed in with, "Unless the method of execution is significant."

Wayne muttered, "Fire."

"Something to consider," said Emory. "Anything else for us, Cathy?"

Cathy opened her arms. "Isn't that enough?"

"Thanks Cathy." Wayne moved his face closer to the phone so that all Emory could see were his eyes and the deep crow's feet channeling from them. "I'll talk to you later."

Emory stared at his blank phone for a moment before deciding to dial another number.

From the passenger seat of Virginia's car, Jeff answered his ringing phone. "Emory? Did I butt-dial you?"

Emory responded, "No, I called you."

"First time for everything. What's up?"

Emory pondered his words before answering, "I heard something disturbing this morning."

"Hang on. I'm putting you on speakerphone so Virginia can hear."

"Hi Emory," Virginia said with a wave, even though he couldn't see it.

"Hi Virginia." Emory was going to ask about Jeff's friendship with Pristine Algarotti, but he didn't want to do so with anyone else listening, so he came up with another reason for the call. "Jeff, are you coming to Barter Ridge today?"

"We're almost there now. Virginia had to drive me because I had a little accident with my car last night."

"What happened?"

"I'll fill you in later. What did you want to tell me?"

"I stayed at my parents' house last night. Wayne took my car back to Knoxville, and he's not going to be able to pick me up today."

Jeff laughed. "Well, that is disturbing, I guess. What's the address? We'll come get you."

CHAPTER 15

EMORY ANSWERED THE door to find Jeff and Virginia on his parents' doorstep. "Hi guys."

Jeff smirked when he saw Emory's outdated, lumberjack apparel. "Are we chopping wood today?"

"I didn't bring any clean clothes with me," Emory explained. "Hang on. Let me just grab my stuff."

As Emory was about to shut the door, Jeff put a hand up to block it. "Hold on, Paul Bunyan. I have to go to the bathroom."

Emory hesitated while he debated denying him entry. He felt their situation had already gotten too personal, but he couldn't think of a reasonable excuse to keep him from the bathroom. "Fine. Come in."

Jeff and Virginia entered, and their eyes wasted little time soaking everything in. "Nice place," said Virginia. "Cozy."

Emory looked to Jeff, awaiting a smart remark, but all he said was, "Bathroom."

"Oh." Emory pointed to a hallway at the other end of the living room. "On your right."

After Jeff left them alone, Virginia said, "This is quite a little town you have here."

Emory told her, "It's not mine anymore."

"Pretty, but I can't imagine what it must've been like for you growing up here."

"What do you mean?"

She ran her fingers across the afghan thrown over the back of the couch. "Small towns have their charms, but the warm smiles and open arms too easily turn to snarls and closed fists for those who don't fit in."

"Okay," Emory said as if he didn't get her meaning, although he knew where she was heading.

She held up her right hand toward him and caressed the air as if she were tracing the outline of his face. "Your facial structure. The high cheekbones and your eyes and hair. You're Native-American – half, I'd imagine. Given the area you grew up in, I'd guess Cherokee."

Emory's shoulders relaxed when he realized he had been wrong about where she was going. "My birth mother's side. You're very perceptive. I've always been pale – a trait from my father – so most people don't pick up on it. But you're wrong about Barter Ridge. Even if they did know about that, I doubt I would've had any problems related to it. I don't think small towns are really like that anymore."

Virginia shrugged. "What do I know. I'm originally from Atlanta."

Her dismissiveness gave Emory the distinct feeling that she was keeping him occupied as a distraction. He glanced toward the hallway. "I wonder what's keeping Jeff."

Virginia whispered, "I think he had to go number two."

Emory wasn't buying it. He stepped into the hallway and noticed the bathroom door wasn't closed. He eyed Virginia from beneath a furrowed brow and went to investigate. He found Jeff inside his old bedroom, sitting on the bed and playing with Sophie. "What are you doing?"

Jeff flashed him a guilt-free smile. "You think I was going

to pass up an opportunity to see where you were reared?" He stood and looked around the room. "Key points of information about who you are as an adult can be revealed from a visit to your childhood bedroom. From this room, I can see why you're so high-strung."

"What do you mean?" Emory scanned the room for how he would reach such a conclusion. "I'm not high-strung."

"Okay, Stradivarius, why is there no fun in this room? Where are the toys? Where are the posters of your celebrity crushes?"

"I didn't have any. Now can we go?"

Jeff gave Sophie a final pat on the butt before heading to the door. On their way out, Emory grabbed the denim jacket and the trash bag of dirty clothes from the living room, prompting a laugh from Jeff. He nodded to the jacket, along with the clothes Emory was wearing. "So did you fancy yourself a cowboy when you were younger?"

"They were Christmas presents. I didn't pick them out." Emory shooed them out of the house.

The three investigators piled into Virginia's car – she in the driver seat, Jeff in the passenger seat and Emory centered in back. As she was about to start the car, she asked, "Guys, where are we going?"

"Good question." Jeff looked at Emory through the rear-view mirror.

Emory replied, "Knoxville. I need to get my car."

Jeff laughed. "We're not going back to Knoxville right now. We just got here." He pointed to Virginia and himself. "We're going to investigate this case. You're welcome to join us."

Emory shook his head. "I can't work with civilians on a murder case."

"Then get out," Jeff told him. "We'll come back for you when we're done."

Grabbing the door handle, Emory hesitated. He couldn't let

this cocky PI get a full day's worth of investigation ahead of him. Besides, he needed more information about his relationship with Pristine. "Fine. I'll go with you, but I'll conduct my investigation separately."

Jeff rolled his eyes. "Whatever. We need a place to start. Do you have an explanation yet for Rick Roberts?"

Emory responded, "I can't comment on that."

Jeff whirled around to face the stubborn man in the back seat. "Seriously? I know you can't claim the reward, but we can. I promised to stay out of your way. The least you could do is be a little more Wiki with the information so we don't all spend the day spinning our wheels."

As Jeff stared at him, Emory became transfixed by his crystal green eyes, and his fortitude quaked. *Why does he have to be so beautiful?* Emory's lips cracked apart to say, "Potassium permanganate."

Jeff looked at Virginia, who wasted no time pulling her phone from her purse and researching the chemical compound.

Since the cat was out of the bag, Emory decided to tell them what he knew. "It was delivered through his tea, and it reacted with the stomach acid to cause the fire."

Virginia found some information online, which she started reading aloud. "Potassium permanganate is commonly used to wash carbon dioxide, which is used to make—"

All three finished the sentence, "Mineral water."

Jeff slapped the dashboard. "To the water factory."

"No, we can't go now," Emory told them. "It's closed today for Britt's funeral."

"Even better! We'll have free reign." He gave a nod to Virginia. "Let's go."

Emory grabbed his shoulder. "We're not going to break in."

"I don't know about you, but I'd rather go when Victor's not looking over my shoulder. I know he's the client, but I haven't ruled him out as a suspect."

Virginia took her hands off the gear shift with it still in the park position. "Guys, figure it out. I don't want to sit here all day listening to you bicker."

Emory insisted, "It's illegal."

"You're an investigator. Logic trumps legal. We have a murder weapon that probably came from that building, and if it did, whoever wielded that weapon more than likely works there. Maybe there's something in that factory that would connect the murder weapon with the murderer. If so, we could catch him today before he has a chance to strike again. Isn't that a good enough reason to work around the law just a smidge?"

Emory countered, "It's not a smidge. It's utterly and completely breaking the law."

"Emory, do you want to solve the case or not? Virginia and I are going today, so if you don't want to be part of that, I suggest you get out of the car now."

"I just can't." Emory again grabbed the door handle, but this time, he opened the door and put one foot out.

"Wait!" Jeff jumped out of the car and blocked him from getting out. "I have an idea. How about this: When we get there, you hang out in the car with Virginia for a minute without looking at the building. After a couple of minutes, get out and go try the front door, which I'll have unlocked by then. When it opens, you just assume that someone forgot to lock it, or you claim you didn't know the place was closed today."

Emory shook his head. "That's ridiculous."

"You've been there. They don't keep the front door locked during the day. You'll have plausible deniability, and Virginia and I will corroborate it."

Emory brought his foot back inside and closed the door without saying anything. "Just drop me off at the sheriff's station."

"Fine, but the factory's on the way, so we're going there first." Jeff returned to his seat, giving Virginia the go-ahead to drive.

While Jeff and Virginia discussed the details of their planned break-in, Emory thought about the information Scot had given him. *If Jeff really is friends with Pristine, they might've cooked up this scheme to get Britt's money. He could be sabotaging the investigation at every turn. Is that why he's sticking close to me? Is he setting me up?*

Emory brought up another reason the break-in was a bad idea. "What about video surveillance? Are you going to bypass that somehow?"

"What kind of detective are you?" asked Jeff. "Didn't you notice there were no video cameras anywhere? At least there weren't from the lobby to Victor's office."

Emory corrected him, "I'm a special agent."

"Well, special agent, in my line of work, we notice details like that."

"So do thieves." Emory turned his eyes to the window to keep from looking at Jeff in the rearview mirror. He saw a pink laptop on the seat beside him and realized it looked familiar. He held it up for Jeff to see. "Is this Britt's laptop?"

Jeff took a breath. "Yes."

"I thought you were going to return it."

"I am. I just haven't had a chance."

"Now my finger prints are on it." Emory put it back on the seat and began wiping it with his sleeve. "I can't believe I'm sitting in a car next to stolen evidence."

"Oh my god!" Jeff yelled. "Look, would returning it now get you off my back?"

"You can't return it now. The funeral—"

"Virginia, what time is the funeral?"

"Two this afternoon."

"Good. They're probably still at the house, and it's on the way to the water factory." Jeff looked at Emory through the rearview mirror. "Problem solved."

"How is the problem solved? We can't go to the house on the day they're burying a family member."

"We won't. I'll text Ian now and ask him to ride his bike down to the road so I can give it to him. Victor will never know."

Jeff texted Ian, who responded right away that he would meet them. Once they neared the driveway, Ian was indeed there on his bike waiting for them. Without looking around, Jeff told Emory, "If you don't want anyone else to know that you're aware Britt's laptop was in our possession, you better duck down now." Emory complied. When the car stopped, Jeff exited with the laptop and closed the door.

"What's going on?" Emory asked.

Virginia covered her mouth with her hand. "Jeff just handed him back the laptop, and now they're talking about something."

"About what?"

"I'm not a lip-reader."

A moment later, Jeff returned to the car and shuddered. "I hate to say this, but that kid has a real Damien Thorn vibe going on."

Still crouched behind the seat, Emory asked, "What do you mean?"

"He asked all about how Rick Roberts died, and he wanted details – vivid details, like he was into it or something."

Virginia drove back onto the road. "Boys are like that, aren't they? It's all the torture porn movies and zombie shows. Nothing's gruesome anymore."

"Well, he creeped my shit."

Emory arose from the back seat. "You think he's a suspect?"

"Oh come on." Virginia chuckled. "He's a little kid."

"You know I don't cross anyone off my suspect list until I have undeniable proof of their innocence." Jeff pointed to the back seat with his thumb. "Not even Mr. TBI Special Agent back there."

"Me?" Emory asked. "Why am I a suspect?"

"You weren't until I found out you're from this town. For all

I know, you knew the victims and had some kind of vendetta against them."

"Fair enough," Emory conceded.

Virginia asked, "But why would Ian want to kill his sister?"

Jeff answered, "Planning ahead. With her out of the way, he'll have everything when he turns eighteen instead of just half the family fortune."

"I can't argue with that." Emory gave him a quick pat on the shoulder. "I almost forgot, you said you were in an accident last night?"

"Oh yeah. I caught some guy watching the office last night, and I chased him in my car. By the time I caught up with him, he had put spike strips on the road. Now my car's in the shop."

"Do you think it was related to the case?"

"A case, maybe. We have other ongoing investigations, so who knows."

A moment later, the factory was in sight. Jeff asked Virginia to pull off the road and into the woods, where the car couldn't be seen. Once parked, he looked over his shoulder at Emory. "Are you sure you don't want to come?"

"I'm sure."

"Fine." Jeff patted the messenger bag at his side, exited the car and ran through the woods toward the factory.

After several moments spent in silence, Emory began fidgeting in his seat.

Hearing the persistent squeak of his pants against the vinyl, Virginia told him, "Don't worry. Jeff is very resourceful."

The comment gave Emory an idea. "Pristine Algarotti said something similar about him."

"She did? That's odd."

Emory doubled down. "It didn't strike me that way. They are friends."

Virginia raised an eyebrow at his reflection in the mirror and opened her mouth, but what he heard was a double ping. She checked her phone. "I just got an SOS text from Jeff!"

Emory's phone vibrated in his pocket. "I got it too. What does it mean?"

"It means he's in trouble."

"I figured that, but what kind of trouble? Why doesn't he elaborate?" His eyes returned to the woods, squinting to see the factory through the trees.

"Maybe he can't." Virginia unbuckled her seatbelt. "I have to help him."

"Wait!" Emory paused for a second and sighed. "I'll go."

CHAPTER 16

EMORY STEPPED OUT of Virginia's car and made his way through the short stretch of woods that separated him from the factory. When he had the front door in sight, a semi-truck with the Algarotti company logo on the side chugged up the driveway. He had an idea.

The special agent ran up to the back of the truck's trailer, grabbed one of the door handles and jumped onto the under-ride guard. He rode it to the shipping and receiving area at the back of the factory, jumping off just before the truck reached its destination.

The driver backed the truck into an alcove that led to the loading dock, so that the door to his trailer abutted the rollup door to the dock. Emory peeked around the corner of the alcove and was surprised to see the rollup door open and two employees inside, standing on the dock. *It's supposed to be closed.* The driver jumped out of the cab, holding a drink in a paper cup and a bag from a fast-food restaurant. As the driver walked toward the dock, Emory ran to the cab and dove underneath, crawling under the truck until he was near the back of the trailer. He heard one of the employees greet the driver as Eli. Emory peered out from under the truck to see the two of them shaking hands just before they walked deeper into the shipping and receiving area. He saw the third man getting behind the wheel of a forklift, which was facing away from the truck and near some stacked palettes of water.

Emory rolled out from under the truck and snuck into the building while the forklift driver picked up a palette from the top of a stack and loaded it into the trailer of the truck. Using the palettes and some boxes for cover, he made his way through the shipping and receiving area, and passed through double swing doors into a hallway.

With his next step he heard a rasping like duct tape being ripped off linoleum. Holding his left leg up for a moment, he turned around to see if the sound attracted anyone else's attention before inspecting the floor where his shoe had been. *Tire tracks, I guess from the forklift. It must've run over something sticky.* Emory noticed that his right shoe was also on the tracks. *Crap!* Clutching his fists and gritting his teeth, he inched his heel up trying to minimize the sound, but it just prolonged it. After another glance over his shoulder he proceeded forward, being careful to avoid the tracks.

The hallway had a door on either side, and at the other end, it turned left into what Emory assumed was another hallway. The first door had a small sign designating it as a broom closet, but the second wider door had no such identifier. *I wonder what's in there.* He tried the doorknob to find it locked, but before he could remove his hand, a voice startled him.

"Who the hell are you?"

Emory looked in the direction from which he had just come and saw the man who had been talking to the truck driver. He had a patch that read, "Foreman," on his jacket and a none-too-pleasant face glaring at him.

"I'm…" Emory struggled to come up with an excuse to explain his presence, "with the truck that just came in."

Holding a brown bag, the foreman didn't look as if he believed him. "You riding with Floyd?"

He's trying to trip me up. "No. Eli." As soon as he said the right name, he noticed a marked change for the better in the foreman's expression, but it did little to assuage his nervousness, which prompted him to embellish. "I'm learning to be a driver." He kept going. "I'm Eli's son."

The foreman smiled at him and stepped closer. "You Terry?" When Emory said that he was, the foreman shook his hand. "You're taller than I imagined you'd be."

Emory returned his smile. "I take after my mother." He decided to risk a question, so he nodded toward the room. "Why's this room locked?"

"M' guess is the owner don't want people going in there. Why you want to go in there?"

The special agent gave him the first answer he could think of. "I have to pee."

The foreman laughed. "Wrong hallway." He pointed toward the receiving area and put a hand on Emory's shoulder. "Bathroom's this way. I'll walk you there."

"You don't have to do that."

"It's no problem." The man held up the brown bag. "I was fixing to head there to wash m' hands anyways."

Emory kept cool and decided he would try to find out why the foreman was there when the place was supposed to be closed. "Where is everyone?"

"Boss' daughter died. He closed shop for the funeral." Noticing that his shoes were squeaking, the foreman looked at the tracks on the floor and muttered, "One of these idiots must've spilled that damn flavored water somewhere. Tracked up the whole damn floor."

"Why are you here?"

The foreman pushed the double swing doors, and they were back in the receiving area. "Didn't your daddy tell you about the robberies?" When Emory shook his head, the foreman pointed to the stacked palettes of water that the forklift driver was loading into the truck. "When a shipment's ready to be loaded, we stack 'em over there. But with traffic and icy roads and all, we can't always rely on trucks getting here when they s'posed to, so when we close up in the evening, sometimes the palettes are just sitting there overnight waiting to be loaded. About two months ago, we started having some palettes go missing at night."

Emory clenched his right cheek. *That's burglary, not robbery.*

"Thought we caught who was doing it – an employee – but yesterd'y morning, another palette went missing. If you ask me, the guy we fired stole that one too just to make himself look innocent so he could get his job back. I ain't buying it, though." The foreman pointed to the light green walls. "This whole back area was redone about three months ago, and they still haven't installed the video cameras I asked for."

"Why not?" Emory followed the foreman into a long hallway that smelled like new carpet.

"They tell me they backordered. Anyways, after yesterd'y, I figured me or one of my men got to be here 24/7 in case he comes back for more. I been asking for a while, and now Victor finally approved the budget for a secur'ty guard, so I'm working on hiring someone now."

When he finished speaking, they had walked halfway down the hall and entered the bathroom. Emory forced himself to pee, as the man washed his hands. "After you shake it off, I'll take you to see your dad."

Shit! Emory zipped up his pants and washed his hands. "Do you think you could give me a tour of the factory? I've always been curious about the process for bottling water."

"I should be getting back…" Drying his hands, the foreman paused before acquiescing. "Sure, I s'pose I can give you a quickie."

Once they exited the bathroom, the foreman led him down a different hall to a large metal door. On the other side was an enormous factory room, where all the conveyors and other machinery lay dormant. The foreman stretched out his arms as if he were awaiting a hug. "This is it."

Without a note of insincerity, Emory exclaimed, "This is spectacular. I didn't expect it to be so huge."

The foreman beamed with the pride of a champion thoroughbred's jockey. "Yeah, she's something. Should see her in action." He walked to two U-shaped pipes, about a dinner plate in diameter, with both ends in the ground. "Did you spot the natural spring out back when you was driving up?" Emory said that he had. "It's called Yonder Springs. It's where we get our water to bottle. Now we don't take none from that water you see above ground. We use borehole extraction to pipe the water from the source, underground. That's what these here two pipes are for. He touched one of three curvatures in the wall, which Emory figured were part of the silos that were attached to the building and visible from the main road. "Water is pumped into this filtration system to get out all them impurities." When Emory nodded, the foreman kept walking and talking. "Now we're regulated by the FDA. We follow the IBWA's strict Codes of Practice. That means our water is held to a real high standard for quality." They reached a pipe attached to a box that reminded Emory of the fluorescent lights in the ceiling of the TBI office. "After the water's filtered, it goes through this here ultraviolet system and something called an ozonator to get rid of bacteria. Then it's on to bottling. From the ground to the bottle, our water never touches the open air."

"That's amazing." Emory hesitated before asking a question concerning the only piece of information he wanted to know. "Do you use potassium permanganate?"

The foreman gave him a confused smile. "That's the first time I gotten that question on a tour." He pointed to the silo walls. "We use it in the filtration system." He clapped his hands together. "That's all the tour I got time for. I can show you the bottling process another time. Why don't we head on down to the break room to eat with your daddy."

As the foreman led him out of the factory area and into the hall, Emory tried to think of an excuse to get out of going to the break room. Any excuse. "Thank you for the tour. I really appreciate it. I actually need to head back to the bathroom."

The foreman grimaced at him. "Again?"

Emory could taste the sweat dripping from his forehead to the curl of his fake smile. "Seeing all that water."

"But we didn't even see any water."

"Well, we talked about it a lot."

The foreman plopped the knuckles of his left hand onto his waist. "Just meet us down there then, I guess. You remember where the bathroom is?"

"I do."

As Emory hurried down the hall, he could hear the foreman mutter, "Granny bladder."

Emory's breathing shallowed, and he could feel his heartbeat in his neck. He knew that the two men would be looking for him as soon as Eli heard his "son" was here.

Where the hell is Jeff? He checked every door he came to but didn't see the PI in any of the rooms. He stopped when he heard voices coming from the other end of the hallway. *It's them!*

Emory detoured down a short hallway on his right and then down another. He found himself turned around and had no idea where he was headed, but he kept going. He raced down the hallway so he could get out of sight. To his left he saw a sign on a door that read, "Break Room." *Crap! Is that the break room the foreman was talking about? What if the voices aren't them and they're still inside?* He opted to take a chance. He opened the door, and no one was there. Emory threw himself inside.

The voices grew louder. He slipped between two vending

machines and hid. Would they enter the break room or think it's the last place he would hide?

His heart thumped against his ribcage like an encaged rabid animal. His breaths turned to gasps. *No! Not now!*

His fingers fumbled for the pill bottle inside his jacket pocket. *I can control this. Just relax. Relax.* His breathing calmed, but not for long.

They were there – on the other side of the door!

The pills clinked against the bottle. *Shit!* He wrapped a hand around the plastic to muffle it and let one pill slide down to the opening. He popped it in his mouth and waited for the inevitable. They would come in and find him. Victor would press charges, and he'd lose his job.

I shouldn't have come in here. I shouldn't have come.

CHAPTER 17

ONCE HE HAD arrived at the front entrance of the Algarotti factory, Jeff went to work on the stainless steel lock on the glass front door. From his messenger bag, he retrieved a home-fashioned L-shaped strip of copper and a custom-made pick with a tulipwood handle and aluminum blade. Thirteen seconds after working the lock, he turned the tumbler and opened the door. The lobby reminded him of a credit union office – white walls, grey carpet, fluorescent lights and clear plastic racks with printed collateral. After a quick snarl of his nose, he sprinted to the administrative offices.

He rummaged through Scot's desk drawers, finding nothing of interest until he reached the largest one. Instead of files, he found personal items – toothbrush, toothpaste, razor and a gi, a garment worn for mixed martial arts. *Explains the cauliflower ears.* Closing the drawer, Jeff grabbed a couple of sample bottles of water on top of the desk and stuffed them into his messenger bag. *For the road.*

He decided to check out Victor's office. Before he could head down the hall, however, he saw the door to that office opening.

Jeff bolted into the bathroom. *What the hell? No one's supposed to be here today.* He texted "SOS" to Virginia and Emory. He was about to text more when he heard someone at Scot's desk.

He inched the bathroom door open just enough to see who would be coming from Victor's office. It was Scot. Victor's assistant was now sitting at his desk, typing at the computer.

Great! No telling how long he's going to be there. How am I supposed to get out? He closed the door and texted Virginia and Emory again. "Scot's here. I'm stuck in bathroom near his desk. I could use a distraction."

As the minutes droned by, Jeff kept his ear to the door, waiting for an opportunity to escape. *What's taking them so long? I left the front door unlocked.*

At last, the keyboard tapping stopped. *Is he finally leaving?* Jeff cracked the door again.

Now turned away from the computer monitor, Scot touched his desk in several places as if he were killing ants. He opened the large desk drawer.

Damn! He must've realize someone went through his desk. Or, stupid me, that I took his water.

Scot's eyes darted around the room, and they landed on the bathroom door.

Jeff let the bathroom door close all the way. He stood against the wall, hoping he could hide behind the door when Scot opened it and sneak out while he was checking the stalls for the intruder.

He could hear Scot coming closer. He flattened himself against the wall as much as he could and held his breath. The handle to the bathroom door turned. The door cracked open.

CRASH!

A distant sound he couldn't decipher made Jeff jump. *What was that?*

The door closed once again.

Jeff released his breath in a quiet sigh as he realized Scot had left to investigate the source of the noise. He opened the door a crack, and saw no one around. He stepped out of the bathroom and sprinted to Victor's office.

Jeff walked past the small desk in the corner and glanced at the only thing on it – a photo of Victor and Ian smiling within a white frame. He continued to Victor's desk and rifled through the drawers. He discovered that one was locked. *No problem.* He opened it in one swift motion of his lock pick. "Well, look what we have here." He pulled his phone from his pocket and took a picture of the .32 caliber revolver inside the desk drawer.

As his thoughts flagellated him for his poor choices, Emory realized that he no longer heard voices. *Did they pass by? They must have.* He waited a moment longer before creeping from the break room in search of a way out. *I should've asked him where he planned to go once he was inside.*

He found his way to the lobby. From where he stood, there were three corridors, including the one that he had just walked through. He peeked down the other two – one leading to the administrative offices and one to ancillary offices – looking for any signs of Jeff.

Maybe he's trapped somewhere, hiding like I was. Emory pulled out his phone to see if Jeff had texted again. He had! Emory noticed the time the message was sent as he opened it. *I must've been on the truck. I didn't even feel it.*

The message read, "Scot's here. I'm stuck in bathroom near his desk. I could use a distraction."

Emory pocketed his phone and eyed a standalone display that held an assortment of company brochures. He kicked out one of its legs, and the plastic rack crashed to the ground, fanning brochures across the floor.

Emory ran out the front door and into the surrounding woods, hiding behind a thick pine tree. He peered to the side of the trunk to see if anyone followed him out. Two seconds later, he saw Scot exiting the building. Emory watched as Victor's assistant stood in place and pushed up his glasses to look around for a brief moment before returning inside.

Emory leaned his back against the tree to calm himself, but he yelped when he saw a man now standing in front of him. "Jeff! You startled the crap out of me."

"You came. Thanks for the distraction."

"You're…" Emory gasped. "…welcome." He grabbed at his heart, which was again banging against his ribcage.

"Are you okay?"

"I'm fine. Let's go. Emory's fingers dug into his pec, trying to keep his heart in its place.

Jeff could see the tremor in Emory's hands and the rapid rise of and fall of his chest. He placed his hands on the special agent's shoulders. "No, you're not. Are you having a panic attack?"

Emory nodded.

"Can't you hold it in until we get to the car?" When Emory growled at him, Jeff had his answer. "Forget I asked. Your pills!"

"Took…a pill. Has…hasn't…kicked in yet."

"All right. I've been reading about this. I need to calm you down." Jeff took a deep breath. "Okay. Here goes." He calmed his voice to a soothing tone. "Picture yourself at a beautiful beach on a remote island, gentle waves lapping at your heels as you lie on the white sand, mojito in hand." Jeff waited for a few seconds but heard no change in his breathing and still saw the trembling in his hands. "Okay, what's your happy place?" Emory couldn't answer, so he took a guess. "Imagine you're at a shooting range, having a grand old time blowing the heads off targets one after another. You can't miss. Now imagine your fears, anything that scares you or holds you back, have become the targets. Just like before, you can't miss. You're taking them out one by one until there are no more targets. All of your fears, every little thing that causes you stress, they're all gone. All that's left is the elation over what you've accomplished."

Jeff stopped talking. Emory was no longer gasping or clutching his chest. He grinned and squeezed Emory's shoulders. "It worked!"

"Yeah, it did." Emory smiled as his body relaxed. *Actually, I think my pill just kicked in.*

"I'm the Miracle Worker. You know, you should consider getting that medication in injections. That way, I could just shoot you with a dart gun the next time you have an attack."

Emory sneered at him. "I'll consider it."

"Are you okay to walk now?"

"I'm fine." Emory started back to the car with Jeff at his side. "Who told you this place would be empty today?"

"Scot. Did he see you?"

"Almost. Hey, did you know Victor has a door to the outside?"

"He does? I just remember seeing a closet door in his office."

"It's not a closet." Jeff took out his phone and showed him the photos he had taken. "Look what I found in Victor's desk."

"That's a .32 caliber. The same type of gun that was used to kill Rick's dog."

Jeff scowled at him. "Holding onto that bit of information, were you?"

Emory didn't respond.

"I thought we were partners."

Emory stopped and pointed at Jeff's chest, shy of touching it. "You're not my partner. I have a partner."

"And where is he?" Jeff looked around with his hands spread. "He's certainly not here helping you."

"Helping me what? Helping me by trying to talk me into breaking the law?"

"I hate to have to tell you this, but you did break the law."

"Technically, I didn't." Emory started walking again.

"What, because I picked the lock and you didn't? You know as well as I do that's a bogus argument."

"No. I entered through the back door, which was wide open."

Jeff grabbed Emory's arm. "Stop stealing from my playbook, and get that smug look off your face."

"I'm not smug. I'm just right." Emory jerked free and continued walking.

"You know, this whole helping-each-other-out thing was a big mistake!" Jeff hastened his stride to get ahead of Emory.

"Agreed!"

The PI hurled himself around and jabbed his finger into Emory's chest. "You think you're hot shit because you have a badge. We do the same thing, but you look down on me because I'm not employed by the government. Big deal! I'm you without the badge!"

"Why do you do it?" asked Emory.

"Do what?"

"Your job."

Jeff threw out his arms. "Why do you think?"

Emory explained, "I joined the bureau to help people – to be part of the greater good."

Jeff rolled his beautiful eyes. "You're such a saint."

"I'm not saying I'm a saint, but my reasons are at the very least bordering on altruistic. Yours are greed and, in this case, competitiveness."

"I'm done here." Jeff started walking again. "We'll take you into town, and you can rent a car or hitchhike or take a bus or whatever. I really don't care."

Emory followed a few steps behind Jeff as they plodded through the remaining woods to Virginia's car. The PI dropped and crouched behind a tree, motioning Emory to do the same. Emory complied and stayed low as he made his way forward to see what had alarmed him. Once he was behind Jeff, he could see a truck on the road just above where Virginia parked her car. Virginia was now standing outside her car talking to the foreman.

CHAPTER 18

VIRGINIA HANDED HER keys to the foreman, and he slipped behind the wheel of her car. He drove it toward the road and, as he did, she scanned the woods with frantic eyes.

Jeff whistled like a mockingbird and waved when Virginia looked his way. She put up her hand in a signal for them to stay put. She met the foreman at her car, now parked in front of his truck. He got out of her car and handed her the keys, and the two exchanged some pleasantries before he returned to his truck and drove away. Virginia slipped into her car and texted Jeff that the coast was clear.

Jeff dropped into the passenger seat. "What was that all about?"

Virginia waited for Emory to climb in and shut the back door. "That was the foreman at the water factory. He said he was looking for someone who had broken in, and he thought I might be an accomplice. I told him I had hit an icy patch and was too scared to try driving the car back onto the road."

Jeff put a hand on her shoulder. "Quick thinking."

"Thanks. So what did you two find out?"

Jeff filled her in on his experience in the factory, and when he was finished, Virginia asked, "Emory, did you find anything?"

The PI snorted and answered for him, "Oh, don't ask him. He's too altruistic to help us crime whores."

"Okay, what did I miss?" She looked in the rearview mirror, and Emory diverted his eyes. "Fine. Someone at least tell me where to go next."

Emory answered, "The sheriff's station."

Virginia was the only one to acknowledge Emory when he thanked them for the ride. As he walked toward the front door of the trailer, he noticed a truck parked beside the sheriff's in the tiny parking lot. It was the same truck the foreman at the water factory was driving when he stopped to help Virginia.

"Crap!"

Emory about-faced. He saw a coffee shop across the street and decided he'd wait there until the foreman left. With a pull on the glass-paned door, he smelled the sweet caramel of grinding coffee beans, and he took a deep whiff as if he expected his lungs to absorb the caffeine. Behind the counter, he noticed Britt Algarotti's best friend. "Tati. I didn't realize you worked here."

Tati stopped scooping coffee into the large paper filter long enough to offer a smileless greeting, "Hi Agent—"

"Rome."

Her eyes rolled up and down his plaid shirt and faux-fur-lined denim jacket. "I almost didn't recognize you." She topped off the filter and dropped it into the brew basket of one of the coffee makers. "What can I get for you?"

"Just a plain coffee." He looked at the clock on the wall behind her, which read half past noon. "Why aren't you at school?"

Tati placed a cup in the coffee dispenser and pushed the button. "I took the day off to go to Britt's funeral."

"Why aren't you there?"

Her eyes dashed toward the opening door and three new customers. "I'm leaving in fifteen minutes. I normally work in the afternoons, right after school, so I had to switch shifts today."

Emory nodded and handed her money for the coffee. "Are you doing okay?"

Tati snarled at him. "You sure are asking a lot of questions."

Emory brushed off her tone with a friendly laugh. "It is kind of my job."

"Well, you're keeping me from mine." She nodded to the newcomers, who were standing behind Emory, waiting to be served.

Emory looked behind him and back at her. "Sorry." He grabbed his coffee and sat at a small table by the window, facing the sheriff's station. He spent the time in between sips going over the case notes and pictures on his phone. When he was three-quarters done with his drink, he saw the foreman exit the building. *Finally!* Downing the rest of the coffee, he got up to leave but stopped after a hand touched the crook of his right arm.

"Agent Rome." Tati released her grip when he faced her. She was now wearing a white, quilted coat and on her way out.

"Tati, what is it?"

"I'm sorry about earlier. It's just a bad day. I didn't mean to take it out on you."

Emory smiled at her, appreciative of the apology. "That's okay. It's not a day you should be experiencing so young."

"Thanks for understanding." The pale skin surrounding her numerous freckles reddened. "I'll walk out with you."

Emory opened the door for her. Once outside, their icy breath intermingled as they said their goodbyes. Tati walked down the street to her car, while Emory stepped over a blackened dune of snow to cross the street.

Emory's father greeted him as soon as he entered the station. "Is Wayne with you?"

"Just me."

"Well, I'm glad you're here. Come on into my office. I want to talk to you."

Emory followed his father and closed the office door behind him. "What is it, Dad?"

The sheriff leaned against his desk and waited for Emory to sit before speaking. "There was a break-in at the Algarotti factory today."

"Really?" Emory asked in his most innocent tone.

The sheriff crossed his arms and glared down at his son. "You want to tell me why the description of the intruder I was given matches you to a T – right down to that shirt and your size fourteen boots?"

"He could tell my shoe size?"

"No, that part came from me," the sheriff growled. "I'm the one who bought them for you. Now what on Earth would you, an officer of the law, mind you, be doing breaking into a business that was closed?"

"I didn't technically break in. The door was open."

"Stop with the justifications!" Sheriff Rome's wrinkles dropped from his forehead to center around his squinting eyes. For the next nine minutes, he lectured his son about following the letter of the law, a lecture that ended when Emory apologized and promised not to repeat the transgression. The sheriff said that he would accept the apology and make sure the case ended there but added, "Now they think this intruder might have something to do with the water thefts over the past few weeks, so you best avoid contact with whoever saw you today."

Emory held up his right hand. "I will. I promise. About the thefts, what do you know?"

"They thought it was an employee, and they fired him, but we didn't have enough to arrest him. A fella named Charlie Claymon."

Emory's ears perked up at the name. "Claymon? As in Dan Claymon, Britt Algarotti's ex-boyfriend?"

"The same family. Charlie is Dan's father."

"Scot Trousdale told me that Dan pulled a knife on Victor the day before Britt died and threatened him."

"He did? No one reported it." The sheriff cupped his chin in his hand. "You think he was seeking revenge for his dad getting fired?"

"I'd bet on it. I wouldn't doubt if that's why he and Britt broke up." Emory stood and looked his father in the eyes. "Dad, we need to bring him back in. We need to talk to him and his father. Separately."

"You can't interrogate the minor without a parent present."

"Then get his mother to come too. You take one, and I'll take the other."

The sheriff scuffed his foot at the floor. "Fine. We'll try it your way."

CHAPTER 19

THAT AFTERNOON, DAN Claymon entered the sheriff's station with his parents in tow. The teenager unzipped his brown leather jacket as he nodded to Emory. "'Sup, Fast and Furious?"

Emory was unable to conceal a grin at the nickname bestowed upon him. "Hi Dan."

Sheriff Rome clapped his hands once. "Thank y'all for coming."

As if they had designated a speaker ahead of time, the male Claymons looked to Abigail, the matriarch, in her denim dress, faux rabbit coat and galoshes. "You're welcome, Sheriff, but we're a bit confused about what we're doing here."

Sheriff Rome and Emory had discussed the need to put them at ease, which could help minimize the effort needed to separate them, so the sheriff spoke in his folksiest tone. "Well, we just wanted to talk to Dan some more about Britt."

Abigail's eyes squished together, and her pallid skin flushed. "We want nothing more to do with that horrible family."

Dan scowled at the sheriff. "I already talked to you anyway."

Emory adopted his father's tone and mannerisms, relaxing his shoulders and adding a little extra twang to his enunciation. "We've had some more questions come up that we were hoping you could help us with, if you don't mind, since you knew Britt so well. It would really help us out." He waved his left arm toward the interrogation room.

The Claymon men looked at Abigail, who huffed and nodded. As the family followed Emory, the sheriff acted like he had a last-minute thought. "Charlie, could I speak with you alone for a minute?"

Without a word, Charlie let his wife and son go with Emory while he followed the sheriff to the break room.

In the interrogation room, Emory sat in a folding chair across a white portable banquet table from Dan and Abigail. The teenager hunched forward with his forearms resting on the tabletop, while his mother rested against the back of her chair, her shoulders at attention.

The special agent started by introducing himself to the matriarch. "Mrs. Claymon, my name is Emory Rome. I'm with—"

Abigail put her hand up to interrupt him. "Rome? Are you any relation to the sheriff?"

Although he was uncomfortable with sharing personal information, he believed answering would get them started on the right foot. "He's my father. I'm a special agent with the Tennessee Bureau of Investigation, and we're here looking into the murders of Britt Algarotti and now Rick Roberts."

"Mr. Roberts?" Abigail placed a hand on her son's forearm. "My son certainly had no reason to kill Mr. Roberts!"

Dan pushed off the table with a sideways glance at his mother. "He didn't say that."

Defensive tears pooled in her eyes. "You think I don't know what people are saying? He loved that girl. He would've never hurt her. It's not in him!"

Dan touched his mother's hand to calm her before turning his attention to Emory. "We dated for eight months. I loved her." His head dropped. "Now, I can't even go to her funeral."

"Why not?"

"Victor had that asshole assistant of his call me up to let me know that my presence would not be welcomed."

"I'm sorry to hear that. So why did you and Britt break up?" The teenager looked down at the table in silence. "Was it because your dad was let go from the water factory?"

"He wasn't let go," Dan said, mocking Emory's tone. "He was fired over a lie! Dad never took anything from anyone that wasn't rightfully his. Britt wouldn't even defend him. She said she didn't want to get in the middle of it. Can you believe that? She sat at our dinner table a hundred times. She knew my dad, and she refused to defend him. I guess it's easy for someone with money to sit on the sidelines while others struggle to get by."

Abigail touched her son's shoulder. "He didn't do it."

Emory kept his focus on Dan. "Didn't you confront Mr. Algarotti about the firing?"

Abigail came to his defense. "Of course not." She looked at Dan and her assuredness seemed to evaporate. "Dan?"

"I just wanted him to listen to me, to realize what he was doing to us." Dan's eyes glistened as a tear dripped down his cheek. "Where's Dad supposed to go when the place he's worked at for eleven years called him a thief? Nowhere! Mr. Algarotti will deny it, but I know the only reason they singled out my dad, without any proof whatsoever, was because he didn't like the fact that the son of one his employees was dating his daughter. That's why I went to see him. I told him that I would never talk to Britt again if he would give my dad his job back. Mr. Algarotti just blew me off."

"Is that when you threatened him with a knife?"

Over his mother's gasp, Dan insisted, "It wasn't a knife. I picked up a letter opener from the desk."

Abigail dropped her hand from her mouth. "Daniel."

Dan slapped the table. "I did it for dad."

"He wouldn't want you—"

"I know. I know. I wasn't thinking. Agent Emory, I've done some stupid things, but I've never killed anyone. No matter how angry I got. I was pissed at Britt, sure, but I would've never laid a hand on her. I loved her."

In the small break room of the sheriff's station, Charlie Claymon sat with his forearms resting on a round table and two vending machines at his back. He wiped away his black stocking hat to reveal dark brown hair, thinning at the crown, and he squeezed the hat as he told Sheriff Rome, "I don't know how much more I can say about it. What would I get by stealing bottled water? We drink well water and always have."

The sheriff said, "You could've sold it."

"Are you kidding?" Charlie buried the dirty fingers of his left hand into his hefty beard somewhere in the vicinity of his jawline, grating the silence as he scratched his face. With flourishes of grey in the mats of brown hair, the beard seemed tangled in his leaden wool jacket and the top buttons of his mottled brown shirt like Spanish moss draped on an oak tree. When his fingers reemerged and returned to the table, he again spoke. "All the water that was stolen probably adds up to about five or six hundred dollars. That'd be nice to have, but it ain't worth losing my job over."

"No one ever saw you take it. Maybe you thought you were too good to get caught."

"No one saw me 'cause I didn't do it! They blamed it on me since I was the last one on the docks when they went missing. That ain't proof! That's circumcisional."

A snicker snuck from the sheriff's mouth before he could stop it.

Charlie jerked his head back. "What's so funny?"

"I'm sorry." Sheriff Rome got ahold of himself. "I think you meant circumstantial."

"Whatever you call it. Anyway, if someone was looking to sell it, who would be crazy enough to buy bottled water from the back of a truck?"

"You got me there. I have no idea." The sheriff shifted his body forward to lean on the table. "Listen, the missing water isn't really why I wanted to talk to you."

"Well then, what is it?"

"Charlie, how angry are you at being fired?"

Charlie leaned forward, glaring at the sheriff. "What kind of question is that?" He pounded a fist on the table.

Although Charlie's face was now a few uncomfortable inches from his own, Sheriff Rome didn't alter his expression or scoot back. "Were you angry enough to take it out on...Britt Algarotti?"

Charlie's bushy eyebrows met over his bloodshot eyes. "What are you asking? Now I'm being accused of murdering that girl? Did Mr. Algarotti say that?" He jerked his body out of the chair, sending the back of it slamming against one of the vending machines – the glass of which would've broken if the chair had been of sturdier make. He pounded his fist on the table again. "I ain't a thief, and I ain't a murderer! If I was gonna get revenge on anyone, I would've done it on him or that damn foreman. Not some girl. Don't try pinning that on me!"

Charlie Claymon stormed into the interrogation room and threw open the door, roaring at his family members, "We're leaving! Come on."

Abigail and Dan didn't say another word. They followed

Charlie from the room, and a moment later the three exited the trailer.

Sheriff Rome asked his son, "Well?"

"I'm kind of torn. I don't think Dan had anything to do with the murders, but I'm not certain enough to eliminate him as a suspect."

"Well, I'm certain about Charlie."

Emory looked at his father, as if he were about to reveal Charlie as the murderer.

"He's not the water thief."

One corner of Emory's lips pinched into his cheek. "Is he a murderer?"

The sheriff thought about it for a second. "I can't answer that. A man accused and punished for something he didn't do…" He shook his head.

Emory glanced at his watch and realized that he needed to leave if he were going to catch the last bus to Knoxville. "Dad, I have to head out."

"You're not staying?"

"Wayne's picking me up," Emory answered – a half-lie since Wayne would be picking him up from the bus station once he arrived in Knoxville.

One of the desk phones rang, and the sheriff saw there was no around to answer it. "I better get that."

Emory took the opportunity to leave. "You're busy. I'm going to wait for him outside."

"Okay, Son. I'll see you tomorrow?"

"I'll be here." Emory waved to him once before walking out the door and hurrying to the bus station.

CHAPTER 20

AS THE BUS pulled into the Knoxville station, Emory spotted Wayne's decade-old, garish-green SUV in the parking lot. Stepping onto the pavement, he buttoned his denim jacket and rammed his hands into the pockets. *I think it's colder here than it was in Barter Ridge, even without the snow.* Hurrying to the frog mobile, he could see the grin on Wayne's face before he opened the passenger door, and once he did, he heard the laughter.

"I'm sorry, mister, but the posse's gathering at the ranch."

"I blame you for this." Emory pointed to his clothes with both hands. "You left me there."

"What, you look fine…partner. I can't remember ever seeing you without a suit on." He turned the engine and pulled out of the parking lot, still laughing.

Emory forced a change in subject. "Where's my car?"

"I parked it at the office last night and had Mandy pick me up."

"How'd your court date go?"

"It went all right. The defense attorney tried his best to trip me up, but I held my own. So you said you talked to the boyfriend again?"

"I did, and Dad talked to his father."

"His father? Why?"

Emory filled him in on the conversations with the Claymons, the water theft and the potassium permanganate's use in bottled water manufacturing, but he kept quiet about his trip to the water factory. Once apprised, Wayne grunted twice. "Looks to me like if we find the thief, we find the killer."

"I don't know about that."

"What? That's a logical assumption."

Emory averted his glare by keeping his eyes fixed on the passing buildings. "They could be parallel lines."

"Okay, you're saying that like I should immediately understand where you're going, but I have no idea what you mean."

"When do parallel lines intersect?" asked Emory.

"Parallel lines? They don't."

"That's all I'm saying. Events that happen simultaneously aren't necessarily related. I mean, unless you consider time the relation."

Wayne slapped the steering wheel with each word when he asked, "What in the holy hell are you saying?"

Emory had to look at him now. "Remember the murder of that college football player? We spent most of the time investigating his girlfriend's ex-boyfriend because she had a restraining order on him."

"It was a reasonable assumption that he had something to do with the murder."

"It was right to look into him, but our focus on that one possibility obscured the fact that the evidence suggested a female killer. I think we would've caught his cuckoo neighbor sooner if we had let ourselves take a three-sixty view of his world."

Wayne's voice grew aggressive as he grumbled, "You thought we were on the right track too."

Emory remembered it another way. The younger agent had been with the TBI for two months when they were assigned the case, and he wasn't yet confident enough to question Wayne's investigative process. Instead of arguing right now, Emory decided to ease the building tension in the car. "You're right."

The statement seemed to deescalate the tension, as Wayne's voice softened. "I'm still putting my money on the water thief."

"That's fine, but I'm not ready to make that connection yet."

"What about the butterfly effect?"

Emory frowned at his reflection in the side window. *That's random.* "What about it?"

"You know, an event that seems like it's not related to another turns out to be."

Emory nodded to appease him. "So what happened with Rick's wife?"

Wayne chuckled, "She's a…What do you call those women who date young guys?"

"A cougar."

"Yeah, she's a cougar." He grinned as he said the word. "Get this, her new boyfriend is a former student of her husband's."

"A skater?"

"No, he said he had him for science class." Wayne released a bellowing laugh before delivering his impending joke, "And then she had him for recess."

Emory half-laughed to be polite, and then it struck him. "Science."

"What about it?"

"I thought he looked familiar. Rick Roberts was a chemistry teacher in high school when I went there."

"You mean you're just now remembering him? High school was like last year for you." Emory's age was a wellspring of derision for Wayne, one that never elicited more than a polite smile from his partner.

My god, has he got the giggles? "I wasn't in his class, so he wasn't that familiar to me."

"Now that you mention it, I'm surprised you don't know everyone involved in this case. You did grow up in that little town."

"I was an introverted kid, and I wasn't popular." The admission stung more than Emory realized it would. "I do remember wishing I were in Rick Roberts' class. He always took his top students to the state science fair. Mrs. Cooper, my crappy science teacher, taught line-for-line from the textbook and never did anything to encourage her students with scientific ambitions."

"You wanted to be a scientist?"

Emory pulled away from the conversation when he realized he had shared more about himself in the past few minutes than he had in the previous year. "Just a fleeting interest."

"I think it was more than that. The pretty boy dreamed of being a nerd." Wayne laughed yet again.

Wayne's amusement aggravated Emory, who took a vow of silence for the remaining few minutes to the TBI station. When Wayne pulled up to Emory's parked car, the younger special agent didn't wait for the car to come to a complete stop before he opened the door and prepared to step outside.

"Are you going back there this weekend?"

"Probably."

Wayne frowned as he handed Emory's keys back. "Well, don't crack the case without me."

Emory recognized the contemptuous countenance before him now. Wayne was annoyed over the fact that he didn't stop working at five o'clock on Fridays when he had an open case to solve. Saturday and Sunday were family days for Wayne, a scheduling conflict his partner didn't share. "I can't promise you that."

"Whatever." Wayne offered an apathetic wave. "I'll see you on Monday, but keep me posted on any developments."

Emory shut the door. Waiting for Wayne to drive away toward the setting sun, he went inside the building instead of getting into his car.

Apart from two other special agents working at their desks, the office was quiet. Once seated in front of his computer, Emory logged in and opened the portal to the Tennessee Fusion Center, an information-sharing program among state and federal law enforcement agencies. He visited the Homeland Security section and searched for Jeffrey Woodard on the TSA no-fly list. Sure enough, he found the name, but when he clicked on it, the reason given for his inclusion was, "[Redacted]."

"That's odd." Emory spoke as he typed the words, "Why is this information redacted?"

The computer responded with the text, "Insufficient security clearance."

"Crap."

CHAPTER 21

WEARING A NIGHTGOWN, Lula Mae was brushing her hair in the master bathroom when she saw her husband sitting at the foot of the bed, putting on his boots. "What are you doing?"

"I'm going to drive by the water factory one more time."

"But it's so late."

"That's the point, Lula Mae. All the thefts occurred at night."

"I thought you already knew who the thief was."

"I'm rethinking that. I'm positive they pointed the finger at the wrong guy, which means whoever it is, he's still out there." He stood and gave her a kiss. "I'll be back shortly."

"Be careful, Nick."

Jeff was cleaning off his kitchen counter when his phone rang. He walked to the coffee table to answer it, glancing at Bobbie as he passed by her sleeping on the couch. "Hello. Hi August." He grabbed a pen from his desk and wrote notes on a legal pad. "What's the license number? Okay, I'll see what I can find out." Seconds after the conversation with one of his regular clients ended, his doorbell rang. He looked out the window and saw Emory below standing in front of the door to Mourning Dove Investigations.

A moment after Emory rang the doorbell to Mourning Dove Investigations, Jeff opened the office door. "What do you want?"

Still wearing the clothes from his former home, Emory blurted out, "I'm sorry." The expression on Jeff's face, however, refused to change. "I've never broken into a place or anything like that. It stressed me out."

"So stress turns you into an ass?"

Emory tilted his head and raised his right shoulder. "Sure. Let's go with that."

"Are you stressed now?"

"A little bit. Honestly."

"Then we better get you something to calm your nerves." Jeff waved him inside to the reception area. As he headed toward the bookshelf door to his office, he asked, "What kind of man are you?"

What kind of question is that? Emory followed him through the door. "What do you mean?"

"Vodka? Gin? Whiskey?"

Jeff stepped in front of the bookshelf beside his desk and pulled on the Nancy Drew book, The Secret in the Old Attic. The bookshelf was another hidden door that led to a narrow room with two copper staircases. One staircase spiraled up to a second floor, while the other went down, Emory presumed, to a basement.

"Gin."

Jeff ascended the nearer staircase. "That stuff's nasty."

"What is this space?"

"This place used to be a speakeasy. When I bought it, this

part was hidden behind a five-foot-tall painting that opened like a door. He pointed to the other stairs. "That leads to where the bar was." He pointed up. "And this is where the prostitutes did their business. Now, that one goes to our storeroom, and this one goes to the living room in my apartment."

Emory followed him into his apartment. "It's really an amazing place."

Jeff smiled at last. "Thank you. I've gone into major debt getting it the way I want, but I had a clear vision in my head, and I wasn't about to compromise." He made a beeline for the kitchen. "Martini or with tonic?"

"Tonic."

Jeff mixed drinks for them both. "So tell me you didn't hitch."

"What?"

"From Barter Ridge."

Emory shook his head. "Bus."

Jeff handed him a gin and tonic and clinked the glass with his own vodka cranberry. "Cheers."

After taking a sip, Emory coughed and sputtered, prompting Jeff to ask, "Are you okay?"

"That's a strong drink."

"Sorry. I like them that way." Jeff focused his laser-green gaze on Emory's seared brown eyes. With cranberry-wet lips, Jeff said, "I forgive you."

Emory's vocal cords knotted within the binds of Jeff's stare. When he finally opened his mouth, he could only wiggle them free enough to utter, "I…" He gulped his drink for lubrication and ended up choking again.

Jeff took the drink from him and placed it on the counter beside them. "Let's go out."

Freed once Jeff looked away, Emory asked, "What?"

"It's Friday night, and we both need to blow off some steam. When's the last time you went to a club?"

"I'm not into the bar scene."

"I know a place you'll love. It's not like the others." He looked down at Emory's clothes. "First, we need to fix what you're wearing."

"We can swing by my place so I can change."

"No need." Jeff stepped within a few inches of Emory and compared their bodies. "We're the same size, basically. I have plenty of cool clothes you can wear."

Emory faced down to avoid Jeff's eyes. "I couldn't do that."

"It's no problem." Jeff headed into the bedroom. "I'll find you something."

Emory reached for his gin and tonic but opted against taking another sip of the powerful drink. "You have any water?"

From the bedroom, Jeff told him, "There's some cold water in the fridge."

Emory preferred room temperature, so when he saw a couple of unopened bottles on Jeff's desk, he decided to take one. He flipped open the top and took a giant gulp.

Jeff returned from the bedroom carrying a pair of designer black jeans and a jersey-knit rust-colored shirt with long sleeves. "What do you think of this look?"

Emory frowned at the selection. "It's not really my style."

"I know. It's perfect." Jeff placed them on the couch for him. "I also have a pair of great boots for you and a jacket."

"Sounds...good. Oh, I forgot to tell you that I started looking into your problem with the TSA."

"You did?" Jeff gave Emory his undivided attention. "What did you find out?"

Seeing how delighted Jeff was that he had followed through on his request made telling him that he didn't have much to report even more difficult. "Your name is on the no-fly list, but the reason for it was redacted."

"Why?"

"I don't know. I've never seen that before. You have no idea why you're on it? No connection with any person or organization that could have ties to terrorism?"

"Nothing." Jeff held up his right hand. "I swear."

"Don't worry then. I have some friends in the Tennessee Homeland Security office. We'll get to the bottom of it."

"Thank you." Jeff flashed him a warm smile. "We better get ready. I'll dress in the bedroom if you're okay changing in here."

"Sounds great to me." Once Jeff disappeared behind the bedroom door, Emory changed clothes and transferred his wallet and pill bottle into the pocket of the pants he was wearing. He piled his old clothes onto the couch, hiding his keys and his holstered gun underneath them.

Jeff opened the door and stepped out holding a pair of black boots and a navy linen jacket, which he placed on the coffee table. "You look great. I knew that combo would work for you."

Emory didn't even look down at his own attire, as his gaze was locked on Jeff. He was wearing a clover-green polo shirt that made his eyes pop, like a pair of lightning bugs hovering on a windless summer night. The elastic bands of the short sleeves squeezed against his striated biceps in a lopsided battle to maintain their shape and, although not meant to be tight, his dark jeans couldn't conceal the sculpted contours of his muscular legs.

"Damn," Emory thought, and then he realized he said it out loud. "I need to go to the bathroom."

Jeff pointed. "Right in there."

Emory retreated to the bathroom, closing the door behind him. He dug out his anti-anxiety medicine from his pocket and took one pill, downing it with the rest of the bottled water.

Sheriff Rome turned his truck onto the driveway of the Algarotti Smoky Mountain Springs factory. He killed the headlights, depending instead on the diffuse amber glow from the staggered lampposts to guide him. He drove around to the back of the building, past the natural spring and to the loading dock – just a quick round before he went home to crawl into bed with Lula Mae. When he turned the back corner, however, he noticed something alarming.

A black van was parked at the dock, and the rollup door in the building was open maybe two feet. The sheriff shifted into reverse and parked his truck out of the line of sight. He exited the vehicle and turned the volume down on the radio attached to his belt. Drawing his gun from its holster, he crept toward the rollup door.

Peering inside, he could see no one except a man lying facedown on the floor about thirty feet in front of him. Sheriff Rome squeezed under the door and hurried to the man. He turned him onto his back and realized it was the foreman. He touched his neck for a pulse. It was faint but there. On the ground next to him rested a broken coffee cup. *Did he have a heart attack?* He reached for his radio, but a powerful jolt arced his back and curled his arms.

The sheriff fell onto his side and rolled onto his back, his muscles convulsing. He saw someone wearing a black ski mask standing above him, holding a stun gun.

Placing the weapon on the floor, the stranger picked up a bottle of purplish water with an open sport top, which he forced between the paralyzed sheriff's lips. The bottle's contents gushed down his throat.

Once the bottle was empty, the man again hit the sheriff with the stun gun. As he convulsed, the back of his head banged against the floor in rapid succession until he lost consciousness.

CHAPTER 22

A S THEY STEPPED out of the Uber, Jeff explained to Emory, "This is a mixed club of universal acceptance. They play experimental music that's a fusion of folk instruments and trance – unlike anything you've ever heard before."

Emory could hear Jeff speaking, but he felt no need to respond. He stared at the neon sign above the door to their destination, "If Tomorrow Comes."

Jeff grabbed his arm. "Are you okay?"

"What?" Emory made vague eye contact with him. "Yeah, I'm fine."

"You seem a little...off."

Emory looked like he was going to speak, but the sound didn't come for several seconds. "I feel, I don't know, weird. Guess I'm nervous."

Jeff laughed and moved his hand to Emory's shoulder. "You'll be fine. I'm here."

After a short wait in line, the two left Knoxville behind and entered a fantasyland. As Jeff pulled him through the crowd, Emory's eyes danced around the club to take in the whole spectacle. Knotty wood walls reached up to a ceiling of unnatural blue, streaked by laser spectrum lights in frenetic succession. Bar pods shaped like perfect dew drops were interspersed on the leaf-colored floor, and inside each pod stood a crimson-shirted bartender.

Emory's gaze shot to the stage, which looked like a pier that had been built in the wrong place. The word "Timbrance" glowed above the performers, and he assumed it was the band's name. Apart from the female singer, dressed like a lake nymph, the remaining members played instruments – an electric dulcimer, a synthesizer, an accordion and Cherokee drums. The ethereal yet driving beat impelled the dancers on the floor. Couples of same and opposite sexes, as well as singles and groups, moved together like budding fields bending to opposing winds.

"Wow!" Emory exclaimed, but he couldn't even hear himself over the music.

Jeff turned a happy face toward him. "What do you think?"

"It's really ama-a-a-azing!" Emory yelled back in a tone both animated and odd. His eyes drifted to the wait staff, who wore iridescent uniforms as they glided through the crowd like fairies, bringing nectar for the visitors to their forest sanctuary.

"Are you sure you're all right?"

"I'm great." Emory didn't want to say it, but he wasn't nervous. In fact, he was on the verge of euphoria – as if his blood cells had stopped flowing and started dancing through his veins. He was focused yet adrift, the same as when attempting to accomplish even the simplest task within the fluidity of a dream.

Jeff said something to him, but he had no idea what it was. He nodded anyway as Jeff left his side.

Emory started watching the band from the edge of the dance floor, which was silvery blue like a mountain lake with a giant yellow strobe light hanging overhead to simulate the sun. He found himself fixating on the spidery fingers of the dulcimer player as he taunted the melody inside the silky strings. The rhythm permeated Emory's skin and attached to his muscles like strings on a marionette, moving them with each confident pull of the beat.

He had forgotten all about Jeff by the time he popped up with a drink in each hand.

Jeff handed him a gin and tonic. "Looks like you're ready to get on the floor."

Emory sipped half the drink with a single suck on the straw and shook his head. "I don't dance."

Jeff looked down at Emory's hips pivoting on his legs. "You might need to tell your body that." He grabbed Emory's drink and placed it alongside his on a nearby table.

"Hey, I wasn't finished with that."

"Let's dance." Jeff took his hand and led him to the floor. Emory didn't want to go, but he seemed unable to make his body stop walking. Once they reached about one-third of the way into the crowd, Jeff stopped to face his partner, releasing his hand. He began to translate the music's rapid tempo into a charmingly masculine dance that pulled Emory's lips into a sweet grin. Emory danced with moves harmonious to Jeff's, prompting a matching grin. Emory's attention shot up to the streaks of laser light overhead. He lost himself staring at them. Eventually Jeff put his hands on Emory's face and turned his attention back to him.

As he watched Jeff, Emory thought about Wayne's suspicions. *Could Victor have had another reason for hiring him, this hyper-hot PI? Is he friends with Pristine? Is he my friend now? God, look at him. Why do we keep spending time together? Is he keeping tabs on me, on the investigation?* Emory's head spun. Without warning, he slipped from the dance floor and zigzagged to the front door.

Once outside, he lost his balance and had to put a hand on the burly bouncer's chest to keep from falling. The bearded man, who looked like a scary mountaineer, placed a steadying hand on Emory's shoulder and asked, "Are you okay?"

"I'm fine. Fine." Emory stood on his own.

The bouncer took out his cell. "Stay here. I'm going to call a ride for you."

Emory took a few steps and waved at him. "That's okay. I'm going to walk."

Jeff bolted from the club. "Where are you going?"

"I need to go home now." Emory's eyes looked everywhere but on Jeff.

Jeff ran in front of him and forced him to stop walking. "Why?" Emory swayed away from him. "Are you drunk?"

Emory shook his head and slurred, "I don't understand. Why are we here?"

"We were dancing. Would you look at me, please?"

Emory focused on him as best he could. "From the moment I first saw you, you know, when you smiled at me, it was like you had decided our fates."

That statement brought a confused smile to Jeff's face, a look Emory could no longer resist. With both hands he pulled Jeff's face to his and kissed him full on the mouth. As soon as their lips parted, Emory told him, "God, I hate your eyes."

Jeff scowled at him. "What?"

"Your eyes, they make me do things I shouldn't want to do."

"Hey guys." Jeff and Emory looked at the bouncer, who was pointing his thumb toward the door of the club. "You should get back inside if you're going to do that. Not too safe out here."

Jeff waved to him. "We're just going to head out now."

Emory pushed away from Jeff. "I'm not going anywhere with you until you tell me about Pristine!"

"You know, you are totally confusing me tonight. What about Pristine?"

"Why didn't you tell me you're friends with her?"

Jeff's face froze like a child caught in a lie. "We should get you home."

"I can get myself home."

"No you can't. Your keys are at my place."

The bouncer held up his cell phone. "Ride's coming now. He's right down the street."

As Emory thought about what to do, he stared at the bouncer and told him, "You know, you have a great beard."

The bouncer snickered at the remark. "Thanks buddy."

Jeff waved at the arriving cab. "Time to go now." He helped Emory into the back seat and got in the other side.

During the short ride, Emory nodded off, and his head rolled until it came to rest on Jeff's shoulder. His next conscious moment came when Jeff slapped him awake once they arrived at Mourning Dove Investigations. Jeff walked behind him up the spiral staircase and helped him to the couch. When Emory saw his clothes where he had left them, he remembered something Jeff said earlier. "How did you know I left my keys here?"

Standing in front of him, Jeff didn't answer his question. "You seem more than drunk to me. What are you feeling right now?"

Emory thought for a few seconds as his head bobbed side-to-side. "I feel..." He squinted like he was trying to think of the right words. "Really weird. I've never done drugs, but I imagine it would feel..." With sudden realization, he looked up at Jeff through half-closed eyes. "Did you drug me?"

Without hesitation, Jeff answered, "Yes."

Panicked, Emory looked for his gun underneath the pile of clothes. He found the holster and reached for the gun, but it wasn't there. "What did you do to my gun?"

"Why? What are you planning to do with it? You should rest."

Emory fought his way to his feet and tried to leave.

Jeff wrapped an arm around him and forced him to the bed. He pulled off his boots and clothes, except for his underwear, and made him lie back.

"No," Emory protested and tried to get up, but he was so woozy now, he could no longer keep his eyes open. He could feel something tightening around his wrists.

Sheriff Rome awoke in freezing darkness with the roar of running water above his head. He could move, but he found the act of ordering his body to do so almost insurmountable. His mind tangled itself into strings of random, unfinished thoughts that seemed beyond his control. He struggled to open his eyes, and when he did, the information filtering through a single slit of vision took him more than a minute to process.

He was lying in the snow with his back to the sky and his head turned to his right. He tried to lift his face from the ground, but he couldn't keep it up. The few seconds of elevated vision did allow him to see the back of the water factory. He now realized he was in the woods behind it, somewhere near the natural spring. He also noticed that the black van was gone.

The sheriff heard something that panicked some clarity into his head – the yipping of coyotes approaching from the woods!

He willed his right hand to slide over the snow to his waist. He ran his fingers along his belt to find the gun in his belt holster. It was gone.

The yipping grew louder.

With his right hand, he pushed against the ground with all his might. His elbow buckled twice, but he kept pushing until he rolled onto his back. He bent his right knee above him and reached a shaky hand toward his ankle. His spatial perceptions were deceiving him, so he missed his ankle three times before connecting.

The coyotes growled from mere yards away.

The sheriff found the pistol hidden inside his ankle holster. He fired three shots in the general direction of the coyotes before blacking out again.

CHAPTER 23

SATURDAY MORNING EMORY awoke yawning, but when he tried to cover his mouth, he found he couldn't move his hands. He looked above his head to see why. "What?" He refocused his eyes to make sure he was seeing what he thought he was. Sure enough, his hands were tied to the iron headboard with neckties. He tried to jerk himself free without success. "What the hell is going on here?"

"You're awake." Jeff stirred from a chair in the corner of the room, a quilt draped over him like he had slept there through the night.

"Jeff." Pieces of the night before started dropping into Emory's head. "Untie me!"

Jeff threw the quilt aside and walked over to the bedside. "How are you feeling?"

"Vengeful," Emory snarled. "Untie me now!"

"All right. Keep your shirt on." Jeff smiled at his bare-chested captive as he freed one of his hands. "I figured you'd be in a crappy mood this morning."

Emory shot his free hand to the bound one and tried untying it while Jeff made his way to the other side of the bed.

"How many of those pills did you take last night?"

Emory stopped what he was doing to face Jeff. "My pills? You're blaming me?"

Jeff finished untying the second knot for him. As soon as he did, Emory leapt from the bed and rammed Jeff back into the wall. He grabbed his collar with both hands. "You drugged me, you son of a bitch!"

Jeff drove his forearms between Emory's, forcing him to release his grip. "Don't blame me for your drug use."

Emory shot a right hook to Jeff's chin, knocking him on his ass into a corner. "I've never done drugs in my life!" With a blood-red face, Emory glared at the fallen man.

Jeff wiped blood from his mouth and let out a little laugh. "Well, that's not exactly true, now is it, Mr. Anxiety?"

"Those are prescription, asshole!"

"They alter your mood, just like any street drug. Look, I'm going to stand up now, and I'd appreciate it if you could refrain from any more sucker punches." Jeff steadied himself with a hand on the nightstand and rose to his feet, while Emory remained in a boxing stance. "I knew you were on something last night, and I just figured you took too many of your pills. You did say you were stressed."

"You're just trying to absolve yourself." Emory's anger was not the least bit abated. "I swear, I've never seen anyone who could charm people so effectively to get what he wants, and I encounter sociopaths on a regular basis."

Jeff's lips stretched into a blood-laced smile. "You think I'm charming?"

"It's not going to work on me now. I don't remember a lot about last night, but I remember that you admitted drugging me."

Expecting another strike, Jeff put his hands up to block Emory. "You asked me if I drugged you, and I said, 'Yes.' Sarcastically. It was a ridiculous question, and I gave an equally ridiculous answer. I swear to you on my honor."

The special agent huffed at the thought of Jeff having any honor.

"Okay, on Virginia's honor."

"I don't know her well enough."

Jeff dropped his smile. "The point is, I didn't do it. I'll take a lie-detector test or whatever you want me to do to prove it."

Emory lowered his fists. "I just don't know if I can really trust you."

"That's okay. Most times, I don't trust myself."

Emory thought about it for a few seconds. "So you didn't roofie me?"

"I assure you, Hester Prynne, your honor is intact. No, I didn't roofie you."

"Well, I was drugged. My pills don't do that to me. And how was I supposed to detect sarcasm in the state I was in?" Emory started walking away, but he shifted back to Jeff. "Wait a second. Why'd you tie me up?"

"You kept wanting to leave, and I couldn't let you drive the way you were." Jeff put an arm around Emory's shoulders and led him to the living room. "I wanted to take you to the hospital, but I was afraid you would get into trouble with your job. I thought the best course of action would be to put you in bed and watch over you."

Emory sat on the couch. "A bit extreme, tying me up, don't you think?"

Jeff grinned at him. "I'm an extreme guy. Hey, do you want some coffee?"

"Sure." Emory smelled under his arm. "Ooh, I stink."

Jeff nodded toward the bathroom. "You shower. I'll get you some fresh clothes."

Seeing his old clothes on the couch, Emory remembered his gun. He searched through them and found the empty holster. "Jeff, where's my gun?"

On his way to the kitchen, Jeff took a detour to the old-fashioned radiator against the wall. He turned a knob on it and pulled one side away from the wall, revealing that the radiator was hinged like a cabinet door. Behind the radiator, a safe was embedded in the wall. "When you went to the bathroom, before we left last night, I started wondering where you left your gun. I found it under your clothes and put it in here for safekeeping." Jeff opened the safe and handed the gun to Emory.

"Thanks. What do you do when it gets cold?"

Jeff pointed to a vent in the ceiling. "I had central air put it when I bought the place." He continued to the kitchen to make coffee. "I've been thinking. Most drugs administered orally, assuming it was orally, take about half an hour to start kicking in. When did you notice that you were feeling different?"

Emory paused for a moment. "I think on the way to the club."

"So you would've taken it here at my place or just before you came. Did you eat or drink anything around that time?"

Emory tried to retrace his steps. "The last thing I ate was at the bus station in Barter Ridge about three hours before we left for the club. After that I went to the office and didn't have anything there. I came here, and had the drink you made me."

Jeff found the bottle of gin and bottle of tonic, and placed them onto the counter. "We should get these tested."

"What about the ice?"

Jeff shook his head. "I had the same ice. Anything else?"

Thinking further, Emory remembered one more item. "I took one of my pills before we left."

"Could someone have switched your pills?"

"I don't see how. I took one at the factory yesterday, and I was fine. If someone did, it had to be between then and when I came here last night, but I know I had the bottle with me the whole time."

Jeff put out his hand. "Give them to me. We should have

them tested to be sure. Maybe they weren't all switched." Hesitating, Emory handed him the bottle from his pocket. "Will you be okay until you get more?"

"Sure," Emory responded, although he was anything but.

"Did you take it with your gin and tonic?"

"No, I had one of your bottled waters."

"Where's the bottle?"

"In your recycle bin."

Jeff looked in the bin and saw four bottles of water. "Do you happen to remember which one it was?"

"It was grape-flavored."

Jeff found one bottle of grape-flavored, empty but for a little backwash. He put it on the counter with the other items. "I hope that's a big enough sample. I should get a full one, just in case." He looked in his refrigerator for more flavored waters. "All I have left is plain."

Emory pointed to a bottle on his desk. "You have a grape one over there."

"I do?" Jeff's mouth opened as he realized where that particular bottle had come from.

"What is it?"

"At the factory yesterday, I took a couple of bottles from Scot's office."

"Why would they have drugged water on their sample table?"

"I didn't get it from that table. I got it from Scot's desk." Jeff snapped his finger. "Britt. Oh my god."

"What about her?"

"Rick told me someone spiked her drink at her last competition."

"Is that what happened to her? I saw the video."

Jeff pointed at Emory, and his eyes brightened. "What if it wasn't spiked? What if it came that way?"

CHAPTER 24

AFTER CONVINCING JEFF that he was okay to get behind the wheel, Emory peeked at his reflection in the rearview mirror and groaned at what he saw – bloodshot eyes, blotchy face and hair matted to his head. "I look like afterbirth."

"Now that's disgusting." Jeff gave him the once-over. "Not untrue, but disgusting."

Emory started the car. "Thanks."

"It's not your fault. I guess the shower didn't take." Jeff chuckled and patted Emory on the shoulder. "I'm just kidding. I don't think you could look bad if you tried. And you're certainly trying."

Emory couldn't keep the corners of his mouth from perking up. "Kick me when I'm down."

"I'm done now." Jeff scooted his seat back. "So this medical examiner friend of yours will test everything we have for drugs and keep it a secret for you?"

"She would if I asked."

"Good. You definitely don't want the TBI to find out you took drugs."

Emory slapped the steering wheel. "I didn't take drugs. I was drugged. And she's not going to have to keep it a secret because I'm obligated to report it."

"Are you crazy? There's no proof you didn't take it willingly."

Emory patted his chest. "There's my word."

"Are you sure that's enough?"

"Of course it is."

"You know, sometimes doing the right thing is the wrong thing to do."

Emory waved a finger at him. "I'm not going to be a disciple of your fuzzy morality."

"Just think of this then: If it is in the water, how are you going to explain where you got it?"

"What do you mean? I'll tell the truth. It came from the Algarotti factory."

"But you got it from me."

"And you got it from the factory."

"Don't you see? You just have my word for that and, at least with your people, mine doesn't carry the weight of yours. There's no proof that I didn't drug it myself."

"I'll back you. Oh…" Emory pinched his lips together. "They'll know you broke into the factory because it was closed that day."

Jeff shrugged off that concern. "I'll just say that I got it the day before."

"You can't do that. The date could prove important."

They were silent in thought for a moment until Jeff snapped his fingers. "I've got it. I'll say I went through the back door, which was open, right?"

"Why would you've gone in back?"

"I wanted to check out the cool spring behind the factory. I saw the back door was open, so I made a natural assumption that the factory was open. Instead of going all the way back to the front…There's the story."

"No matter what, you always find a workaround."

"What's wrong with that? Besides, it's the least I could do to help you out." Jeff smirked at him. "Especially after that kiss you gave me."

"What?" Emory's face blanked as the memory flashed back to him. "I was under the influence."

"You can't use that excuse. If you had gotten behind the wheel and hit someone, you would've been responsible for your actions. You couldn't say it didn't count because you were under the influence."

"If I weren't responsible for intoxicating myself, I wouldn't be responsible for any of my actions resulting from it. Whoever drugged me would be."

Jeff crossed his arms and looked forward. "Now who's found a workaround?"

Emory ignored the question in favor of a subject that had been nagging at him. "I've got to know something."

"What is it?"

"Are you friends with Pristine Algarotti?"

"Who told you that?"

"That doesn't matter. Is it true?"

Jeff uncrossed his arms and fidgeted in his chair before bringing his right foot up to rest on his left knee. "We're not friends, but I did know her before."

Finally, the truth! "How did you know her?"

"She's a former client – one of my first." Jeff widened his eyes in a classic move to appear more innocent. "You need to know I'm not happy about this, but when I started, I took any client I could get my hands on, regardless of what the investigation entailed. Hell, if I'm being completely honest, I still do today, but I'm trying to quit."

"What was the job?"

Jeff shrugged as if it were no big deal. "Pristine wanted to marry a rich man, so she hired me to find one for her."

Emory's mouth opened, but his next words came as a delayed reaction. "Are you saying that you got her and Victor together?"

"Yes, although Victor doesn't know that. He had never met me before you and I went to his office the other day."

Emory hit the steering wheel. "I knew she was lying when she told me she married him for love."

"There's more." Jeff's gaze fell to the floor. "Besides being rich, Pristine's only criterion was, in her words, 'Someone I could stomach looking at in bed.' She didn't necessarily care if the man was single. She wanted me to widen the pool by including men who could be...stolen." He took a deep breath. "I came up with a list, including pictures. Victor was on the list because I knew his wife didn't have long—"

"Oh my god." Emory gasped.

"I know. I know. I guess I just validated your opinion of PIs."

"No," Emory replied, but his tone was unconvincing. "So how did you manage to get them together?"

"That was a little tough. I had to figure out a good way for them to meet that wouldn't appear like she was after him. Since Victor has absolutely no social life whatsoever, the best way for them to meet, outside of a car accident, was through work. The only opening the water factory had was for a communications coordinator – someone to give tours, update their website and other stuff like that. I fixed her resume to state that she was a highly effective coordinator at a brewery, where I had a friend who would serve as a reference and confirm that she had been employed there for three years."

"Why? What was Pristine's real job?"

"She was a waitress. Anyway, she got the job at the Algarotti factory, and that was the extent of my work with her until I got the call from Victor's assistant for this job." Jeff paused, perhaps waiting for Emory to say something. "I hate what I did, and I would never do something like that today. I swear to you, I only want to take good cases – ones with a good purpose." He let out a laugh. "Maybe I should run any potential cases by you first. You could be my sounding board."

Emory wasn't amused, keeping his eyes on the road and off Jeff. "I can't be your Jiminy Cricket. Besides, who am I to judge?"

Cathy Shaw removed her latex gloves as she dictated her final comments concerning the autopsy she had just performed. "COD: traumatic injury to the frontal lobe caused by impact with the dashboard. Failure of airbag deployment a major contributing factor." She told the cadaver before pulling the sheet over his face, "Your family is about to come into some serious money."

"Cathy."

She looked over her shoulder to see who had called her. "Emory!" She rushed to give him a hug but stopped just short, putting her hands up instead of around him. "I should wash my hands first." She stepped over to the sink. "So good to see you in person. I like the outfit, by the way."

"Thanks…" Emory didn't admit the clothes weren't his.

As Cathy dried her hands, she noticed he wasn't alone. "Who's this?" she asked with an amorous smile. Jeff grinned and told her his name.

"Really nice to meet you, Jeff. You know, with that cut on your lip, you've got a real rough-pretty thing going on."

"Well thank you. And you can thank Emory for the busted lip."

Emory explained, "He's a private investigator working the same case as us."

"Oh? Where is Wayne?"

"You know he doesn't work weekends."

"Must be nice. I work so many hours, I'm developing Stockholm syndrome for my boss. So do you have another body for me?"

"I do," Emory responded. "Mine."

Cathy glanced at Jeff and back at Emory. "I don't understand."

"I was drugged last night, maybe with MDMA."

Cathy threw a hand to her mouth. "Oh my god. Are you okay?"

"I am now. Jeff helped me get through it."

"How did it happen?"

"We're not totally sure," answered Jeff, holding up a cloth bag containing the items that might have been tainted. "Here are the most likely delivery methods." He placed the bag on a table and pulled the bottled water from it. "My money's on this." He gazed into Cathy's eyes like a mesmerist. "Listen, Cathy, is there any way you can keep this quiet – just report back to Emory."

"That's not necessary," Emory insisted.

Jeff threw up his palm to Emory but kept his eyes on Cathy. "At least until he has a chance to think about reporting it himself?"

Cathy fell under Jeff's spell. "With those eyes, I bet you get away with murder."

"Jeff, seriously, I'm submitting a complete report. I've got nothing to hide."

Jeff shrugged. "Fine. I hope you're right."

"I need your hair." Cathy pulled her vision from Jeff to look at Emory. "I mean your hair, Emory. A few strands plucked to test for toxins, poisons."

"What about the items we brought?" Emory asked.

"If I know exactly what you took, it'll be easier to look for that specific drug in these." She began taking the items from the bag. "Ooh, gin. Someone had a party and didn't invite me."

Emory plucked some hair from his head. "No party. Just us."

Cathy looked at both of them and grinned.

As Emory turned the ignition in his car, Jeff entered the passenger side and handed him the bottle of pills he had removed from the bag. "Here you go. I took them out."

"Why'd you do that?"

"There's no need to have them tested unless she doesn't find anything in the other things we brought her. I'd still get a new prescription."

Emory nodded. "Thank you."

"So where to next?"

Emory was about to answer him when he heard chiming from his phone. It had died the previous night and was now charging on the arm rest between them.

"Damn, you missed a lot of calls."

Emory checked his call log. "It's Mom. I wonder what's wrong." He called his voicemail, and Lula Mae's shaky voice played over his car's speakers.

"Emory, it's your mama. Something happened with your dad. He was attacked, and he's at the hospital. I need you here."

Other than a gasp, Emory froze in his seat.

Jeff popped out of the vehicle and hurried to the driver side, opening the door. "Get out," he ordered. "I'll drive." Jeff helped him out of the car to the passenger side and sped through the ninety-minute drive to Barter Ridge in an hour.

CHAPTER 25

EMORY BOLTED INTO the hospital room and found his father propped up in bed with a bandage around his head. "Dad, are you okay?"

Sheriff Rome smiled and said, "I'm fine, Son," in rhythm with the beeping heart monitor.

Emory gave him a gentle hug, grateful to find him lucid and awake, but the older man still winced in pain. "I'm sorry."

The sheriff waved off his concern. "No, it's okay. I'm just sore all over."

Emory jumped when a hand grabbed his arm, and he turned to see his mother's tear-stained face.

Lula Mae hugged him. "I'm so glad you're here,"

Emory glanced at the chair behind her. "Mom, I didn't even see you." He broke away and grabbed the back of his dark brown hair. "What happened?"

Sheriff Rome related the details of the previous night, and Emory's anger swelled when the story reached the physical attack on his father. "He forced me to drink something – had a grape flavor to it. It must've been spiked."

The water! Emory clenched his fists at his side.

"I've never felt like that, the way I did when I woke up outside – like I didn't have control of my body."

Lula Mae rubbed his shin through the blanket. "It's a good thing he was able to fire that gun. I might never have found him."

"You found him?"

The sheriff grinned. "You know your mama. Can't sleep without me there."

"His restless legs vibrate me to sleep," she said with a sarcastic smile. "When he didn't come home after an hour, I started to worry and decided to go looking for him. I drove around the factory, and I heard gunshots. My heart was just pounding. I saw the flash when he fired the last one. I didn't know if it was him or…Then I saw him." Lula Mae's throat went hoarse, and tears filled her eyes.

Emory put an arm around his mother as she took the sheriff's hand and squeezed it. "Dad, who were you firing at?"

"Not who. What. When I woke up, I heard coyotes coming at me from the woods."

"Oh my god."

"I reached for my gun, but it wasn't in my holster. Whoever did this to me took my gun. Thank goodness I always have Loretta with me. That's my—"

"I remember," said Emory. "Loretta the Beretta."

"Anyway, I fired a few shots in the general direction. I don't know if I got any of them, but it must've kept them at bay."

Lula Mae told Emory, "I didn't see any when I got there."

"They were there, I tell you. I didn't imagine them."

"Dad, do you have any idea who attacked you? Anything to go on?"

"Well, I feel silly for saying this, but it really did happen so fast. My deputies are at the factory now going over the place. You should talk to the foreman. He was attacked too. Worse off than I am. Maybe he saw more than me. A couple of deputies tried to talk to him this morning, but he was still unconscious. Lula Mae, where'd they say he was?"

"Just down the hall. I'll take you there."

As Lula Mae led him out of the room, Emory panicked. *I can't interview the foreman. He'll recognize me as the intruder at the factory. What will he say when he sees me again? How am I supposed to explain it?* Along the way, he saw Jeff in the waiting room. "Mom, I need to talk to someone first." He nodded to Jeff, who started to walk their way until Emory motioned him to stay put. "You can just let me know which room it is and get back to Dad."

"Okay, honey." Lula Mae pointed down the hall. "I don't know the room number, but it's the last one on the left."

"Thanks, Mom." Emory left her and walked to Jeff.

"How's your dad?"

"He's going to be okay. Listen, I need your help." Emory gave him the highlights of his father's attack.

"He was drugged too? There seriously is something in the water here."

"Now Dad wants me to talk to the foreman to see if he has any helpful information."

"But won't he recognize you?"

"Exactly. I think Dad forgot about that. Would you talk to the foreman?"

"Of course."

"I appreciate it. Here's what I need you to ask."

Jeff stopped him with an open palm. "I know how to conduct an interview."

Emory wanted to say more to ensure his own questions were answered, but he held back. "Okay." He then jumped when he heard his mom calling from behind him. "Mom, what is it?"

Lula Mae looked to Jeff. "Hello."

"Mom, this is Jeff Woodard. He's a private investigator who's helping with the case."

"Very nice to meet you, ma'am. I'm so sorry about what happened to your husband."

"Thank you. The doctor says he'll be okay, but we'll be staying here overnight. Emory, would you be able to take care of Sophie until tomorrow?"

"Of course."

"There's plenty of food for you in the fridge. Sophie hasn't even been fed today."

"I'll take care of it." Emory remembered he wasn't alone. "Ah, Jeff rode down with me."

Jeff told him, "Don't worry about me. If you don't mind, I could just borrow your car tonight and come back tomorrow."

Lula Mae spoke before Emory could respond. "I don't know how you boys stomach all the driving back and forth. It'd make me a nervous wreck. Why don't you just stay at our place? We have plenty of room, and you both have important work to finish here."

"Thank you for the hospitality," said Jeff. "And Mrs. Rome, I promise you we're going to find the son-of-a-bitch who did this to your husband."

Emory was mortified that Jeff would curse in front of his mother, but Lula Mae smiled at the PI. She gave him a sweet hug and kissed Emory on the cheek before leaving them alone.

Jeff said to Emory, "I don't really have to stay if you're not comfortable."

Emory shook his head. "You heard my mother."

"Okay then. I have a witness to interview."

As the two investigators left the hospital, Jeff related to Emory everything the foreman had told him. "He said he had just gotten a cup of coffee, trying to stay awake, when someone attacked him with a stun gun from behind. He has a pacemaker, and he thinks something happened to it that made him pass out. He didn't see a thing."

"Same as Dad."

"I wonder why your dad wasn't killed."

Emory glowered at him. "That's an odd thing to say. Did you want him to be dead?"

"Of course not. You're missing my point. The foreman's not dead either."

"Oh, now I get it."

"Do you really?"

"Of course not."

"Whoever did this didn't seem to want them dead."

"Dad could've been killed by coyotes."

"True, but that's a variable that couldn't have been predicted. The person who did this dragged your dad out of the way so he could finish his business. He didn't have to worry about the foreman because he wasn't about to wake up. Britt and Rick were killed. Why stop there?"

"But those murders were planned, methodical. The attacks at the factory were spur of the moment. Either the killer refuses to commit a murder without forethought—"

"Or the whole water situation isn't directly related to the murders." Jeff held up Emory's keys. "Where to now?"

"After we feed Sophie, I want to check out the water factory – legitimately this time."

CHAPTER 26

EMORY DROVE TO the back of the Algarotti factory and parked by the receiving area, next to two sheriff's cars. Jeff pointed out the yellow tape encircling a small area in the adjacent woods, and the two surmised that was where the sheriff had been dragged. They walked into the factory through the wide-open rollup door and found three deputies talking and looking around. Emory knew two of them well. The third was Deputy Harris, the one who had kicked him out of his father's office the other day.

"Hi guys," Emory said with a wave. "Can you bring me up to speed?"

The youngest deputy hurried to block their path. "You can't be in here."

Deputy Loggins, a short man about the same age as the sheriff intervened. "You two haven't met?"

"Not officially," Emory responded.

"Harris, this is Emory Rome, the sheriff's son. Emory, this little know-it-all is Deputy Harris, our very first college graduate on the team."

Deputy Harris shook Emory's hand. "Nice to meet you, but you shouldn't be in the crime scene, even if you're family."

As the other two deputies snickered, Emory displayed his badge. "I'm with the TBI."

"You're the TBI agent?" Deputy Harris nodded at his co-workers. "They told me you were the son in real estate."

"My dad only has one son."

Harris glared at the other deputies, who were now belly-laughing. "Thanks guys." He extended a hand to Jeff. "I guess you're his partner."

Jeff neither confirmed nor denied, but he shook his hand. "Jeff Woodard."

Deputy Harris explained, "We're working as fast as we can to document everything so they can open this area back up."

Jeff asked, "What have you found so far?"

The deputies took turns pointing out where Sheriff Rome and the foreman were attacked and reconstructing their theories of how the events had played out. When they finished, Emory snapped some pictures with his phone and glanced at the double swing door that led to the wide hallway and the large, unmarked door he had tried to open the day before. He asked the deputies, "Have you searched anywhere else?"

One of the deputies pointed toward the rollup door to the outside. "We roped off the area where your dad was found, but we haven't had a chance to investigate it yet."

Deputy Harris chimed in with, "I did notice whoever put him there took the time to sweep over his tracks with a branch, so there are no usable footprints."

Emory raised his hands out to his side. "What about the rest of the factory?"

"What about it?" Deputy Harris asked.

"The whole place is a potential crime scene."

The deputy looked at Emory like he was stupid. He pointed with the palms of his hands to the floor. "The crime scene is over here. Both victims were attacked here, and then the sheriff was dragged outside."

"There could be other victims somewhere in the factory,"

Deputy Harris shook his head. "I already thought of that. No one is unaccounted for."

"According to who?" asked Jeff.

"The owner," Deputy Harris answered. "He also told us to confine it to the immediate area where the incident occurred and to get it done as quickly as possible so they could reopen the dock."

"Victor might be able to account for all the employees, but my father wasn't an employee, and he was attacked here. There might be someone else. We need to search the whole factory for other victims."

Deputy Harris took Emory aside to tell him, "I know this is emotional for you, given your connection to the victim." He waved an arm toward the other deputies. "We're all upset about what happened to the sheriff. But you need to put your emotions aside. If you did, you'd understand we don't have a right to search outside the immediate crime scene without a search warrant."

Maintaining listening distance, Jeff butted in to ask Deputy Harris, "Do you want to be responsible for someone dying just because you refused to look around?"

The deputy sighed and crossed his arms. "Fine. I'll see about getting us a warrant."

While the deputy radioed for a warrant, Jeff led Emory away. "Okay, spill. What are you up to?"

"Taking a page from your book." Emory pointed to the double doors. "Down that hallway is a locked, unmarked door. Even the foreman didn't know what was on the other side."

"What do you think it is?"

"I don't know. It could be nothing, but my gut's nagging at me."

Jeff nodded. "That's good enough for me. I'll call Victor to see if we can get a key by the time the search warrant arrives."

Forty minutes later, Deputy Harris returned with a search warrant in hand.

Emory's first question was, "The warrant's for the whole building, correct?" When Deputy Harris nodded, Emory headed for the unmarked room "Good. I know where to start."

Deputy Harris tried the doorknob. "It's locked."

Jeff told him, "I tried tracking down the key, but no one here has one for this particular room."

"No master key?" Harris asked.

Jeff shook his head. "I've left messages for Victor and his assistant, but they haven't returned my call."

"Then we'll search the rest of the place and come back. Give him more time." Deputy Harris led the other deputies away, but Emory and Jeff stayed behind.

Emory banged a fist against the door. "Dammit!"

Jeff touched Emory's back. "It's okay. It shouldn't take long for them to get back here."

"Patience is not one of my virtues."

Jeff dropped his hand and examined him. "From where I stand, you have plenty of virtues."

Emory fought back a smile. "This door's pretty solid. And wide. We need a way to open it in case we don't get the key."

"Why don't I just pick the lock?"

"You can't do that. Anything we might find would be inadmissible."

"We could just take a quick peek and lock it back."

Emory hardened his face. "No."

"Fine. So what does the TBI do when you need to look inside a place and there's no one to let you in?"

"Assuming we have a warrant, we follow the knock-and-announce policy and then wait a reasonable time for a response. If none is forthcoming, we have the right to forcibly enter."

"So it's better to break the door down, cause all that damage, than to pick the lock and cause none?"

Emory shrugged. "It's the law."

Jeff knocked on the door. "Hello? Emory Rome from the Tennessee Bureau of Investigation!"

"What are you doing?"

"Knocking and announcing," replied Jeff before returning his attention to the door. "I have a warrant to search the premises. Open up!" He asked Emory, "What's a reasonable time for a response?"

"Usually fifteen seconds or so."

"Keep listening, and I'll be right back."

"Where are you going?"

Jeff didn't answer as he disappeared behind the double doors leading to the receiving area. He returned a moment later with a crowbar in hand. "I found this near where the forklifts are parked. Has anyone responded yet?"

"No."

"Well, it's been more than fifteen seconds."

Emory hesitated but took a step back. "Go ahead."

Jeff placed the beveled end of the crowbar into the crack between the door and the jamb, and he wrenched the door open, separating the door knob housing from the wood in the process.

After turning on the light, Emory's shoulders slumped. The room was rectangular, forty feet by twenty feet. It contained several industrial shelves filled with file folders, outdated computers, countless ledgers and even boxes of floppy discs.

Jeff said, "Well, I'm not sure what we were expecting to find, but I'd have to say this is disappointing."

Emory nodded. "It's a records room." He took out his phone and snapped photos of the entire area.

"Why are you taking pictures? There's nothing to see."

"Experience. You don't always spot the clues at first glance. This gives me a chance to review the scene later for anything I might've missed."

Jeff pointed to the floor. "There's something odd. Tire tracks." He looked back at the door. "I guess it is big enough to drive a forklift in here."

Emory took pictures of the tracks and followed them to a wall lined with shelves.

The next moment Victor pounced into the room like someone catching an unfaithful lover in the act of betrayal. "What are you doing in here?"

Without missing a beat, Emory answered, "Investigating the assaults that occurred at your factory."

Victor pointed to the floor as the deputies entered the room. "They didn't occur here!"

Jeff chimed in with, "'Here' is a subjective term."

Deputy Harris handed Victor the warrant. "Mr. Algarotti, we obtained a search warrant to see if there were any other assault victims on the premises."

Victor told him, "There's obviously no assault victim here."

Keeping a calm voice, Emory responded, "Mr. Algarotti, we had no way of knowing without checking it out. We did call you and left a message."

"I needed a nap, for god's sake! Excuse me for not answering the phone for a couple of hours during the most stressful week of my life!"

Emory headed to the door, followed by Jeff and the deputies. As Victor walked out, he noticed the damage caused during entry. "Look what you did to my door!" He pointed an angry finger at Emory. "I'm sending you the bill for the repair!"

Emory followed Jeff down the hallway, but slowed his pace so he could hear Deputy Harris apologize to Victor.

Victor took one more look at the room and muttered, "Huh," before flicking the switch.

"What is it?" Deputy Harris asked.

"Nothing," said Victor "Just funny how places seem bigger when you're younger. I used to come to this room all the time. My first job here was filing, among many other menial tasks."

In the receiving area, Emory and Jeff talked for a moment to the other two deputies before going to the place in the woods where Lula Mae found her husband the previous night. They ducked under the yellow crime tape and hadn't taken a step before noticing the compacted snow where Sheriff Rome had been left. Emory took pictures of the ground, including the patch of red snow from the wound at the back of the sheriff's head. He looked at the natural spring behind the barbed wire fence, which was just a few feet away.

Jeff pointed to the ground. "Over here."

Emory joined Jeff and saw numerous tracks in the snow. "Coyotes."

"Look how close they got."

Emory's eyes shot to where his father was found and retraced the short distance from there to the tracks. "I'm going to kill whoever did this to him." He began walking back to his car.

Jeff hurried after him. "Where to now?"

"You're not going to like it."

CHAPTER 27

J EFF SPENT THE ride to the Algarotti house trying to dissuade Emory from his planned confrontation, but the TBI agent's resolve was proving to be immutable. Emory told him, "The way Pristine met her husband is an important clue that has to be investigated."

"I told you that in confidence. You'll break my client-investigator privilege."

"Is there honestly such a thing?"

Jeff threw up his hands. "It's more like a code really."

"Then to paraphrase Alan Turing, that code's about to be broken."

Jeff pulled down the windshield visor and checked his reflection in its mirror. He snaked his fingers through his thick brown hair, tousling it into charming anarchy. "Why do you even have to bring it up? Pristine can't be the one behind everything."

"What rules her out?"

The PI pushed the visor back up and stared at the dashboard. "I didn't know Victor Algarotti's complete financial situation two years ago when I singled him out for Pristine. What if, when she found out the money wasn't his, she decided to kill Britt so her husband would continue to have control over it? The murder would be, in essence, my fault."

Emory glanced at him, but something else caught his attention—a boy pushing a bike down the road. "Is that Ian?"

Jeff's downcast demeanor vanished when he saw the youngest Algarotti struggling to walk his bike. "Looks like Damien's chain came off." He smirked at the boy's misfortune. "He's got a long walk ahead of him." When Emory turned on his hazard lights, Jeff asked, "What are you doing?"

"Helping him."

"He doesn't need us. He has demon-possessed Rottweilers for that."

"Stop it. He's just a kid. What do you have against him?"

"He gives me the creeps. I know you weren't there, but I told you about the conversation we had when I returned Britt's laptop. He seriously lit up when talking about details of Rick Roberts' death. Sorry for the pun."

"We're helping him." Emory parked a few yards in front of Ian and got out of the car. "Ian! Do you need some help?" Ian looked at him as if he couldn't quite place who he was. "Remember me. I'm Emory Rome with the TBI."

Ian nodded but told him, "I don't take rides from strangers."

"You're right. Why don't you call your dad and ask if it's okay for me to give you a ride. That way, he knows who you're with."

The thirteen-year-old pulled his phone from his pocket and brushed his blond bangs from his eyes with the sleeve of his jacket. "I'll text him."

Emory looked around, uncertain how to pass the time as they waited for a reply from Ian's father. "So it feels a little warmer today."

The phone dinged, and Ian told him, "Dad says it's okay."

Emory loaded Ian's bike into the trunk, and the boy scooted into the back seat. "Hey," he greeted the back of Jeff's head.

Jeff lowered the car's visor and looked at Ian through the attached mirror. "Hey."

Emory slipped behind the steering wheel and eased the car back onto the road. "Ian, where are you coming from?"

"Just riding around."

Emory smiled in the rearview mirror. "I noticed the smaller desk in your dad's office. Is that yours?"

"Yes. I work for Dad after school."

"What's it like working with your father?"

"It's okay."

Emory realized that Ian, in typical teenage fashion, had a disdain for elaboration when it came to questions from adults, so he gave up on the conversation.

After several moments of uncomfortable silence plodded by, Jeff broke it with a question of his own. "Junior high was kind of tough for me. How do you like it?"

"I'm not in junior high."

Jeff's face cracked into a grin. "Did you get held back?"

Ian's sudden glare slapped the smile off Jeff's reflection. "I'm in high school."

"Oh, you skipped a grade?" Emory asked.

Ian sighed and rolled his eyes. "Two grades."

Jeff and Emory glanced at each other. They asked no other questions during the final two-minute drive to the Algarotti house.

The two men had no sooner pulled Ian's bike out of the back of the car when the front door to the house flew open and Margaret, the Algarottis' elderly maid, ran out screaming. Flying out the door behind her, a crystal goblet grazed Margaret's left ear before smashing onto the driveway, shattering into sharp, sparkling pieces. Hot on her heels, Pristine Algarotti hurried from the house, fumbling with an arm full of crystal goblets. "Pack up your shit, and don't ever come back!" she yelled as she hurled goblet after goblet at her surprisingly evasive target until only one remained. Margaret ran along the driveway in front of the Alga-rottis' house and turned the corner toward what Emory remembered to be the maid's house in back.

Pristine swung around and at last noticed the three people watching her. "I can't stand thief-ry!" She then looked at Ian as if she were about to apologize to him.

"Are you okay?" the boy asked.

"I'm fine," she answered in a more relaxed tone. "Why don't you go inside, and I'll make us lunch in a bit?" With that, Ian parked his bike on the porch and disappeared inside the house. Seeing the men's faces, Pristine's face again contorted into rage. "She had the nerve to steal one of my crystal glasses." She held up the only remaining goblet.

"Why would she steal a glass?" Emory asked.

Pristine looked at him as if he had asked the stupidest question she had ever heard. "This costs more than she makes in a month."

Jeff asked, "If you care so much about the glasses, why did you break them?"

In a hissy-fit, Pristine threw the last goblet to the ground, shattering it. "It's the principle!"

The PI looked at the shattered glass and then at its destroyer. With a bemused smirk, he said, "Touché."

Emory let loose a small snicker before getting control of himself, but it was enough to send Pristine fuming toward the door. He tried to stop her with, "I…We need to talk to you."

She grabbed the doorknob and turned around to face them. "What, are you two working together now?"

Emory looked at Jeff, who answered, "Marathoners in the same race."

She snarled, "Why the hell are you running by here?"

Emory responded, "We have some questions—"

Pristine started shutting the door. "I'm done with that."

"They're about how you met your husband," Emory blurted out.

Pristine looked at Jeff as if searching for a sign of assurance that he hadn't divulged the truth. His tilted brow and slight shrug seemed to give her an answer. Stepping aside, she waved them into the foyer. "Why don't you come on in and make yourself uncomfortable, like I am right now." Once inside, she told them, "Parlor," as if they should've known where she wanted them to go.

The men walked into the parlor and saw the glass from at least two broken goblets near the bar and a couple of sofa pillows on the floor. Jeff nodded to the pillows and whispered, "Margaret probably used them as a shield from the glass-flinger."

"Look at this mess." Pristine sidestepped the glass. "I've told Victor we need more servants."

"How do you know Margaret took it?" Emory asked.

"I found it in one of her drawers when I was looking through the maid's house out back…" Pristine just realized she had no more crystal glasses. "Great. Now I have nothing to put my protein drink in." She eyed the metal mixing cup. "I'll just make a bigger one."

Jeff asked, "You suspected she was stealing?"

As she talked, she mixed her protein drink in the blender, adding water from a glass bottle, ice and three scoops of protein powder instead of her normal one scoop. "No, I had no idea until I saw it there." She added a generous pour of Tennessee honey whiskey to the blender. "It's our property. I have every right to go in and look whenever I want."

Emory told her, "Uh, not really."

Pristine talked over Emory to finish her explanation. "I came back here to confront her, and she started lying."

Emory held up his finger. "On that subject, could you tell me why you lied about the basis for your marriage?"

In lieu of an immediate answer, Pristine kept her eyes on the blender, covered it with the lid and turned it on. Emory watched her stolid face – assuming she was using the noise from the grinding ice to give her enough time to formulate an answer. Once the noise ended, she poured the drink into the mixing cup. "I have to say, Jeff, I'm pretty damned pissed that you betrayed my confidence. Isn't it illegal for you to share information about your clients?"

"Not illegal," Jeff told her. "More of a broken code."

Emory tapped his foot a couple of times. "Pristine, answer my question."

She glowered at him. "You're being disrespectful to me in my own house."

"If you'd prefer, we could move the conversation to the sheriff's station."

Pristine's expressions teetered between anger and concern, as if she were uncertain of her next words or the manner of their delivery.

Jeff joked, "Too bad you're all out of throwing glasses."

A tear rolled down Pristine's cheek as she appeared to settle on concern – for herself, no doubt. She again delayed her response, this time by sucking in a quarter of her protein drink through the straw. After a deep exhale, she responded, "From your judgmental tone, I can tell you're not questioning my marriage. You're questioning my ethics." She took another drink and meandered from behind the bar. "Our chance encounter did require a gentle prodding of fate, but is that really so unethical? Before you think I want an answer, that question was hypothetical."

Emory told her, "I think you mean rhetorical."

"Whatever. Mr. Rome, I realize my limitations. I know I'm not talented at anything. I'm not capable of becoming rich on my own. The only way I could ever be rich, without breaking the law, was to marry into it." Pristine waved off an imaginary fly. "Now I know you think I'm justifying all those preconceived notions you have of me, but you're wrong. I didn't lie to you. I love my husband now, and I loved him when we married. That's all that counts."

"Okay." Jeff glance at Emory. "I think we've got the story from there."

"Does Britt count?" Emory asked.

Pristine swallowed more of her protein drink. "Are you suggesting I had something to do with the death of my stepdaughter?"

"She and Ian are all that stand between you and your dream, being married to a truly rich man."

Pristine's face began to twitch, and she changed direction as if she were looking for something in the room that she just couldn't find. "When you're in love, money doesn't matter." Her hands shook.

Believing he was making her nervous, Emory couldn't keep his lips from curling into a subtle smile of satisfaction. He was about to ask a follow-up question when she asked one of her own.

"What about her coach? What would I gain by killing him?" Pristine tried to place her mixing cup on the bar, but her hands were shaking so much, she knocked it over. "I think you need to do your job and investigate all the evidence so you can find the real…"

Pristine's neck jerked back, and her spine arched. Muscle convulsions overtook her body. Jeff ran to her as she fell back, catching her before she hit the floor. "Pristine!" He looked up at Emory, who was now standing over her. "What's wrong with her?"

CHAPTER 28

EMORY DIALED 911 on his cell phone as he told Jeff, "It looks like a reaction to poison." When the operator answered, Emory said he believed he had a potential poisoning victim, and he described Pristine's symptoms.

As Pristine's convulsions persisted, Jeff cradled her head in his hands to keep it from banging against the floor. Emory continued talking to the operator while he ran to get a pillow, which he handed to Jeff to place behind her head. He asked the operator, "Should we try to make her throw up?" Once he heard her answer, he shook his head at Jeff.

Pristine's convulsions came to an abrupt stop. Jeff checked for a pulse in her neck. "She's still alive."

Emory let the operator know, and she told them to just keep her comfortable until help arrived. He hung up the phone and called Victor to let him know. Cupping his hand over the phone, he whispered to Jeff, "He's on his way."

Jeff glanced at the ceiling. "What about Ian?"

"I'll go check on him. Are you okay here?"

"I'll stay with her."

Emory left the parlor and walked up to the second floor. At the top of the stairs, he saw a long hallway with several doors in either direction and a red runner rug bisecting the burnished hardwood floor. He didn't know where Ian's room was, so he started with the left hall and listened for movement. The first door he came to was closed. He put his ear to it, just shy of touching, and moved on when he heard nothing. He then passed by a room that had been converted into a home gym, complete with a treadmill, a few machines and pink dumbbells. *Must be Pristine's.* The next door was open, which he found surprising because it was Britt's bedroom. *That's odd. A parent in mourning will typically shut off a dead child's bedroom to preserve its essence.*

Emory walked into the lavender-hued room and looked around. Among the trophies, medals, competition photos and jewelry boxes cluttering the tops of the furniture was her laptop where he presumed Ian had returned it. He opened one of the jewelry boxes and found a few costume pieces comingled with the finer ones. "Probably from Dan Claymon," he muttered about the inexpensive items. He opened the smaller jewelry box and found condoms inside. "Probably for Dan." He picked up a small framed picture of Victor and Meredith, the children's mother, holding a baby Britt following her birth. *Apart from some crow's feet, Victor looks pretty much the same. I hope I age so well.*

Emory's eyes wandered around the room, landing on a poster-sized picture inside a gold frame that, instead of hanging on the wall, was lying on top of the bed. "Wow," he whispered in reference to the beautiful shot. It was a black and white photo of Britt looking over her shoulder at the photographer as she walked toward the lake where she would later die. The trees and ground were covered in snow, and she had skates hanging from her shoulder. Her smile was radiant and sweet with no hint of sadness, yet that's all Emory felt as he stared at it. He snapped a picture of the photo with his phone.

"That's the picture we had at her funeral," a woman said from behind him.

Startled, Emory jerked around to face the doorway, where Margaret – the now jobless maid – stood. "Margaret. The door was open."

The old woman nodded. "I keep shutting it, and someone keeps opening it again."

"What are you doing here?" he asked in as delicate a tone as he could.

She nodded to the half-full grocery tote in her right hand. "I came through the back to get some things I left over here."

Emory wondered if they were her belongings, but he left it alone. "This is a great photo."

Margaret stepped into the room. "That's the last picture of her taken alive. Tati, her best friend, fancies herself a photographer, and Britt was her favorite model. She took pictures of her the weekend before she died. She had that one blown up and framed, and gave it to Mr. Algarotti." Margaret admired the picture, shaking her head. "She was such a beautiful girl. She didn't belong in this family."

"What do you mean?"

"Nothing." She turned from him and headed toward the door. "I should go."

"Could you tell me where Ian's room is?"

Margaret pointed toward the direction from which he had come. "He's on that side." She left him and headed back down the stairs.

Could Margaret have poisoned Pristine? Closing the bedroom door, he walked down the hall, listening at each door before opening them to see if the room behind it belonged to Ian. He reached a door and heard the squeaking of a chair on the other side. "Ian?" he called, knocking on the door. "I need to talk to you."

"Just a minute," Ian told him. The squeaking halted, replaced by the sound of rustling plastic followed by a drawer shutting. A few seconds later, Ian cracked the door open, wearing a robe and clutching it closed at his abdomen. "What is it?"

Emory saw a blank computer monitor on the desk next to the bed. "Uh, I'm sorry to tell you this, but there's been an incident with your stepmother."

"What's wrong?"

"We believe she's been poisoned."

"Oh my god!" Ian opened the door wider like he was going to rush to her, but Emory stopped him with a hand to his shoulder.

"An ambulance is on the way." *I should give him a task to occupy him so he doesn't have to see her in her present state.* "You could really help out by packing an overnight bag for her, anything she might need while in the hospital."

Ian nodded. "Okay." He hurried down the long hall to the master bedroom.

Once Emory saw the boy had disappeared behind the master bedroom door, his curiosity got the better of him. He slipped into Ian's room. Walking past the padded blue footlocker at the foot of the bed, he went to the desk. The computer monitor had been turned off, so he powered it back on. What replaced the black screen sent his hand to his gasping mouth.

Splayed across the entire screen was a collage of pictures – all of Victor Algarotti. Some were of Victor by the pool in his swim trunks, but most were taken while he seemed to be asleep in bed. The covers of the bed had been lifted from the lower corner to expose his right, hairy leg and high enough to reveal that Victor slept in the nude. The light in the picture appeared to come from another source instead of a camera flash, perhaps the hallway or the master bathroom.

Emory snapped pictures with his phone as he scrolled through several of the photos until he was startled by a sudden movement behind him. He poked the monitor's power button to shut it off and turned around to see Ian standing in the doorway.

Holding a pink overnight bag in his hand, Ian asked, "What are you doing?" with accusatory eyes flaming from his face.

Emory had no idea how long Ian had been watching or if he had just reached the door. He decided to act as if it were the latter. His eyes darted from Ian to the blue duvet draped over the bed. The paned sunshine that illuminated one corner of the bed gave him an idea.

He pointed to the window that was to the side of the desk. "Admiring your view." Emory turned his head to look through the window, to which he had paid little attention before, and was relieved to find that it did indeed offer a nice view. "The mountains are spectacular."

Emory started toward the door. "It's a lot different from the bedroom view I had as a kid – a bunch of hemlock trees. Is that the bag?" He took it from Ian, whose expression remained unchanged. "Thank you for doing that."

Emory headed down the hall toward the stairs. He looked back at Ian, who seemed stuck in place. "Come down when you hear the ambulance leave."

"I need to change," Ian told him with frosted tongue before retreating into his bedroom and shutting the door.

Hearing an approaching siren, Emory hurried down the stairs and out the front door. Once the ambulance stopped, he escorted the emergency medical technicians to the parlor. Jeff moved away as they took over Pristine's care. A moment later, they carried Pristine out on a gurney, and the ambulance departed.

Emory pulled some plastic baggies from his jacket pocket and told Jeff, "I need to bag everything she put into her protein drink."

"Need any help?" Jeff asked, although he knew what Emory's answer would be.

"I have to do it myself."

"Understood." Jeff walked around the parlor for any clues while the special agent worked.

Once Emory zipped up his last baggie, he told Jeff, "You know, now that this house is a crime scene, I'd like to conduct a thorough search—"

"That's not going to happen," Victor growled as he stormed into the parlor.

Emory tried to explain. "Your wife was just poisoned here."

"In this room. Isn't that what you told me?"

Jeff said, "This is where she passed out, but we can't be sure it's where she was poisoned."

"I'm not going to have you rummaging through my house and tearing each room apart on a snipe hunt." Victor noticed the baggies on the bar. "Was it in her protein drink?"

"Possibly," Emory answered. "Did anyone else ever drink this?"

"Just Pristine." Victor's eyes welled. "Why is someone trying to kill off my family?"

Emory responded, "We don't know, which is why I need to search the house."

Victor nodded toward the baggies. "I suggest you check what you have first. If you don't find it in there, you have my permission to return and look for it. Where's Ian?"

Ian appeared behind his father, dressed and holding a hairbrush. He walked it over to Emory. "I forgot to pack this. She loves to brush her hair."

"Thank you, Ian." Emory took the brush, which had several pulled strands of hair weaved among the bristles, and stared at it for a brief moment before stuffing it into the overnight bag, which Victor then commandeered.

"Ian, wait for me in the car." The boy obeyed his father. "Gentlemen, get your stuff, and I'll walk you out."

Emory picked up the evidence. "I have to say, Mr. Algarotti, I've never met anyone who has lost a loved one and then put up so many roadblocks to determining why."

"You're looking in the wrong place! My home? No one here

could've done that to Britt. And now to Pristine. Who's left? Me? Ian?" Victor turned to Jeff. "I'm paying you to find the truth." He pointed toward the front door. "The truth is out there. My daughter was beautiful, successful and rich – qualities that taken alone could rile jealousy in the purest hearts, but put them all together?" He waved them to the door. "Let's go."

Emory and Jeff walked outside, followed by Victor, who locked the front door and didn't say a word to them on the way to his car.

Jeff asked, "You want to go to the hospital?"

Emory stepped off the porch. "To tell you the truth, I want to call it a day."

CHAPTER 29

ONCE THEY LEFT the Algarottis' house, Emory and Jeff drove to Noah's Market to pick up some groceries before heading to the Romes' house. As they shopped, Emory told Jeff about what he had found on Ian Algarotti's computer.

Jeff's reaction mirrored Emory's when he learned about the pictures. "Oh my god! Dirty pictures of his own father?"

The duo received disapproving looks from three shoppers, including a prudish woman who reversed her cart to avoid them. Emory shushed Jeff. "Keep it down."

"Sorry, you caught me off guard. So Ian's got daddy issues."

Emory steered the cart into one of the checkout lines. In a tone just above a whisper, he asked, "Do you think that could've led him to murder?"

"You mean, if he was jealous of the attention his big sister was getting? I guess it's possible, but you'd need a lot more to go on than candid nudes of your dad."

The older couple in line ahead of them and even the cashier threw them chastising glances. Jeff smiled, but Emory kept his face down all the way through the checkout and to the car.

Once they were driving away, Jeff asked, "If Ian did kill Britt in a fit of jealousy, why would he kill Rick Roberts?"

"I don't know."

They continued talking about the case until they arrived at the house. While they were bringing in the groceries, Lula Mae called to apprise Emory of his father's condition.

As Emory spoke on the phone, Jeff greeted Sophie, who accompanied him on a self-guided tour of the house – the parts he hadn't seen before. When the tour wound back to the kitchen, Emory hung up the phone.

"How's your dad?"

"He's fine. He'll be home in the morning."

"Listen, I don't know that I feel comfortable sleeping in your parents' bed."

"You can have my room, and I'll sleep in there," Emory said as he emptied the grocery bags.

Jeff nosed around the kitchen, starting with the refrigerator. "Ooh, peach juice. I love that stuff."

"Have some."

"Maybe later." Jeff closed the door. "Do you want me to help with dinner?"

"Just go make yourself comfortable. I'll have it ready in about forty-five minutes."

Jeff opened the cabinets and stopped when he found a bottle of Malbec wine. "What are you making?"

"Mustard chicken with asparagus and Greek potatoes."

"Sounds ambitious."

"I like to cook. I don't get a chance to do it much anymore. Cooking for one just isn't...fulfilling." He saw the bottle in Jeff's hand. "There should be a bottle opener in that drawer to your left."

Jeff found the opener and screwed it into the cork. "Where did you learn to cook?"

"I used to help my granny, and when I came to live here, my mom taught me what she knew."

Jeff popped the cork from the bottle and put both on the kitchen counter. "That's an odd turn of phrase. What do you mean, when you came to live here?"

Emory whisked the mustard, flour, herbs and spices inside a bowl. "The Romes aren't my birth parents. My granny raised me most of my childhood. My mother was a bit of a vagabond, a free spirit. She had a passing fling with a man and ended up pregnant. Thankfully, she had the good sense not to raise me herself and left me with her mother, my granny. My mother would show up occasionally, sometimes staying for a few months, but she would always leave – like she was on the run. When I was twelve, she died in an accident. My granny was killed in a fire three years later."

"I'm sorry." Jeff placed a consoling hand on Emory's back.

Emory stopped scraping the whisk around the bowl for a few silent seconds. "Let's talk about something else."

"Fine." Jeff dropped his hand back to his side. "So how did you end up with the Romes?"

"That's a story for another time." Emory nodded toward the wine bottle. "There are glasses in the cupboard over there."

Jeff retrieved two wine glasses and filled them a quarter each, handing one to Emory. The PI dipped his nose into the glass and inhaled. "Mmm. Like black cherries and cracked pepper warming on an oak plank in the sun."

Emory sniffed, and he could feel his face redden at his inability to distinguish the aromas. "It smells good."

Jeff clinked his glass against Emory's. "Cheers."

After an initial sip, Emory and Jeff's eyes lingered on each other to the point of loitering. Like a swinging pocket watch held by a hypnotist, Jeff's sparkling green eyes mesmerized Emory. The special agent tilted his face to one side but couldn't break his gaze.

"I should get dinner ready," he muttered. He blinked, turning away before letting his eyelids rise again. "Go relax."

"As you wish." Jeff tipped his glass to him and left the kitchen.

Once Emory had the chicken and potatoes in the oven, he set the timer and wandered from the kitchen. He found Jeff in the living room, which glowed orange from the crackling fire he'd built in the fireplace. Jeff sat on one of two sofa cushions now on the floor, and he rested his back against the front of the sofa with his legs under the coffee table.

"What are you doing?" Emory asked.

"It was a little chilly in here." He tapped the top of the coffee table. "I thought this would be a better place to eat than the kitchen table. Is that okay?"

"Yeah, it's nice." Emory couldn't tell whether the sudden heat radiated from the fire or percolated through his skin from his over-beating heart. "Dinner's cooking. I'll steam the asparagus when it's closer to done."

"I'll do the dishes then."

"You don't have—"

"No argument from you." Jeff patted the empty cushion. "Sit down."

Emory placed his wine glass on the coffee table next to Jeff's. He kicked off his shoes and plopped down beside him, nodding toward the fireplace. "You do good fire."

Jeff clenched his fist in the air, causing vast tributaries of veins to ripple around his forearm. "Just call me Icarus."

"Well, if you're done stealing from the gods."

"I never said that. The gods are hoarders of magic, and I've got sticky fingers."

Laughing, Emory pointed at the PI. "You owe me something."

Jeff rested his elbow on the sofa and waved a hand over his body. "What do you want?"

"I've told you a lot about me, but I know next to nothing about you."

Jeff gave him an incredulous look. "For the record, there's no measurement system in the world that would quantify what you've told me about yourself as 'a lot,' but what do you want to know?"

Emory turned away from the fire and crossed his legs to sit facing Jeff. "Start with where you grew up."

Jeff added an extra twang when he told him, "Well, I was born and raised in Bristol, right on the state line. Our house was in Tennessee, but our backyard was in Virginia. I moved to Knoxville for college, and I never left." A log snapped in the fireplace. Jeff smirked at Emory and inched closer, almost within kissing distance, but he retreated, returning his back to the couch and facing the flames. "I lied to you."

"Really? Where are you from?"

"No, not that. A few days ago." Jeff tightened his jaw. "I didn't major in criminology."

"Why would you lie about that?"

"You had already questioned my credentials. I figured you'd respect me more if you thought I was a serious student of the craft."

"Did you even go to college?"

The question elicited a snarl from Jeff. "Yes, and I graduated – if you can believe that."

Emory placed a hand on Jeff's knee. "I'm sorry. I didn't mean anything by it. I just didn't know how deep the lie went. So what was your major?"

"Don't laugh."

"I won't. I promise."

"Hotel management."

Emory's expression didn't change, except for a minor twitch of his eye. "Hotel."

"I know I told you I was going to Australia for a vacation, but

I was actually going for a job interview at this incredible resort in Melbourne."

Emory's eyebrows ticked up. "Huh."

"What?"

"Nothing."

Jeff rested his hand over Emory's. "You're thinking something. What is it?"

"All right. I was just wondering how expertise in hotel management qualifies you to be an investigator."

Jeff retracted his hand. "It doesn't, but thank you for putting it so nicely."

"I'm sorry. I didn't mean it the way it sounded. I was trying to figure out the segue from that to private investigator."

"Like I told you before, I love mysteries. Being a PI was always a fantasy job for me, something I imagined being when I was a kid. Hotel management was a real job that would take me to fantastic places, wherever I wanted to go, as long as it was far away from here. When that fell through, I went back to the fantasy."

A chime sounded from the kitchen. Emory jumped to his feet. "Time to steam the asparagus."

About ten minutes later Emory sauntered back to the living room and placed two full plates on the coffee table. He held his breath as Jeff raised the first forkful to his mouth, and the PI moaned as the tines slipped from his tightened lips. "Do you like it?"

Jeff beamed at him. "It's wonderful."

Emory exhaled into a smile.

As the two ate, the conversation turned to work when Jeff asked, "What was your most difficult case?"

"Most difficult?"

"One that threw you for a loop."

Emory needed little time to rank the one that impacted him most. "All right. There was this one really sadistic killer who enjoyed humiliating his victims before he would let them die. I won't go through all of them, but one person he decided to kill was an old woman. He made her drink a potent morning glory tea—"

"Morning glory? Is that poisonous?"

"The seeds have d-lysergic acid amide, a cousin of LSD. He waited for her to finish it, and then he watched this sweet, gentle woman descend into madness. He laughed at each ridiculous thing she said and every bizarre thing she did. She tore off her clothes and clawed herself bloody trying to release her soul. All the while he's pissing himself laughing so hard."

"How do you know all this? It's not like you were there."

"He described it all to me in vivid detail like he was telling a long-winded joke with no real punchline."

"So you did catch him."

Emory cocked his head to one side and clenched his right cheek. "So to speak. Anyway, back to that day. He hid when I arrived, and I didn't realize he was there until it was too late. I rushed to help the woman, and he hit me from behind. I woke up lying on the cold cement floor of the basement bathroom with something crackling in my ear. I pushed myself up and saw that the door was on fire, and there was no window for escape. Above me, I could hear the woman screaming in agony, and I knew she was on fire."

Jeff gasped. "Oh my god. What did you do?"

"I grabbed the porcelain cover from the back of the commode and hurled it through the door, breaking it into flaming kindling. I wet a towel and threw it over my head and shoulders. When I jumped from the bathroom, I ran through a tunnel of fire to a spot without flames, and I saw the fire hadn't spread to that corner of the basement – although the entire ceiling above me was burning. The wooden stairs up to the house were gone, but I saw a small, ground-level window above a shelf beside me. I climbed the shelf, wrapped the towel around my fist and broke out the window."

"Holy shit." Jeff waved a hand like he was erasing a chalkboard. "Okay, this isn't the dinner conversation I had in mind." He gulped a little wine and returned the empty glass to the coffee table.

Emory rested his hand on Jeff's rock-solid thigh. "Sorry. Didn't mean to get so serious."

"Oh, I don't mind serious." Jeff anchored his gaze to Emory's eyes. "I can do serious." He caressed his shoulder before cupping the back of Emory's neck, drawing his face closer.

Emory raised his hand to Jeff's side and twisted his body to bring their chests together. Their lips met, and the two lost each other in a kiss that was awkward at first but soon fell into an exultant rhythm. Tasting the wine on Jeff's tongue, Emory now picked up on its elemental pleasures.

Emory was the first to pull away, just far enough for their lips to part, but Jeff was the first to speak. "Damn."

Smiling, Emory glanced at the discolored bump on Jeff's mouth. "How's your lip?"

Jeff touched the spot where Emory had punched him that morning. "Totally worth the pain."

Emory swept in for another kiss, but he pulled away as soon as their lips touched. "Wait. I can't do this."

"Do what?"

Emory returned to his own cushion and motioned at the space between them. "This. It makes me nervous."

"Wait, are you a virgin?"

"No, of course not."

"Then what's the problem?" When Emory didn't respond, Jeff released a heavy sigh. "What's in your head right now? Spit it out."

"All right! I've been so focused on my career, I've let my personal life basically atrophy. The point is I'm not sure I'm…good."

"Like I told you before, you intrigue me, Emory Rome. I just want to experience you, whatever form that takes." Jeff grabbed his arms. "As for the atrophy, I took some physical therapy classes in college. I can trigger that muscle memory for you."

Now grinning, Emory pushed himself off his cushion and straddled Jeff to deliver a vigorous kiss.

Jeff's fingers brushed against the handcuffs attached to Emory's belt, and he pulled them off. "Ever use these outside of work?"

Emory's eyebrows peaked. "I'm going to want to use my hands."

"I didn't mean you."

"I don't think I want you restrained." Grabbing the handcuffs, Emory flung them over his shoulder, and he heard them clang to the floor somewhere near the fireplace.

Emory pulled Jeff down to horizontal on the cushion. Their hands grappled for the other's flesh, reacting with savage aversion to any clothing that kept them from it. Shirts ripped, and pants were kicked to the sidelines. Pressing every square inch they could against each other, the two men rolled onto the hardwood floor, each fighting for dominance until one submitted.

CHAPTER 30

EMORY STARED AT the ceiling of his old bedroom, at the tiny phosphorescent stars he and his dad had painted years ago. They were faded now, but they still comforted him. Jeff lay sleeping at his side, breathing on a shared pillow like a neck-tickling breeze on an exertive night.

Although Emory sensed sleep lurking nearby, he couldn't quite find it. He pulled his naked body from beneath the covers and exited the room with such a light footfall, Sophie didn't miss a single step in her dream running at the foot of the bed. He drifted into the living room, the cozy space glowing in the faint embers of a fire that roared with a ferocious fever just two hours earlier. He collected his clothes scattered about and dressed himself again, along with his shoes. He saw his holster hanging from the arm of the couch, thought about putting it on but didn't feel like carrying the extra weight. He retrieved his jacket from the back of a chair in the kitchen and left the house.

Emory walked over the fading snow and through the moon-glimmered mist to the fence at the edge of the woods. He took a moment to smile at the handful of visible stars before resting his forearms on a lateral plank and facing the hazy trees. Eyes wide open, he reveled in his current elation. "Jeff," he whispered.

Emory had known he wanted the handsome PI from the moment he first saw him through the windshield of his car, but he was not the type to give temptation a second thought, much less surrender to it. Each encounter with the green-eyed man had started with a conscious effort not to think of him in that way. Concentrate on the work, no matter how difficult he made it. Now those efforts were moot.

Thoughts of work slammed the door open to anxiety. *What will tomorrow be like? How will we work together? What's going to happen once this case is over? Was tonight just a one-time thing? Should it be? Oh god, it's happening – just what I was afraid of.* Emory had mastered his life and had it under control, but his actions tonight had made him vulnerable to self-doubt, like rust eating at unpainted steel. *What the hell have I done?*

Emory didn't have long to contemplate. A woman's scream pierced through the fog. His first instinct was to reach for his gun, which wasn't there. He cursed himself for leaving it in the living room, but no matter, he had to act. He leapt over the fence and raced into the woods.

Without a flashlight, he had to slow his pace after a few steps. His eyes were now dependent on the deceptive moonlight diffusing through the fog, but even that light couldn't penetrate the soupiness below his knees. Each step from here on out had to be gauged on the probability of hidden obstacles.

Speed-walking deeper into the woods, he heard the distant cooing of a mourning dove. He stopped to listen for anything human, and he could hear faint rumblings coming from the same direction as the bird's call. He pursued the voices, stumbling over tree roots and the occasional pine cone as he course-corrected more than once. Even when the voices became more distinctive, he couldn't understand a thing they were saying.

Emory saw a glow up ahead, and as he moved closer, he entered a small clearing. In the center stood a modest shack with a double-sloping roof attached on its longest sides. Erected adjacent to the house was a barebones outhouse. Light spilled from the only window on the side of the house. Emory crept closer. As he peered through a lower corner of the window, he could see it wasn't a home at all, but a church.

He saw a woman in front of a pulpit, writhing on the floor like a possessed sidewinder. Encircling her were seven men, each with one hand on the woman and one hand raised as if taking an oath. Another man danced around the seven men while clutching three rattlesnakes in his right hand. Each time the dancing man passed a table, he drank a clear liquid from a mason jar atop it. In the pews, congregants performed a choreographed modern dance – many with eyes closed and gripping a Bible in an angry fist, while some flailed their arms above them like they were swatting at a flying terror. Except for the woman being *healed*, everyone inside the church was chanting nonsensical languages.

As he watched, a face popped up before him. On the other side of the glass, a woman with dark eyes and a scornful glare was looking into his eyes!

Startled, Emory stumbled back from the window, tripping over his own feet and falling onto his butt. Hearing something from his right, he jerked his head around. A scowling man approached him from the outhouse. The man didn't say a word, but he was stomping his way closer.

Emory jumped to his feet and bolted for the woods. He could hear the snow crunching as the man pursued him.

Within seconds, Emory tripped over a root and went tumbling forward. He parted the thick lower layer of fog as he crashed to the ground. He turned himself around, but the approaching footsteps gave him no time to get to his feet and run.

Emory lay himself down with his back on the ground and allowed the fog to pour over him. He could hear the man just feet away now, but the fog that now concealed his body also kept him from seeing where the man was. *Please, don't step on me!* A boot clomped down within inches of his head. He squeezed his eyes shut.

The man stood still for a moment, waiting for any sign of movement. When none came, he turned around and walked back the way he had come.

After several undisturbed minutes, Emory's head and upper body rose from the fog like a zombie from the grave. He looked all around before rising to his feet. He started walking back to his old house when a flashlight's beam slapped him across the face.

Emory raised his forearm in front of his eyes to shield them from the perfusing light.

"What are you doing?" the light bearer asked.

"I was…" Emory began before the voice clicked in his head. "Jeff?"

Jeff shined the light onto his own face. "Who else would it be?"

"What are you doing here?"

"Uh-uh. I asked you first."

"I was taking a walk."

Jeff cocked his head to the right. "Don't lie to me."

"How did you find me?"

Jeff pointed the flashlight down and stirred the fog with his foot to expose the snowy ground. "I followed your tracks. From all the zigzagging, I thought you might be out here with a bottle of whiskey in your hand."

"No drinking. Just fresh air." Emory started walking again. "Let's go home. I hate it here. Bad things always happen in the woods."

"Okay, but you still haven't told me what you were doing."

As they retraced their steps, Emory told him everything that happened, after which, Jeff threw an arm around his shoulders.

"I'm glad you're okay. I woke up, and you weren't there. I started to worry."

"You were worried?"

Jeff pinched together his index finger and thumb. "Just a little bit. You are my ride home."

The next morning, Jeff again woke up alone – except for Sophie, who was snuggled under the blanket with her head hogging the pillow. The dog opened her eyes a moment after Jeff, and the two found themselves in a staring contest. Sophie broke it when she closed her eyes for a big yawn, prompting a laugh from Jeff. "Not a morning person?"

He got out of bed and walked into the living room, where he found Emory on the couch reading a book. "What's your aversion to beds?"

Emory smiled up at him. "Good morning. How'd you sleep?"

"Great." He leaned over the back of the couch and kissed Emory. He ran his hands down Emory's wet hair. "You showered already?"

"Yeah, and I'll make us breakfast in a second."

Jeff plopped his naked body on the couch beside him and glanced at the cover of Emory's book. "The Bible? Atoning for our sins?"

Emory snickered. "You're on your own with that. No, I'm just doing a little research. Listen to this: 'And these signs shall follow them that believe: In my name shall they drive out demons; they shall speak with new tongues. They shall take up serpents; and if they drink any deadly thing, it shall not hurt them; they shall lay hands on the sick, and they shall recover.'"

"Is that the passage snake handlers use to justify their practices?"

"It is. I think they coined the term, 'literally.'"

Jeff groaned. "I hate when people say that. They almost always use it incorrectly. I want to make saying 'figuratively' a thing just so people will be correct when they use it."

Emory placed the book on the floor. "You should get dressed. My parents could be home any minute."

"Damn. Why didn't you tell me?" Jeff hopped up and scrounged around the room for his clothes. "Can I take a shower?"

"Of course."

Jeff picked up the long-sleeve pullover shirt he had worn the day before to see that it was now ripped in two places. "You killed my shirt."

Emory smirked at him. "You can always pick out a shirt from my old clothes."

"From your old wardrobe?" Jeff pointed at him. "That was your intent all along, wasn't it? My poor shirt was collateral damage in your plan for revenge."

"That's not true. It's an unexpected perk. Paul Bunyan."

Jeff picked up the rest of his clothes. "All your old clothes can't be that bad. I'll find something that I can make look good." With determination, he eyeballed Emory as he left the living room.

"Good luck!" Emory yelled after him, laughing.

When Jeff entered the kitchen about twenty minutes later, he found Emory setting the table with breakfast. The PI was wearing a bowling shirt with a retro design. The short sleeves were, of course, tight around his biceps, and he had the top two buttons undone, exposing the hairy trench between his pecs.

Emory's eyebrows perked up. "Wow, it looks good."

"Not bad, huh?"

"I don't remember that shirt."

"It's your dad's." Jeff sat at the table. "That's okay, isn't it?"

Emory sat next to him. "Oh yeah, I'm sure it's fine." Seconds later, he added, "Maybe just keep your coat closed when we pick him up."

Jeff took a bite of his eggs. "I thought your mom was driving him home."

"She called while you were in the shower. They're releasing him a little later than they thought, so Dad told her to go on to church without him."

"She didn't ask you to go with?"

Emory took a sip of peach juice. "I told her I went last night."

CHAPTER 31

SHERIFF ROME PACED in his hospital room, his eyes ping-ponging between the floor and his packed suitcase by the door. Checking his watch yet again, he returned to the bed and pressed the call button.

Without the sheriff saying a word, the nurse on the other end told him, "Your doctor will be here shortly."

"Why can't I just go?" the sheriff asked.

"We can't discharge you until the doctor signs the order. Please be patient."

"I've been patient, and I'm getting tired of it." When the woman didn't respond, he dropped the call button and returned to pacing. After two laps, he looked relieved to see his son and Jeff enter the room. "Emory."

"Hey Dad." Emory gave him a hug. "How are you feeling?"

"I'm fine. Ready to get out of here." The sheriff extended a hand to Jeff. "Mr. Woodard."

Shaking his hand, Jeff told him, "I'm glad you're doing better."

"Thank you. I just want to go home now, but the doctor hasn't discharged me yet. I'm sorry to make you guys wait."

"Oh we don't care about that," Jeff said. "Right, Emory?"

Emory was deep in thought and didn't respond, so Jeff elbowed him. "Emory, are you okay?"

Emory snapped to attention. "Huh? I'm fine. Dad, would you mind if we came back in just a few minutes? I have an errand to take care of."

The sheriff shook his head. "I'll be here."

Jeff followed Emory into the hospital hallway. "What was that about?"

"Pristine's here. I want to visit her." Emory looked over his shoulder at the nurse station. "Wait here, and I'll be right back."

Emory walked up to the station, identified himself as a TBI special agent and asked for Pristine's room number. The nurse assistant at the desk gave him the room number and said, "There's a note here that she asked not to be disturbed by anyone but family."

"Do you really think she meant to keep out the person trying to find whoever put her in the hospital?"

The nurse assistant frowned as she took a moment to think. "No, I guess not."

When Emory returned to Jeff, they said in synchronicity, "I know which room she's in."

Confused, Emory asked, "How do you know?"

Jeff pointed to Victor's back just before he turned the corner and disappeared. "Victor just left it."

"Can you do me a favor and keep him occupied? I'll text you when it's all clear."

"Will do." Jeff pursued Victor down the hallway.

Emory approached Pristine's room and peered inside the open door. It wasn't a private room, but the bed closer to the door was unoccupied. The lights were dim, and the TV was on but almost inaudible. He could see the shape of Pristine's legs under the blankets, but he couldn't see her face to tell if she were awake or not. He decided to risk it. He stepped inside the room and touched the doorknob to the bathroom. After a brief pause to listen for any movement on her part, he opened the bathroom door and slithered inside, closing the door behind him before turning on the light.

He saw her makeup bag on the sink and her nightgown hanging from a hook on the door but not what he was looking for. *Damn.* Turning off the light, he stepped in silence from the bathroom and guided the door to a quiet close.

Emory waited for a moment and still heard nothing from Pristine. He stepped deeper into the room. When her pillow came into view, he saw that she was sleeping with her face turned toward the window. He also saw the object he sought on her bedside table. He crept closer until he was able to pick up the hairbrush. He pulled several strands from it, and as he began exiting the room, he retrieved a baggie from his pocket. The crinkling sound it made when he opened it seemed to echo throughout the room.

"Victor, is that you?" Pristine asked from behind him.

Emory stopped in his tracks.

CHAPTER 32

AT THE HOSPITAL in Barter Ridge, Jeff waited by an elevator, watching the numbers above the door light in descending order until it came to a stop. *Victor got off on the first floor.* Rather than wait for the elevator to come back up, he found the adjacent stairs and ran to his destination. Once there, Jeff scanned the lobby for Victor but didn't find him. He saw a directional sign for the cafeteria and spotted a clock. *It's brunch time.* He walked down the hallway and found Victor in the cafeteria line, so he jumped in a few people behind him.

Seeing only breakfast items being served, Jeff said to the server, "I just had breakfast. Do you have any lunch items?"

The small woman with a sweet granny-face pointed her spatula at the clock behind her. "Not until 10:30." The time on the clock was 10:21. "Would you care to wait?"

Jeff saw Victor paying for his food, and he didn't know if he planned to take it back to Pristine's room or eat there. "No, I'll just take a pancake."

The woman looked confused. "Just one?" When Jeff nodded, she handed him a plate with one silver dollar pancake. Jeff hurried to the cash register with the plate, ignoring the server as she held up a packet. "Don't you want your syrup?"

Jeff paid for the pancake and rushed into the dining area. Relieved to see Victor seated at a table, he sauntered through the large room, pretending to notice his client only when he was upon him. "Victor?"

Victor had been staring at his untouched food before he heard his name. "Mr. Woodard, what are you doing here?"

"I'm visiting the sheriff. Do you mind if I join you?"

Victor began to say, "I'd rather be alone," but he only got the first two words out before Jeff sat down.

Jeff unbuttoned his coat and hung it on the back of his chair. "How is Pristine doing?"

"Better." Victor's demeanor was unlike any previous meeting Jeff had with him. The sternness in his face had softened, and he had a slight bend to his back, as if defeated. "Thank you for asking. Do you have any idea who's doing this to my family?"

"I'm very close, but I can't discuss the case."

Victor stopped what he was doing to sneer at the PI. "You work for me."

"I know, but I've been working intimately with the TBI, sharing information to help us get to the bottom of it. Truth be told, I've given them a lot more information than I've received from them – and much more valuable information. No matter, I don't mind helping them. After all, we all want the same thing. Since we are sharing information, though, they've made me promise not to discuss the case until it's concluded."

"Fine." He stabbed a clump of his scrambled eggs. "I heard about Coach Roberts. He died in a house fire?" When Jeff nodded, Victor shook his head. "Terrible. Did his entire house burn?"

"It was contained to a really small area."

"The news said it might not have been an accident."

"Definitely not."

This revelation piqued Victor's interest. "Do you think it had something to do with Britt?"

"We believe so." Jeff clenched his jaw when he realized he was sharing too much. "Can I ask, what convinced you that Charlie Claymon was your water thief?"

"Why are you concerned about that?" Within two seconds, his confusion morphed to anger as the knuckles around his fork grew white. "You think Charlie Claymon killed my daughter? And tried to kill my wife?"

"No." Jeff raised his hands to calm him, hoping to avoid more eyes turning their way. "Whoever stole the water might be involved, but we don't think Charlie is even the thief."

Victor released the fork, which clinked onto his plate. "I was afraid of that."

"What do you mean?"

"I wanted to fire him the minute I found out his son was dating Britt. Of course that wouldn't have been just cause. When the foreman mentioned him as a suspect, I seized the opportunity." Victor shook his head. "I just want it all to stop. How much tragedy can one family endure before we're completely broken? You know, my first wife, Meredith, she was a wonderful woman. I know it's cliché, but the moment we met is the instant I fell in love with her. From the beginning, she had this incredible inner light, and when the children came along, they just magnified that brilliance inside her. We had a wonderful life together. Britt has so many of her qualities, but she was daddy's little girl." Victor let loose a chuckle. "Ian was Meredith's special guy – followed her around everywhere. I wish he had more time with her.

"When I found out she wasn't going to recover, I retreated to the office even more, so I wouldn't have to see her like that. I know it was cowardly. It's something I'll always regret. One evening I was sitting in my office, bawling at my desk, when this new employee walked in for a meeting that had slipped my mind. She asked me what was wrong and listened to me wallow in my misery. She pulled a flask from her purse and offered me a drink.

Next thing I know, we're drunk and having sex in my office. After that, she came by regularly to comfort me. I wasn't looking for someone to replace my wife. Hell, I didn't think it was possible. She wasn't even gone yet, but I fell in love with Pristine, almost as hard as I had fallen for Meredith all those years ago."

Jeff gripped the table, his heart punching his ribs like a speed-bag. He knew that the encounter Victor described was not one of chance. He could no longer pretend that he hadn't played an important part in the downfall of a strong marriage. If Victor hadn't been staring at his food, he would've seen the guilt splayed across his face like fluorescent graffiti.

With tears now flowing, Victor continued, "I had always been honest with Meredith, but I kept the affair from her. I didn't want to add to the pain of her remaining days. After she died and her will was read, I realized I had been unsuccessful in my deception. She could always see right through me, to my soul.

"Britt was a lot like her mother – beautiful, larger than life. When Meredith died, Britt just blossomed, like her mother's life force had shifted bodies. She was so elegant on that ice. Her mother was good, but Britt was so far beyond that. She would've been an amazing woman. Ian went the opposite route. After his mom died, he just wasn't as outgoing as he once was. He clung to me like he was afraid I was going to leave him next. His personality retreated inside himself. At least he gets along with Pristine. He'll come out of his shell one of these days." Victor stopped as if he had exposed himself to the bone and couldn't go any further. "Sorry. I've droned on."

"Don't apologize," Jeff said. "I'm sorry...for all that you've had to go through. We'll find the one behind it. I swear, you're not going to lose anyone else."

197

In Pristine's hospital room, Emory kept his back to her as he tried to think of how to respond.

"Victor?" Pristine called again. "Who's there?"

Emory stuffed the hairs he had taken from her hairbrush into the baggie and buried it inside his jacket pocket. He forced his lips into a smile and turned to face her. "You're up."

"Detective Rome. What are you doing here?"

"Special agent. I came by to see how you were doing and ask if you had any information that might help us figure out who did this to you."

Pristine's lips moved to one side, as if she were deciding whether or not to believe him. "Why didn't you answer when I first called to you?"

"I thought it was the TV." Emory yanked the conversation to a different subject. "How are you feeling?"

Pristine looked at her blanket. "I'm weak but better. They said I'm lucky to be alive."

"Have they determined the poison?"

"The doctor found strychnine in my blood. How on Earth did I get strychnine in me? Do you know?"

"The tests haven't come back yet, but we suspect it was in your protein powder."

"No one touches that but me." Pristine's eyes turned wild with fear. "You've got to help me. Someone's trying to kill me!"

"I want to help," Emory assured her. "To do that, I need you to be completely honest with me."

"Are you suggesting I haven't been?" A glimmer of Pristine's former self returned.

Emory ignored her question. "Do you have any idea who would want to kill you?"

"I don't know. I guess our old maid's not overly fond of me now, but she'd never be capable of this. Honestly, I don't have any enemies. I don't get out much, and the friends I do have are more like beggars who only talk to me when they need something. No, no one comes...to mind." Pristine looked as if the culprit had appeared before her, ready to inject a fatal dose of poison into her IV.

"Pristine, what is it?"

"Nothing," she answered in a manner both soft and unconvincing.

"If you have any suspicions, you need to let me know."

Pristine tightened her face. "I told you I don't know. Do you have anything else?"

Emory frowned at her, wondering what she was hiding. "I suppose not. I'll let you get back to resting." He left the room and texted Jeff that he was done.

Leaning against the fence behind his parents' house, Emory flipped through pictures of the Algarotti factory storeroom. The sun had dropped just enough for the treetop's shadows to reach the phone in his hands.

"There you are."

Emory turned toward the voice to see Jeff plodding through the snow.

"Your mom's home from church and is making lunch. And your dad said I could keep this cool shirt."

"So he did notice."

Jeff rested an elbow on the fence. "What are you doing?"

Emory pocketed his cell phone. "Cathy called. There was strychnine in Pristine's protein powder, enough to kill her ten times over."

"Wow. She's lucky to be alive."

"She also finished testing the items from your place. The bottled water I drank was drugged."

Jeff pounded the fence. "I knew it! With what?"

"She didn't know exactly, but she thinks it's a derivative of MDMA that's been altered to stay stable in water for an extended period of time."

"That explains your reaction to it."

Emory pushed his eyebrows together. "Have you taken ecstasy before?"

Jeff shrugged. "Once or twice. Didn't you experiment any in high school or college?"

"No, high school wasn't any fun for me."

"Really? I loved it."

"I figured."

"Was it difficult being back there when you arrested Britt's boyfriend?" Jeff laughed. "Is it true what they say about revisiting childhood haunts? Did it look smaller than you remembered?"

"It actually was." Emory's smile morphed into a gasp. "Wait a second."

"What is it?"

Emory pulled his phone back out and searched for a picture. He paused for just a moment before running toward the house. "Come on. We need a warrant to search the factory again."

CHAPTER 33

AS THEY EXITED the car, Jeff said, "You realize if you're wrong about this, Victor's going to fire me."

"Let's hope I'm not then." Emory tried the front glass-paned door to the Algarotti Smoky Mountain Springs factory and found it locked.

Jeff nodded toward a young uniformed man sitting in the lobby, watching TV and eating a dripping meatball sandwich. "Looks like Victor finally hired a security guard."

Emory knocked on the door and held his badge to the glass. The startled young man placed his dinner on the seat and walked over to open the door.

"What can I do for you, officers?" asked the guard, fluorescent lights shining off his over-gelled black hair.

Emory handed him a document. "We have a warrant to search the factory again."

"Wh…What?"

Emory noticed the name on the guard's badge. "Clarence, are you the only one here?"

Clarence nodded. "It's Sunday."

"We need to see the records room," Emory said as he headed that way.

Clarence stepped in front of him. "Wait, you can't come in. Please. Today's my first day. I don't want to get fired."

Jeff smirked. "There's a lot of that going around."

Emory asked, "Would you rather be jailed for interfering with an investigation?"

"Well, no." Clarence stepped out of the way. "I don't even know where the records room is."

"That's okay. I do." Emory proceeded down the hall with Jeff at his side, and the security guard following.

The guard pulled his cell phone from his belt. "I'm calling my boss."

"Please do," Emory replied as the guard began talking on the phone.

"God, I hope you're right," Jeff muttered.

Clarence told Emory, "My boss wants to know what's this about."

"Tell him we're looking for narcotics."

"Narc…Drugs?" The guard told his boss on the phone, "That's what he said."

When they reached the records room, Emory said, "New door."

Clarence covered his phone to tell them, "The door guy was here earlier."

Jeff tried the doorknob. "Locked." He looked at the guard. "Did the door guy give you a key?"

Clarence told his boss, "Sir, I gotta go. They want me to open a door for them." The guard hung up his phone. "He's calling the owner."

Emory's only reaction was, "Open it."

Clarence looked at the door and frowned at the two men. "This don't say record room."

"It's the right room," Emory insisted. "Do you have the key?"

"They gave it to that other guy, the one who works here. Sam...Stuart..."

"Scot?" asked Jeff.

"That's it!"

Emory's eyes locked on Jeff's, and he could tell they were thinking the same thought. "Scot's our guy."

"Wait!" Clarence held up a black key on the key ring chained to his belt. "I do have a master key."

"Will it work?" Jeff asked. "It's a new door."

The guard laughed. "Big places like this always install locks with the same master core. And those locks can all be opened with the same master key." He inserted the key and tried to turn the tumbler, but it wouldn't budge. "That's weird. It should work."

Emory nodded to Jeff, signaling him with his expression. The PI asked, "Are you sure?"

Emory shrugged and pointed his hand toward the guard. "The key doesn't work."

Jeff headed toward the receiving area. "God, I hope you're right."

"Stop saying that. You're making me nervous."

Clarence asked, "What's he doing?"

"Finding a key that works."

"Oh," Clarence muttered.

Emory knocked on the door and announced himself.

The security guard told him, "There's no one in there."

"Just a formality."

A moment later, a roaring sound caught the attention of the two men by the records room. They both faced the double swing doors and saw Jeff charge into the hallway in a forklift.

Emory's mouth dropped. "Oh my god!"

Clarence shook his head and waved his arms. "No, you can't do that! Seriously. It's my first day!"

Jeff stopped shy of the records room door. "The crowbar wasn't there. Should I?"

Emory stepped back. "Do it."

The skinny guard gasped and clenched his fists as Jeff rammed the forklift through the door. He drove inside a few feet before parking it and jumping out of the cab. Emory flicked a switch to illuminate the small room, lined with metal shelves full of file folders, ledgers and other archived materials.

Clarence put his hands on his hips in a cocky stance. "Well, it don't look like there's any drugs. What made you think there'd be something in here?"

Emory explained as he passed the shelves, touching various items, "Something the owner said. When Victor Algarotti saw this room yesterday, he said it seemed smaller than he remembered from when he was younger."

The guard said, "Yeah, I've heard that before, that places look smaller when you're older."

"It's not because you're older. It's because you're physically bigger. Victor was in his twenties when he started working here, and from a picture I saw of him, he looked the same as he does now – same height, same build."

Jeff asked, "So why would the room look smaller to him?"

"Exactly, so that got me thinking. When I flipped through the pictures I took of the room, I noticed something odd." Emory pointed to the forklift tracks on the floor of the records room. "You see the tracks?" After the two men nodded, Emory pointed to where the tracks ended. "See how they end at the shelf against that wall?"

The guard said, "Someone must've backed into it."

Emory shook his head. "That's what I thought at first, but look at the shelf and the wall."

Jeff inspected the metal shelf where the tracks ended and then the wall behind it. "There's no damage to either."

"Not a scratch," said Emory.

"Maybe the shelf wasn't there, and the forklift stopped just before it hit the wall." Clarence grabbed the shelf and tried to move it. "It's attached to the wall. Could've just been attached recently. There's no telling how old them tracks are."

Emory stepped on one of the tracks, and he felt a slight stickiness when he raised his shoe. "The tracks are fresh. Two days ago, the foreman commented on the same sticky tracks in the hallway like they were new."

Clarence grimaced at him. "I didn't see no tracks in the hall."

"They must've been mopped up by whoever cleans this place, but they didn't have access to this room." Emory turned on the flashlight feature of his cell phone and looked under the shelf. "The tracks continue, looks like all the way to the wall."

"There's a hidden space!" Jeff exclaimed.

Emory returned to his feet. "I think so. The foreman also told me they had recently refurbished the back area. Either something was put in there to stay for good—"

"Or there's a secret door." Jeff put his hands on hips. "We need to find the trigger to open the door."

All three started pulling on ledgers and other items on the shelves, but Emory soon stopped to look at the massive amount of materials stored on the shelves against the wall and throughout the room. "This is going to take forever."

He abandoned the wall and jumped into the forklift. "Stand back!" Jeff and Clarence jumped out of the way as Emory turned on the vehicle. He raised the arms five feet, floored the gas pedal and crashed into the shelf-covered wall. The forklift crumpled the shelf and punctured two manhole-sized breaches into the wall.

As Emory backed the forklift, Jeff squinted into one of the holes. "There's definitely something back there!"

Emory repositioned the arms and hit the wall again, repeating his actions until the opening was large enough to walk through.

He turned off the forklift and joined Jeff and Clarence as they were about to crawl over the rubble.

"Oh my god!" Victor screamed from behind them. He was standing in the doorway, eyeing the damage to the new door. "Again?" His gaze turned to the gaping hole in the wall. "OH MY GOD!!"

Standing nearest to the door, the guard froze in Victor's glare. He responded in staggered grunts before forcing his mouth shut. Clarence handed the search warrant to Victor and pointed an accusing finger at Emory and Jeff. "They served me with a search warrant."

Refocusing his glare onto the other two men, Victor told them, "That doesn't give you the right to damage at will." Mouth open and shaking his head, Victor stamped toward them, and he handed Emory a folded paper he had brought with him. "This is yours."

"What is it?" Emory asked.

"The bill for the last door. Expect another one tomorrow." Victor looked to Jeff for an explanation. "Now tell me what on Earth is going on here."

Emory asked, "You put Scot in charge of your recent renovation, correct?"

"So?"

"My guess is he took the opportunity to cut this room in half."

"Why would he do that?"

"Let's find out." Emory turned on his phone's flashlight and led them into the secret room.

When they entered, a motion-detecting light turned on. Once his eyes adjusted, Emory did a three-sixty and estimated the original storeroom was about sixteen-hundred square feet. He whispered to Jeff, "Strange coincidence, don't you think?"

"What?"

One of Emory's eyebrows rose above the other. "I've encountered two hidden rooms in a week. The other was in your office."

Jeff threw a hand to his chest. "What, you don't think I have something to do with this, do you?"

"Like I said, it's a strange coincidence." Emory shrugged and walked away.

Victor touched some antique equipment shoved against one wall. "I had forgotten all about this. It's some of the original machinery and tools my father-in-law used when he started the company. I kept meaning to build a museum room off the lobby, but I never got around to it." He passed a coffin-sized glass case, which displayed the original drill Connor Ashley, Meredith Algarotti's father, used to bore a well into Yonder Springs. A picture of Connor by the first well leaned against it on the floor.

Emory focused his attention on two long metal tables in the center of the room. They were littered with a wide assortment of lab supplies – beakers, test tubes, a digital scale, Bunsen burners and a centrifuge. "This place looks like a high school chemistry lab."

Jeff glided past a group of five propane tanks toward eight palettes of Algarotti water – cases of grape-flavored water. Someone had cut the shrink wrapping down the middle of each case and taped it back together. "This water's been tampered with. Victor, how many palettes have been stolen?"

"Twelve, I think."

"Where are the rest of them?" Jeff muttered.

Emory strolled between the tables, giving alternating glances to the items on top of each. He saw a lab apron draped over the room's only barstool, and on the table surface above it, he found a lab notebook, a stapled printout of step-by-step instructions for the manufacturing of MDMA and a black light. He put on his gloves to pick up the notebook and thumb through it. "Scot kept a record of his attempts to make ecstasy and then modify it." He put the notebook down, and his hands moved to the next object. "Why does he need a black light?"

"Maybe he has underground raves here," Jeff joked.

Emory scanned the room until he saw the light switch on the wall. He asked Clarence, "Would you mind hitting the manual button on that light switch?" Once the guard did, the room pitched into near-perfect darkness.

"What are you doing?" Victor asked.

Emory turned on the black light and flashed it around the room until he saw points of illumination near where Jeff was standing. "What's that?"

Jeff walked to the points of light and grabbed one, causing a squeaking sound as he did. He held it up for others to see. "It's a bottle of water. Each one has a luminescent smiley face emoji painted on it to mark it."

"Turn the light back on," Victor ordered, and a second later, it was on again. Fuming, he approached a map of the Southern states hooked onto the wall. Numerous cities had a green triangle beside them, and three of them – Knoxville, Nashville and Memphis – had been circled with a red marker. "Our distributor map." As the other men came to him, he explained, "The triangles are cities where we deliver our water."

Clarence gawked at the map. "Wow, that's a lot of cities."

"What are the circles?" asked Jeff.

Victor faced them. "I have no idea."

Emory had seen similar maps in previous drug busts. "Those are the locations where he has a distributor for his product."

"What are you talking about?" Victor asked.

Emory explained, "He's using your trucks and water to get his product out."

"What product? What is all this?"

Jeff answered, "Scot is spiking some of your water with a drug similar to ecstasy, which would make it easier to distribute to users without being detected."

"He put drugs in my water?!"

"Not all of it," Emory told him. "Just the stolen water. I think he has an accomplice at each of the circled sites who could pick up the water marked with a smiley face and sell it at local clubs."

Victor leeched his palm onto his forehead. "This will ruin my company."

Jeff waved toward the water. "There are three cities circled, but four palettes are unaccounted for."

Emory said, "The van the sheriff described seeing here wouldn't have the capacity for four palettes. My guess is it picked up one of the palettes to give samples to his distributors and maybe others he's trying to recruit. Victor, were deliveries being made to any of the circled cities this weekend?"

Victor thought aloud, "I shut down production on Friday, so we didn't have enough product to ship out yesterday. We just barely made enough yesterday for one truckload to ship out today. With my foreman out, I had to come in myself to open the dock for a little bit before going to the hospital."

Emory asked, "Where was it heading?"

Victor's head dropped. "All three cities."

Emory exclaimed, "We've got to stop that truck!"

"Wait!" Victor shouted before anyone could leave. "You have to keep this confidential. If word got out that any of our water, even stolen water, had drugs in it, our customers would drop us before waiting for an explanation. Promise me this won't get out to the media."

Emory assured him, "We're not going to announce it, but arrests are public record."

Victor snarled at them both, "I want you to get that son-of-a-bitch. Better yet, shoot him!"

"I'm not going to shoot—" Emory started before he was interrupted.

Victor pointed to Jeff. "Wait a second. Didn't you say whoever was stealing the water killed my daughter?"

"I said it *could* be the same person," Jeff clarified.

"I'm going to shoot him myself!" Victor growled before storming from the room.

Emory and Jeff dashed after him, followed by the security guard. As soon as they passed through the broken doorway, Emory looked to his left to see Victor turning a corner to another hallway, heading toward his office. "This way!"

Jeff grabbed Emory's arm to get his attention. "That way. It's Scot!"

Emory looked to his right. Scot Trousdale stopped in his tracks and shot a glance toward Jeff's voice. After a frozen second, Victor's assistant bolted.

"You take Victor!" Emory ordered Jeff, and he pointed at Clarence. "Do not let anyone in this room!"

CHAPTER 34

EMORY TOOK OFF after Scot. He slammed through the double swing doors to the receiving area, where Scot was waiting for him. The shorter man faced him in a wrestler stance, crouched with both hands before him, one holding a stun gun.

Emory almost ran right into the gun, but at the last second, he grabbed the device and tried to wrestle it from Scot's hand.

Scot pushed back hard and Emory landed on his back with Scot on top of him, struggling to force the stun gun to Emory's neck.

Scot squeezed the trigger. Blue bolts of electricity twisted between the electrodes at the head of the device.

Emory clenched his free hand and sent it up to Scot's chin, sending his glasses flying. He punched him three more times before he jarred him enough to weaken him. He pushed the gun back toward Scot's face.

Scot moved more of his weight to his knees, using both hands to push the stun gun back toward his opponent.

Emory tried bucking him off, to no avail. He kicked his knee up until it slammed against Scot's groin. As Scot fell over in pain, Emory grabbed the weapon, blasting a bolt of electricity into his face.

Scot fell to the floor, a red goose-egg welt rising from his left cheek. Nearly immobilized, he tried grabbing at the pain.

Emory stood and caught his breath. He kicked Scot in the balls a second time. "Asshole!" He dropped the stun gun to the ground and stomped on it, smashing it. "I hate these things!" Panting, he jerked around and kicked Scot in the balls once more. "That's for my dad."

Scot groaned in agony. This time he was able to reach the pain with his hands.

Satisfied with his handiwork, Emory reached for the handcuffs on his belt. "Oh crap." He remembered that his cuffs were somewhere in the living room of his parents' house – thrown there the night before.

He walked away from Scot in search of something to tie him with. He didn't notice Scot's glasses before stepping on them, nor did he see their owner working his way back up to his feet.

Jeff lost sight of Victor during his pursuit, but his threat to shoot Scot was a verbal breadcrumb to where he was heading. It reminded him that he had found a gun in Victor's desk when he broke in a couple of days earlier. When he arrived at Victor's office, he turned the knob and ran into the door, expecting it to open. He tried the doorknob again, leaving no doubt that it was locked. He pounded the thick wood with his fist. "Victor! Victor, open up!"

Jeff could hear movement inside the office and the sound of a turning knob – but not the one he was holding. "The other door." He raced to the lobby and out the front entrance. He could see Victor walking from his office's exterior door toward the parking lot. Without calling to him, Jeff ran and intercepted him at his luxury sedan.

"Give me the gun, Victor," Jeff demanded, although no gun was visible.

Victor turned to Jeff. "What would you do if a man killed someone you loved?"

"Exactly what you're planning to do, but Scot didn't kill Britt."

"You said whoever stole the water."

"It was an assumption. I don't know it for certain, and we won't until we have a chance to talk to him. Victor, you know Britt didn't have a choice about how her life ended, but you do. Don't throw your life away on a hotheaded mistake."

Victor hesitated. "Fine. I won't." He opened his car door and slipped into the driver seat. "Do your job," he said before closing the door.

Jeff knocked on the window and waited for Victor to roll it down. "I was serious about the gun. I need it."

"I've given you my word."

"It's not that. I trust you're not going to shoot Scot," Jeff said, although it wasn't true.

"Then why do you want my gun?"

"Rick Roberts' dog was shot to death, likely by whoever killed him."

Victor let out an angry laugh. "You think I did that?"

"I'm not accusing you, but your gun is the same caliber as the bullet that was recovered, and you're not the only one with access to your office."

"Scot!" His eyes rolled up to Jeff. "How did you know about my gun?"

Jeff lied, "Agent Rome told me that you had a gun registered," hoping he did have it registered.

"How did you know I kept it in my office?"

The success from his first lie emboldened Jeff to do it again. "You talked about shooting and ran to your office."

The answer seemed to satisfy Victor, who pulled his gun from inside his suit jacket. Jeff produced a small knit scarf from his coat pocket and used it to take possession of the weapon.

Emory had been looking for a rope or something to bind Scot with for just over a minute when he passed a stack of full five-gallon water bottles that reached halfway to the ceiling. On the other side he spotted another forklift with arms facing him and some tools on a bench. Walking toward the tools, he noticed the rope keychain hanging from the forklift's ignition. *It'll be close, but it might be long enough.* He was reaching for the key when he was attacked from behind.

Scot wrapped his right arm around Emory's neck and pushed his left forearm into the back of his neck, locking him in a sleeper hold. "I'm going to fucking kill you!" Scot screamed into his ear.

Startled, Emory grabbed at the forearm around his neck before he realized what was happening. His other hand tightened around the key, turning the ignition. As the forklift's engine puttered on, Emory kicked at Scot's shin. If he didn't break free within a few seconds, he would pass out from the lack of blood flow to his brain. The kicking wasn't working.

With one hand on Scot's forearm, Emory reached a frantic and aimless hand before him. Grunting, he hit the forklift's arm control, which made the arms of the forklift start to rise. Scot tried pulling him away, so Emory held the steering wheel and turned it. The forklift's arms turned in their direction.

Emory was about to pass out.

The forklift's arms reached eight feet high when they impacted the stack of five-gallon water bottles, piercing several of them and knocking others off the palettes. The water gushed from the bottles onto Scot and Emory like a spring waterfall, drenching them both.

As his feet slid on the floor, Scot lost his grip enough to give Emory a second wind.

Emory used his elbow to jab Scot's left ribcage four times. He butted the back of his head into Scot's forehead.

Twisting around, Emory hurled a fist at Scot's injured cheek, knocking him back into the crumbling stack of water bottles. Emory slipped in the growing puddle, but he was back on his feet just before Scot. He grabbed the neck of one of the fallen five-gallon water bottles, still full, and swung it until it connected with Scot's face.

Scot fell back, landing on a broken water bottle before coming to rest on the floor. He was out cold.

Emory noticed Scot's running shoes. He removed the laces and tied them around the suspect's wrists.

CHAPTER 35

S ANS GLASSES AND sporting a bandage around his head, Scot tapped his handcuffed wrists on the white table in the sheriff's interrogation room. "You've got nothing on me."

Sitting opposite him, Sheriff Rome asked, "Then why'd you run?"

Scot squinted a blackened eye at Emory, who was seated next to the sheriff. "Because he was chasing me! I heard how he chased Dan Claymon through the high school and then roughed him up. I was trying not to be his next victim."

Wearing latex gloves, Emory pointed to the broken stun gun on the table. "Is this the one you used to immobilize the sheriff two nights ago?"

"I've never done anything to your daddy."

Emory held up the notebook he had retrieved from the secret room. "I have your journal right here."

Scot turned away. "I've never seen that before in my life."

"There are fingerprints all over this, some good ones from the cover. It won't take long for us to get the results back, and I'm betting they match yours."

"That doesn't mean anything. I touch all our office supplies because I'm the one who puts them in the cabinet for anyone to take."

"Had that answer all prepared, didn't you?" Emory thumbed through the pages. "You took the precaution of writing in all caps, making handwriting analysis more difficult, but not impossible. You've written in meticulous detail how you modified ecstasy into a new drug, Kama Sutra."

"Kama Sutra?" asked Scot. "Good name, but they should shorten it to Sutra. Druggies can't handle more than two or three syllables. It does sound cool, though, if I were into that sort of thing." Scot used his hands to place his next words on an imaginary sign: "Kama Sutra, the path to carnal bliss," hissing the last word with a grin. His eyes shifted from Emory to Jeff, who was leaning against the wall. "Hey, you two should try it."

Jeff pushed off the wall and got right in Scot's face. "You nearly killed the sheriff! What I'd like to try is breaking that table in half with your snarky face."

Scot laughed and nodded toward Emory. "Your boyfriend got a lucky shot in, or I wouldn't be here."

Emory could feel his father's eyes on him, but he maintained his focus on the suspect.

Scot held up his cuffed hands. "Unleash me, and we'll see how lucky you are."

Emory slammed the notebook on the table. "Look, Scot, we've seen the map, and I've read all your notes. We know your entire business plan."

Jeff backed away. "I find it hard to believe you came up with this on your own. Who are you working with?"

His eyes on Jeff, Scot bounced his pecs a couple of times beneath his cotton shirt. "Don't judge me by my muscles. I don't have an ectomorphic IQ."

Emory told him, "You were smart. You probably waited until you had worked at the factory long enough for Victor to trust you before you suggested renovating part of the factory so you could include a secret room for yourself. The building's old, so I'm sure it wasn't difficult convincing him to modernize it. Is that correct?"

Scot shrugged. "You tell me. It's your fiction."

"Although stealing the water was pretty stupid," said Jeff. "Why take that risk? Why not just buy your own?"

The sheriff responded, "I imagine that was a matter of convenience, and I don't think he could've brought outside water into the plant without raising suspicion."

Emory added, "He also might've thought no one would notice."

Scot snorted and shook his head. "I just love how you guys are talking about me like I'm not here and making all these assumptions. Is that what cops do when they don't have a lick of evidence against someone? Any lawyer would have you laughed out of court with what you got."

"So now you want a lawyer?" asked Emory.

"If you're going to just make up stuff about me, I will. But I didn't do anything wrong, so I'd rather not incur that expense unless I absolutely need to. Victor doesn't pay me that much."

"Why not put that brain to better use?" asked Sheriff Rome. "Why drugs?"

"Like I said, I don't know anything about this. I can tell you it doesn't take a genius to realize if someone was trying to break into the local drug market, you'd only have yourself to blame." Scot made a gun out of his hand and pointed it at Emory.

Emory asked, "What's that supposed to mean?"

"Everyone read about that big drug bust. When you put all those ecstasy dealers out of business, you did two things. You made pills too risky to sell, and you left a void. I would imagine tweakers, like nature, abhor a vacuum."

The sheriff asked, "What are the names of your contacts in Knoxville, Nashville and Memphis?"

"I know a lot of people," Scot responded. "Could you be more specific?"

"Your distributors," Emory clarified.

"I don't have any distributors because I'm not a drug dealer. You have the wrong guy."

"Of course." Emory opened the notebook and began thumbing through it. "Let's take a few steps back then. I really do commend you on your notes. Very detailed."

"I can't take credit for it because it's not my notebook." Scot tried to cross his arms but couldn't with the cuffs on, so he returned his hands to the table.

"Although not very smart." Emory lifted his eyes from the notebook, sneering at Scot as he continued flipping the pages. "Your arrogance is brandished in blue ink on every page – each paragraph, an inch of rope to hang you with."

Scot growled, "How many times do I have to tell you?"

"I know, it's not your notebook." Emory referred to a bookmark he had placed in the book. "You were good about protecting other peoples' identities, including your test subjects. In here, you recounted how you first tried making ecstasy in pill form from a recipe you found online, batch by batch, until you had perfected it. You tested each batch on subjects of opportunity to see if it were safe and had the desired effect. You gave the pills away at random clubs in Knoxville and Nashville and watched as the subjects partied. The first few batches didn't turn out so great. Batch number five was the first one that didn't make them vomit within the first hour." Emory paused to glance at Scot.

"Please keep reading," said Scot. "I'm dying to find out how it ends."

Emory continued, "Once you were confident with manufacturing ecstasy in pill form, you started altering the formula, bit by bit, until you had created something new that was stable in regular water." He turned to another bookmarked page. "The way you described your first test subject for Sutra, I don't need a name. It was Britt Algarotti."

"Britt?" the sheriff asked. He turned to Emory. "Is that what killed her?"

"I didn't kill Britt or anyone else!" Scot insisted.

"This was three weeks before she died," Emory explained.

Jeff snapped his fingers. "The skating competition."

"Now that was funny," said Scot with a grin. "I've watched that video probably a hundred times. Is that what happened? Someone drugged her?"

"Yes, you did," answered Emory.

"I didn't, but I would've had plenty of reason to," said Scot. "Britt would come into the office without so much as a 'hi' to me to go ask Daddy for money. And she had no regard for my things. She was always leaving her duffle bag on my desk. Never asked – just plopped it up there, scooting away anything in its path. I hated that."

"Is that how you drugged her?" asked Emory. "She came in before her last competition, and you put the water in her bag while she was in Victor's office?"

With an incredulous look sweeping over his face, Jeff asked, "What makes a person like you?"

Scot said, "I'm no different than you, Mr. PI. Well, except in that one way." Scot winked at Emory.

Jeff threw open his arms. "You've already admitted you hated her. You drugged her. You're obviously adept at chemistry. It must've been easy for you to plan her murder. Did you watch her from the woods that morning, as she skated on the lake?"

"What?" Scot asked.

Jeff lunged forward and grabbed the side of the table. "Did you laugh when the flames started burning her?"

Emory placed a hand on his forearm. "Jeff—"

"What are you talking about?" Scot asked. "The news said

someone burned her and dumped her in the lake. Are you saying someone burned her *on* the lake?"

"Don't act stupid!" Jeff yelled, pounding a fist onto the table. "I'm sure you felt clever throwing the calcium carbide on the ice—"

"Calcium carbide. Oh my god, that's how she died?" Scot laughed. "That's brilliant! I wish I had seen it."

Before Emory could stop him, Jeff's fist shot from the table to Scot's jaw, knocking the suspect and his chair sideways onto the floor.

Emory threw himself in front of Jeff. The sheriff tended to Scot and yelled to Emory, "Get him out of here!"

Emory wrangled Jeff into the adjoining deputy room and closed the door. "Okay, what was that all about?"

Jeff shook his head and apologized. "He just got to me. That cocky attitude."

Emory noticed that, of the four desks in the deputy room, only one was occupied. Deputy Harris looked up from his computer as if he were interested in their conversation, so Emory lowered his voice to maintain privacy. "That's exactly what you can't let happen. We're profession—" He stopped himself before completing the sentence.

"But I'm not a professional, am I?"

"That's not what I was going to say."

"Yes it is!"

"Fine," Emory admitted. "If you had proper training, you wouldn't lose your cool with a suspect like that and perhaps jeopardize the case with an assault charge. I'm sorry."

"Don't be. You're right." Jeff pointed at the door. "He's right too. I am just like him."

"No, you're not. You'd never purposely harm someone."

"What did I do to Victor?"

"Okay, you set up the meeting with Pristine. Your input ended there. He had every opportunity to end his relationship with her, but he didn't because he fell in love with her. For all we know, she fell in love with him too."

"All right, let's change the subject." Jeff rubbed one of Emory's shoulders. "How are you feeling?"

Emory twisted his head from side to side. "My neck is sore, and the back of my head hurts where I butted him."

Jeff smiled. "I can take care of the neck part for you if you want."

As Jeff reached for Emory's neck, the special agent shook his head and tilted it toward Deputy Harris. "Later."

The sheriff opened the door and escorted Scot from the room. With his lip bleeding, Scot started toward Jeff like he was going to lunge at him, but he stopped himself short and laughed at the PI, who had tensed up in preparation for the impact. The sheriff told Jeff, "Mr. Trousdale has declined to press assault charges against you if you apologize to him."

Jeff brandished a contemptuous look. "Sorry."

Scot smiled and nodded to the water cooler at the other end of the room. "I'm thirsty."

"Sure," the sheriff told him as he began to walk with him.

Scot sneered at him. "I'm not an invalid."

The sheriff looked down at Scot's hands, which were still handcuffed in front of him. He released his arm and rested his hand on the gun in his holster. "Fine, but I'm watching you."

All three standing investigators watched Scot as he walked over to the cooler. With his back to them, he grabbed a paper cup, filled it and drank its contents. When he returned the cup to the spigot for a refill, the others began talking.

Jeff said, "Sheriff, I'm sorry about—"

The sheriff raised a hand to silence him. "You saved me the trouble. Why did he refer to you two as…"

Emory cringed. *Don't say it, Dad.*

"boyfriends?"

He said it.

Emory looked at Jeff, unsure how to respond. Jeff answered for him. "He's just trying to get under our skin."

Emory put a hand on the sheriff's shoulder. "Dad, you should be home in bed."

"I'm fine." The sheriff nodded to Deputy Harris, who was now on the phone. "I'll leave it to Harris after I get Trousdale locked up. Do you think we have enough to book him for murder?"

"There's nothing in the notebook about either murder or the attempt on Pristine's life," Emory answered.

Jeff said, "And I don't think he's going to confess."

Emory nodded. "We need to find something more concrete."

"Just the drug and assault charges for now then." The sheriff kept his eyes on Scot's back, but he couldn't see that the suspect was pressing on the Algarotti logo on the side of the cooler. A tiny drawer popped open, and inside was something shiny and metallic.

Emory patted his dad on the back. "The TBI is looking for the delivery truck, and we'll find his contacts."

"We need to know more about him," Jeff said. "Who was he before all this?"

The sheriff told them, "I didn't know him until about a year or so ago, when he started working for the water factory."

"Wayne is looking into his background."

The sheriff tilted his head toward Scot, who was still drinking water. "I'm placing him back in the holding room. I only have one deputy on today, so I'll have someone transport him to Knoxville in the morning."

"Why wait?" Jeff asked "We're on our way to Knoxville now."

Emory shook his head. "Against regulation. I don't have a partition between the front and back seats."

"Could we borrow a deputy car?" Jeff asked the sheriff.

Emory half-rolled his eyes and answered before Sheriff Rome had a chance. "I'm not allowed to drive one anymore."

"Why not?"

Emory's phone chimed. "I'll tell you later." He read his new text message. "The morning will be fine." He held up his phone. "Good news! The drugged shipments in Nashville and Memphis have been confiscated before any left the building. Knoxville's was already gone, but the special agents have captured Scot's accomplice there and are on their way to retrieve the water."

"That's excellent!" Jeff gave him a pat on the back.

"Congratulations Son." The sheriff shook his hand with the firmness of pride. "I better get Scot."

"I could use some water myself," Emory said, so the two followed the sheriff to the water cooler.

The sheriff took Scot by the arm and began to escort him down the hallway, but the suspect tripped over one of the two empty five-gallon water bottles beside the cooler. Although he didn't lose his footing, he did kick one bottle about a foot away from the other.

With a snarky grin, Jeff commented, "Clumsy for an MMA fighter."

Almost as soon as Sheriff Rome left down the hallway to the holding room, the front door opened. A woman wrapped in a rust-hued woolen coat and holding a baby carrier with a tiny sleeping infant inside walked into the deputy room. A broad smile spread across Deputy Harris' face when he saw her, and he left his chair to say hello. "Sharon, how are you?"

Sharon hugged him with her free arm. "I'm good. I just wanted to bring this little guy by to say hi." She place the carrier on the closest desk.

Deputy Harris touched one of the baby's hands. "This must be little Andy. What a handsome little deputy."

"Isn't he?" Sharon asked. "Lula Mae said Sheriff Rome was here."

Deputy Harris pointed toward the hallway. "He's locking a suspect in the holding room."

Sharon looked where he pointed and saw Emory heading her way. "Emory!" She threw her arms around his waist and gave him a big squeeze. "I heard you were back in town."

"It's so good to see you," Emory said. "Sharon Marcel, this is Jeff Woodard."

As the two shook hands, Emory joined Deputy Harris in admiring the baby. "Sharon, he's adorable. How old is he?"

"Three months yesterday."

"Huh," Emory muttered.

"Sheriff!" Sharon screeched as he entered the room.

The sheriff grinned and hurried to meet her. "Sharon, what on Earth are you doing here?"

"I was going a little stir-crazy, and I thought I'd bring Andy to meet the guys."

With the sheriff and his deputies wrapped up in conversation, Jeff pulled Emory aside and asked, "What's wrong?"

"What do you mean?"

"I saw your face when she told you how old her baby is."

Emory got out his phone and flipped through the pictures. "My dad has four deputies – three men and one woman." He nodded toward Sharon and held up his phone to show Jeff a photo of the shoeprints in the snow around the lake. "Most of the shoeprints around the lake where Britt was found are big, so I assume they're male, but there are two separate sets of small ones – I'm guessing female boots. One set must've belonged to Britt, and I had assumed Sharon was one of the deputies who responded, but—"

"She's been on maternity leave," Jeff finished for him.

"So whose shoeprints are these?"

CHAPTER 36

LEAVING BARTER RIDGE, Emory drove as Jeff read an email on his phone. "Virginia compiled all the online information she could find on each Algarotti family member. Check out this section on Ian."

Emory looked at the phone as Jeff held it for him, and he saw a year-end report card with straight A's except for one C. "He's lacking in science."

"Wait for it." Jeff scrolled the image to the right to reveal the names of the teachers for each class. Beside the subject of science was the name R. Roberts. "Rick Roberts was his teacher and the only one not to give him an A." Jeff paused for a moment. "Could the small set of shoeprints belong to Ian?"

"You think he could've killed Britt?"

"And Rick," Jeff said. "Brothers who hate their older sisters are not that uncommon, and I imagine A's are very important to Mr. I-Skipped-Two-Grades, so if Rick kept him from a 4.0—"

"Point made, but I want more before I go up against Victor to question his son."

"Maybe Britt's best friend could shed some light on the little brother."

"Good idea. That reminds me, could you look up the last time

Barter Ridge had snowfall, before this one? I remember at the lake my dad saying this was the first snowfall of the season, but I want to verify that."

Jeff checked his phone and had the requested information less than a minute later. "Before this past Monday, the last snowfall in this area was back in April of last year."

"Interesting," Emory muttered without moving his lips.

"What is it?"

"We'll find out. Are you in a hurry to get home, or would you be up for talking to Tati now?"

"I want to solve the case," Jeff said. "Do you know her address?"

"I don't."

"I'll ask Virginia to find it." Jeff texted his partner, and as they waited for a response, he asked, "So why can't you drive a deputy car?"

Emory tsked at the question. "Promise not to laugh?"

"I've never been able to keep that promise."

"Fine. I'll tell you anyway. Just don't guffaw."

Jeff chuckled. "It's a fine line, but I'll try not to cross it."

"I came home from college one weekend, right after Jerry Belcher died."

"Who's that?"

"He was the mayor of Barter Ridge for like twenty years, but he was retired when he died. They planned a funeral procession from Whitney Ligon Funeral Home downtown to this tiny country cemetery about ten miles away. Dad was short-staffed, and he asked if I could drive the lead deputy car. So...I did."

"Oh my god," Jeff said with anticipation. "What happened?"

Emory inhaled through his teeth. "I thought I knew the way, but just to make sure, I was following the map app on my phone. Shortly after leaving the funeral home, I lost the signal. I kept driving to where I thought the cemetery was – from the paved road to a gravel road and finally to a dirt road, which was more like a mud road from a thunderstorm that had hit the day before. Well, somehow somewhere along the way, I missed my turn, and I was just getting deeper into a wooded area that was way, way off the beaten path."

"Oh no."

"No one stopped me. They just kept following me like I knew where I was going. Then my car got stuck. The hearse got stuck, and about six other cars did, including the one with the widow."

Jeff covered his expanding grin with his hand. "What happened?"

"We had to get a school bus to pick up all the stuck people… and the body. So those people had to ride the bus with the casket in the aisle all the way to the cemetery. They told me the casket kept sliding up and down the aisle."

With that visual, Jeff started laughing. "Why didn't someone hold it in place?"

"I don't know. I think most of the people on the bus were elderly, so they probably couldn't. I'm just lucky it didn't go flying out the emergency door in back." Emory pointed to Jeff, who was now guffawing. "You said you wouldn't do that."

"Sorry." Jeff put on a serious face.

"My dad had to pay for everything, including towing all those cars, out of his budget. That was one of two times I made the newspaper that he doesn't have framed in his office."

"Can't imagine why."

"The whole thing was mortifying. I didn't come home for six months afterwards. Since then, I've been banned from driving any of his patrol cars."

Jeff rested his hand on Emory's thigh. "Oh, I almost forgot." He produced a gun wrapped in a scarf from his coat pocket. "It's Victor's. For testing."

Emory was surprised to see the gun in Jeff's possession, and he wondered if he had stolen it. "Did he give it you?"

"Yes, he did. I swear. And I was very careful not to touch it, so you could dust it for prints."

"That's great. Maybe put it in the glove compartment for now."

"By the way, what was the other time you ended up in the paper?" As soon as Jeff asked the question, his phone chimed.

Emory asked, "Is that Virginia?"

"Answer my question first."

"That's a story for later. I need to know where I'm driving."

"You know, you're racking those up." Jeff checked his phone. "Tati Burrett lives at 1541 Black Bear Lane."

"Black Bear..." Emory began. "Isn't that the same street as the lake where Britt died?"

"I'm mapping it now." Jeff checked his phone for the difference between the two locations. "Not only is her house on the same street, it's right across the street from the lake."

Emory and Jeff parked in the Burretts' driveway and stepped out of the car. Both men looked across the street toward Cicada Lake. Even though they could gauge about where the lake was, it was at the lower end of a slope, so it wasn't visible from their vantage point and much less so from the single-story house behind them.

"Do you think someone could've seen anything from the house?" Emory asked.

"Maybe smoke, if they happened to be looking in that direction at the time."

The two walked up to the front door, and after Jeff knocked, Tati answered. "Agent Rome. What are you doing here?"

Emory started with introductions. "This is Jeff Woodard. He's a private investigator who's also working on Britt's murder."

Tati nodded to Jeff. "Nice to meet you. You want to come in?"

"If you don't mind," said Emory. "Are your parents home?"

"They're helping out at church." Tati led them to the living room, where the men sat on the couch, while she took a seat in a recliner. "Do you have more questions about Britt?"

Emory responded, "We want to ask you about Ian."

Tati snarled her nose. "Ian? Why are you asking me about him?"

Jeff asked, "Do you know any of Ian's friends that we could talk to?"

"Ian doesn't have any friends."

"How did Ian and Britt get along?" Emory asked.

Tati laughed. "That's an easy one. Britt couldn't stand him. They used to be okay, and by that I mean she could tolerate him even though he was an annoying little brother. When their mom died, he got creepier, and Britt couldn't stand being around him."

Emory said, "Then I'm surprised Britt ever came home. She couldn't stand her brother or her stepmother, and her dad was controlling who she could date."

"I think that's how she became such a good skater. She spent so much time on the ice to avoid going home, she couldn't help but be good at it. Hey, you're not thinking that Ian killed Britt, are you?" Both men hesitated to answer. "He's just a little boy. Believe me, if Ian was going to kill someone, I would think he'd have a lot more people higher on his list than his sister. He was always being bullied by people who didn't like that someone his age was in the same grade."

Jeff asked, "Speaking of school, do you know why Ian got a C in science last year?"

Tati laughed again. "How would I know? I don't keep up with…Oh wait. I know what you're talking about now. I remember that. It was last year. He got caught cheating. Ian never says much, but I think he told everyone who would listen for like days after that he wished Mr. Roberts was dead. Do you think Ian burned down his house?"

"Do you know any details about the cheating affair?" Emory asked.

"No, not really. You should talk to Dan Claymon. They were lab partners last year, and I think it had something to do with him. I don't know. I usually tuned out if Britt was talking about something that wasn't important."

"Thanks for your help. We'll go talk to him." Jeff was about to stand when Emory pulled him back to the couch.

"One more thing before we go."

"What is it?"

"Why didn't you tell me you were with Britt the morning she died?"

Tati's face flushed what little color it had down her neck. "What do you mean?"

Emory showed her the picture on his phone of the shoeprints in the snow around the lake, and he pointed to a small print. "I can't tell for certain, but these prints from the lake look to be about the same size and shape as the boots you're wearing right now."

Now fidgeting on the squeaky leather upholstery, Tati continued deflecting. "Those could be anyone's."

"True." Emory flipped to the photo of the framed picture of Britt he found lying on her bed. "This last picture you took of Britt, the one used at her funeral. You told her family it was taken the weekend before she died."

"That's right."

Jeff held his hand out for the phone so he could see the picture. Once he had it, the screen went blank. He pressed the main button, but nothing showed up.

"There's snow in the picture, but the snow hadn't fallen until the evening before Britt died. The picture you took had to be snapped the morning she died, within minutes I'd imagine."

"I don't see anything," Jeff said.

"Fine," Tati blurted out. "I just didn't want anyone pointing a finger at me, so I didn't say anything."

Emory took the phone and tried to get the picture back up, to no avail. "My battery's dead."

"That's okay." Jeff turned his attention to Tati. "Tell us what happened that morning."

"Nothing. At least not while I was there. Britt called me the night before and said she was ready to get back on the ice. She asked if I would take pictures of her skating with the new snow in the background. She thought they'd be cool shots. I met her at the gate. We stopped after a few feet to take some pictures, and then she started talking about Dan and how upset she was. By the time she was ready to skate, I had to get ready for school. I came home, and she went on to the lake." Tati's eyes glistened with tears. "If I had stayed with her, maybe whoever did this wouldn't have attacked her."

"Don't blame yourself for that," Emory said.

Jeff asked her, "Wouldn't you have noticed her car still there when you left for school?"

"Britt had a free first period. She always got to school late."

"What about that evening?" Jeff asked. "Her father didn't find her until 6 p.m."

"I work at the coffee shop after school. I get home at 8. That's when I heard about Britt."

Emory stood up, followed by Jeff. "Thank you for your time."

CHAPTER 37

JEFF AND EMORY walked up the gravel driveway to the Claymon's trailer, uncertain about the reception they would receive. Emory knocked on the front door. "I hope this family doesn't hold a grudge."

Abigail answered the door. "What do you want?"

"Mrs. Claymon, we're sorry for the intrusion, but we'd like to speak to Dan for a moment."

"When are you people going to leave us alone? No one in my family had nothing to do with anything illegal."

"We're not here about that—" Jeff began, before Emory touched his arm.

"I promise you, we're not here to accuse anyone of anything."

Jeff told her, "As a matter of fact, we've proven that your husband had nothing to do with the missing water at the factory."

Mrs. Claymon's face softened. "What?"

"It was Scot Trousdale," Jeff said. "Victor Algarotti's assistant."

"And he let my Charlie take the blame?"

"He's going to pay for everything he did," Emory assured her. "He's in jail now."

"Does this mean Charlie can have his job back?"

Emory answered, "He'd have to discuss that with the foreman. Could we talk to Dan?"

"What for?"

"We just need a little more information that might be helpful in solving Britt's murder."

A few moments later, Emory, Jeff, Dan and Abigail were all sitting around the kitchen table while Charlie Claymon spoke on the phone in the other room. Dan was telling them, "Yeah, Ian gets picked on a lot. I felt a little obligated to watch out for him because he's Britt's brother."

Emory asked, "Can you tell us what happened last year in Rick Roberts' chemistry class? There was some cheating scandal?"

"Oh, that. Me and Ian were lab partners, which was kind of embarrassing because he's four years younger than me, and we were both taking Chem II. Honestly, though, he carried me in that class. One day we had a lab assignment that we had to finish in class – don't ask me what it was exactly, but it was mixing some chemical with some others and explaining what we were seeing by writing out the chemical equations. I hate chemistry. Ian got it right away and wrote out everything in his lab book with really detailed descriptions, but I didn't get it at all. He started trying to explain it to me, but class was almost over, so he didn't have time. He took my lab book from me and starting writing the chemical equations and the reasons behind the experiment's results. I was watching him while he wrote, trying to understand it. I didn't notice that Mr. Roberts was walking around to check on everyone's work. He saw Ian's lab book closed, and he asked, 'Ian, are you writing in Dan's lab book?' Ian turned white as a ghost and tried to tell him there wasn't enough time, but Mr. Roberts accused him of cheating and took both our lab books away." Dan pursed his lips and shook his head. "I felt so bad for him. The next day, Mr. Roberts handed us back our books with a big red F on the assignment. It wasn't my first F, so I didn't care, but Ian was crushed. For the rest of the year, he didn't even speak anymore in that class, and Mr. Roberts never called on him again."

"That explains the C for the semester," Jeff said.

"Did Ian threaten Mr. Roberts?" asked Emory.

"Not to his face. He sure said it to me enough, how much he wanted him dead. I've never known anyone to hate a teacher that much." As if he just realized what he had said, Dan told them, "I know he was just venting. He wouldn't ever do anything like that. He's just a kid."

Jeff glanced at Emory and then redirected. "How did Britt get along with her brother?"

"He annoyed the crap out of her, so she was kind of hateful to him – always making fun of him and telling him to go away whenever they happened to see each other at school. I don't have a little brother, but I figure that's normal. Plus, I think Britt just hated that he skipped grades and got into high school with her. I think it embarrassed her."

Emory asked, "How did Ian respond to her hatefulness toward him?"

"It didn't seem to bother him. I think he got used to it. He loved his sister." Dan crossed his arms. "I always thought he was kind of nice to have around. He likes doing things for people."

Jeff asked, "Like what?"

"I don't know. Little things. Like with helping me in class. He'd always fix me something to drink when I came over to his house. Things like that."

Charlie Claymon hung up the phone and entered the kitchen with a big grin on his face. "I got my job back!"

Charlie Claymon didn't know it at the time, but his elation would be short-lived.

As they drove away from the Claymons, Jeff told Emory, "I hope Victor doesn't try to weasel out of the reward when he finds out who killed his daughter."

"I don't know. He's thirteen. I know teenagers kill, but they're usually spree or passion killings – not three separate, well-planned murders. He just seems so young."

"Damien was in preschool when he started killing people."

Emory snickered at the comparison that Jeff loved to make. "Damien's not real, and Ian's not the anti-Christ. Look, after everything Victor's been through, I don't want to bring his son in for questioning without being much more certain that he is the one that we're after. If he has anything to do with either of the murders or the attempted murder, we're going to have to prove it before we can touch him."

As the car turned onto the main road, in the opposite direction of the Algarotti house, Jeff told him, "So let's find the proof you need to arrest him."

"I need to head back to Knoxville before it gets too late. He's not going anywhere."

"I'm more concerned with his potential victims."

"Pristine's safe in the hospital, and if he is the killer, I think the last person he'd want to hurt is his father after seeing those pictures."

"I see your point. Hey, would you mind giving me a ride back here tomorrow?"

"Your car still not ready?"

"No, and Virginia's got to be in the office, so she can't drive me."

"You can ride with me, but I have to warn you that Wayne is going to be with me."

Jeff moaned and said, "That's just great. Can't he drive himself?"

"We're partners."

"So you're saying you're stuck with him."

"That's not exactly what I said."

"I've seen you two in action. You can't tell me that he adds anything worthwhile to your investigations. I read the articles on the drug bust. He's a shadow anchor. I bet you would've had that case closed at least a month sooner if he hadn't led you down false paths."

Emory agreed with everything Jeff was saying, but he needed to defend his partner. "He spots some things I don't see."

"Fine, I'll bring him a Where's Waldo? book for the car ride. Is it too soon to call shotgun?"

CHAPTER 38

EMORY AWOKE MONDAY morning in a panic. *I need to check the photos.* He threw the blanket off his body and dangled his feet from his bed to look at the alarm clock on his nightstand. *It's 4:15. I slept almost five hours – and without a narcotic sneaked into my system.*

The night before, after dropping Jeff off and taking a quick trip to the Regional Forensic Center, Emory came home and crawled right into bed – a rarity for him.

I know I'm missing something. One of the benefits of snapping so many pictures during open cases was that his subconscious mind could catch tiny inconsistencies that his conscious eye would need to keep reviewing to recognize. Those inconsistencies would nag at him until conscious attention was paid to it – a feeling that had hit him as he slept.

Emory walked naked from the bed to the desk, pulled his phone from the charger and opened his most recent photo album. Scrolling past the newer pictures, he slowed down at the ones taken at Rick Roberts' house. The special agent flipped through pictures of the rooms until he came to the kitchen, wincing at the charred body on the floor. Seeing nothing new, he backtracked to the bedroom, to the dresser. He zoomed in and checked each framed photo on the dresser top one by one. The white-framed picture stuck out from the others, and as he focused on the photo, he did find something of interest.

It was a picture of Rick Roberts with a group of students at last year's science fair. Each of his three students stood behind a three-by-two-foot table, on top which sat their personal science project. The tables were lined up side-by-side, and taped to the front of each was a sign with the school name and city, the student's name and the name of the project. Rick stood just to the left of his students' three tables, in front of an empty table. Although the table was empty, it did have a sign, most of which was cropped out of the picture. Emory zoomed in further to try reading the sign. All he could make out on the first line was "High School," but on the second line he saw, "Ridge."

"That's got to be Barter Ridge," Emory muttered to himself. "One of Rick's students must not have made it to the science fair for some reason."

He looked at the line below the city and saw, "garotti."

That's it!

Emory showered and dressed but forced himself to wait until 6 a.m. to send separate texts to Wayne and Jeff to arrange pickup times and locations. To pass the time, he checked the online news, soon finding a disturbing local story. Under the heading, "Drugged water panic in Tennessee," was the subheading, "Is your drinking water safe?"

"Crap." He started reading the article to make certain it was about the Algarotti factory, and sure enough, the name of the company appeared in bold, hyperlinked text in the second paragraph. "Crap, crap, crap." The story was accurate in reporting that drugged water was shipped to several cities in Tennessee, but almost everything else was wrong. It misled readers into thinking that the tainted Algarotti water was in the supermarkets, offices and churches – that none of it was safe to drink. "We got it in time," Emory muttered. "How did they…" Even before he could ask the question, he knew the answer. "That damn security guard!"

A moment later, his phone rang, and for the next several minutes, Victor chewed Emory out for letting the story leak. When Emory told him his suspicions about the security guard, Victor let him know that his next call would be to fire Clarence. "Thanks to you, he won't be the last one I have to let go. This will ruin my company!"

When Victor hung up on him, Emory took several deep breaths to relieve some of the tension tightening his torso. "Crap."

An hour later he was picking Wayne up in front of his house. During the short ride to Jeff's office, the older man told Emory what he had found out about Scot's life before he was hired at the Algarotti Smoky Mountain Springs factory.

"Scot Trousdale worked for three years as a manager at a nightclub here in Knoxville called If Tomorrow Comes."

"Seriously?" Emory asked when he heard the name of the club Jeff had taken him to the week before.

"You know the place?"

Emory didn't want to get into details, so he kept his answer simple. "I've heard of it."

"Okay. Well, Scot's planned distributor here – the one we arrested last night – is someone who worked as bartender at the same club. Before that, Trousdale worked retail. He graduated from Tennessee Tech nine years ago with a bachelor's in business. He was arrested once for selling marijuana but was never convicted. Besides peddling drugs, his favorite hobby is fighting. He has a brown belt in Brazilian Jiu Jitsu, and he's competed in some local tournaments – winning some, losing some."

Emory rubbed his sore neck with his free hand. "Yeah, I've experienced that firsthand."

"You got him. That's what's important. From the texts you've sent me, it looks like you've had quite an eventful weekend."

"Yeah, I need to fill in the details for you."

"Wasn't that PI...What's his name again?"

"Jeff." *Who you're about to share a car with. This is going to be a ride from hell. Or to it.*"

"Jeff? What kind of name is Jeff for a private eye?" Wayne laughed, but when Emory didn't play along, he finished his question. "Weren't you two together when the skating coach went up in flames?"

"Yes." *Where is he heading with this question?*

"And again when the evil stepmother almost bought it."

"Yeah."

"Man, people aren't safe when you two are together. You two are like nitrogen and glycerin."

Nitrogen and glycerin? What the hell are you talking about?

Wayne nodded. "Yeah, that's right. I know some chemistry too."

That isn't how you make nitroglycerin. Screw it. Let him have it. Emory gave him a polite chuckle.

"Oh, I forgot to tell you that you were right about Victor's gun."

"It's the one used to kill Rick Roberts' dog?"

"I talked to Cathy this morning, and she told me to let you know. It only had Victor's prints."

"Probably wiped after shooting the dog."

Wayne looked out the window and pointed. "Hey, you missed the interstate."

Emory's lips tightened. "We have a stop to make before we get on the road."

"What stop?"

He waited a second before blurting out, "I promised to give a ride to the PI."

"What?!" Wayne slammed the side of his fist into the door. "Why are you helping him?"

"Because I gave him my word, and I'm going to abide by it. He helped me out this weekend – when you weren't there." Emory knew that statement would anger Wayne more but also play to his guilt for being just a forty-hour-a-week employee.

"Hey, I have a family! Let's see how many damn hours you work when you get married and have kids."

Wayne's retort demonstrated just how little he knew about his partner. "That wasn't my point," Emory said, although it was. "We wouldn't have Scot in custody without him, and the drugs he shipped would be on the street now."

Wayne unclenched his fists but muttered a few grunts. "Tell me everything that happened."

"I will, but we're here." Emory nodded toward Jeff, who was standing on the sidewalk in front of his office.

"Great," Wayne groaned.

Wearing his own clothes now and a wide grin, Jeff jumped into the back seat and didn't hesitate a breath before he started needling Wayne. "Agent Rome. Agent Fuckwad."

Wayne looked over his shoulder and growled at him, "It's Special Agent Buckwald! Dick."

"Ooh, sorry. Emory, can we stop by the bookstore? I forgot to pick something up this morning."

Emory smiled at Jeff's grinning reflection in the rearview mirror. "We don't have time. I was just about to apprise Wayne of everything that's happened over the weekend. Maybe you could fill in any blanks."

"Sure."

"I'm not going to talk about the case in front of this wannabe!" Wayne insisted with an angry thumb jabbing the air over his shoulder.

"Fine with me," Jeff said. "Stay ignorant, Special Agent Fuckwad."

Wayne turned around like he was going to jump over the seat.

Emory threw a hand to his right shoulder to stop him, causing the car to swerve. "Cut it out!"

"I'm going to kick his fucking ass!" Wayne screamed as he turned back around to face the windshield.

Jeff just laughed.

Emory grimaced at the man in the back seat. "You two are acting like children. Wayne, he was there. Jeff, antagonism doesn't encourage results."

"Depends on the results you're after," Jeff muttered.

"Enough! We've got a long ride ahead of us, and I don't know the first thing about being a referee." Emory eyeballed Wayne and then Jeff in the rearview mirror. "I'll begin."

With that, Emory began recounting the weekend's events, including the attack on his father at the Algarotti factory, Pristine's poisoning, their dealings with the Claymons, Scot's plan and arrest, and everything they had learned about Ian. Jeff filled in a couple of gaps, but both of them left out Emory's accidental drugging and everything that happened at the Romes' house. Emory closed by telling them both about the picture on Rick's dresser. "Ian was supposed to go to that science fair, but Rick didn't let him after he caught him cheating. I want to get that picture first thing."

"That's pretty thin," Wayne said. "Would all of that have embarrassed the kid enough to kill his teacher?"

"Humiliation at that age can be crushing, and when it morphs into anger, it can feed a powerful thirst for revenge," Emory told him. "Ian has jumped grades, earning nothing but A's. I imagine a perfect score throughout school was pretty much a given for him, until Rick gave him that C."

Jeff added, "Teenagers' emotions are like a hundred times more volatile than adults. Look at all the school shootings. Almost all of them have revenge for humiliation, real or imagined, as the primary motive."

Wayne was unmoved. "I don't buy it." He told Emory, "You're giving up too easy on Scot. Murder's only a baby step up from manufacturing drugs. We just need to press him harder to get the truth out of him. He's the murderer. Maybe he killed them both because they found out what he was up to."

"If that's true, we should ask Pristine if she knew," Jeff said.

"I think she's still in the hospital," Emory told them. "Maybe we can go there after Rick's."

All seemed to be in agreement with the plan, so as soon as they entered the Barter Ridge city limits, they headed to Rick Roberts' house. On the way there, Emory answered his ringing phone. "Hi Dad. You're on speakerphone. I have Jeff and Wayne with me."

"Good," the sheriff said. "I've got some awful bad news to tell you guys."

"What is it?"

The sheriff clicked his tongue. "Scot Trousdale escaped."

"Escaped?!" Emory exclaimed, and it was echoed by the others in the car.

Jeff threw a hand to his forehead. "Oh my god."

"Wait a second, wait a second here," Wayne said, shaking his head. "The drug dealer and our prime suspect for the murders has honestly escaped from your jail? Oh that's right – you don't have a real jail in this damn town."

Emory shot Wayne a scolding look. "Dad, how did he escape?"

"We're still trying to figure that out."

Emory glanced at Wayne and then back at Jeff. "Okay. We'll be there shortly."

CHAPTER 39

EMORY PULLED HIS car into Rick Roberts' driveway, windows steaming from the heated conversation within. Wayne argued that the only place they should be headed was the sheriff's station to work on finding their escaped suspect, but Emory insisted on sticking with their planned first stop. Jeff didn't have a strong opinion one way or the other, but he sided with Emory.

"I should've driven myself," Wayne said.

"We'll be here five minutes max," Emory told him.

Wayne shook his head. "Our prime suspect has escaped. We need to get to the sheriff's station."

"Why?" Jeff asked. "That's the one place we know he's not at."

The three men filed out of the car and walked in silence to the front door, which was crisscrossed with crime tape. Emory snapped his fingers when he realized, "Dad has the keys."

"Wonderful," Wayne said, starting back toward the driveway. "Let's get to the sheriff's station."

"I'm not leaving without that picture," Emory insisted.

"I have an idea," said Jeff. "We can go through the doggy door."

"Good idea." Emory stood by the front door, waiting for Jeff to act.

"What are you doing?"

"I'll wait here for you to open the door."

Jeff laughed and tapped his own shoulders. "There's no way I can get these shoulders through that opening."

"Again, my shoulders are just as broad as yours."

"Put your back against mine." Jeff turned his back to Emory who did the same, and they both tried to gauge whose shoulders extended further.

"What in the hell are you two doing?" Wayne asked, walking back toward them.

"See," Jeff said.

Emory pulled away. "I think your coat has a half-inch more padding than mine. I'll just do it." He took off his jacket, exposing his grey dress shirt, and handed it to Jeff to hold. He ran past Wayne to the five-foot fence that surrounded the backyard and hurled himself over it.

"What's he doing?" Wayne asked.

"Remember the doggy door?"

Two uncomfortable minutes later, the front door opened, and Emory stood behind an X of crime tape with a ripped sleeve and a three-inch scratch on his right upper arm. Jeff smiled at him. "I told you you'd fit."

Emory wasn't amused. Once they were inside, Emory led them to Rick's bedroom and to the dresser. "There's the picture."

"Why is this one white?" Wayne asked, referring to the fact that all the other frames were dark.

"How can anyone live in such filth?" asked Jeff.

Wayne looked around the room. "What? This place isn't filthy."

Jeff pointed at the dresser. "Look at the dust."

Emory examined the thick coating of dust on the dresser top, as well as the frames and glass. "The white frame is clean."

Jeff told him, "White hides dust better."

Emory put on his gloves and ran a finger over the top of the white frame. "Or it repels it all together." He showed the others that the glove was still clean. He picked up the picture and held it so Jeff could see. "Look at the last line of that sign."

Emory hadn't been able to make out everything in the frame from the picture on his phone, but now he could see in the original picture that the subject of Ian's project ended with the text, "Using Calcium Carbide."

Jeff asked, "Do we have enough now to arrest him?"

Emory told them, "Let's go get Damien."

As soon as Emory parked at the sheriff's station, Wayne hurried to the front door.

Jeff was about to exit the car when Emory told him, "Before we go in, I need to talk to you about something." The special agent moved to the back seat with Jeff.

"What, you want to make out now?"

"Just talk. Scot Trousdale was the manager of If Tomorrow Comes for three years."

Jeff's face dropped. "He was? Do you know which three years?"

"He left there about a year ago, when he came here to work at the Algarotti factory."

"I was going to that club then. I'm surprised I didn't see him there."

Emory waited for more, but nothing came. "That's all you have to say?"

"I'm not sure what you want. I didn't know him from the club, and as far as I know, the first time I met him was precisely when you met him for the first time."

"Someone who looks like Scot, you didn't notice at the club?"

Jeff scoffed, "Scot's not that hot. Why? Do you think he is?"

"No...I mean he's certainly not unattractive. That's not the point. Don't you find it odd that, not only was Victor Algarotti's current wife a client of yours, but his assistant worked at a night-club you frequent?"

"Odd maybe, but a coincidence definitely."

"Fine." Emory grabbed the door handle.

Inside the sheriff's station, Wayne was already discussing Scot Trousdale's escape with Sheriff Rome and two deputies when Emory and Jeff entered. The sheriff nodded to his son and told Wayne, "We've been trying to figure out what happened."

Deputy Harris' flushed face gave his blond hair a strawberry tint as he explained, "I clocked out at six last night. I checked on him before I left, and he was in bed. I was planning to drive him to Knoxville myself when I clocked back in this morning."

Deputy Loggins looked up to the other men, making eye contact with each. "I've been here since six last night, pulling a double. I got suspicious around five when I checked on him through the window because he hadn't moved all night. I decided to go in the room for a physical check, and that's when I found out it was just the blankets and pillows. It had to have happened before my shift."

"There's no way," Deputy Harris insisted. "He didn't go missing on my shift!"

Emory asked his father, "Could we see the room?"

"Of course." The sheriff led them past the water cooler and down the hall to the holding room.

As the others continued down the hallway, Jeff stayed at the cooler. "Hey guys," he said but didn't capture their attention. "Guys! One of the empty water bottles is missing." The men turned around, but only Emory backtracked to Jeff.

Deputy Harris gave him his how-stupid-are-you? glower. He told him in the most condescending tone he could muster, "The delivery guy took it yesterday."

Jeff pointed to the remaining empty bottle. "Why would he take only one of the empty bottles? And why didn't he leave a full bottle for you?"

Emory faced Deputy Harris. "When did the delivery guy come?"

"Yesterday," the deputy repeated.

"Before or after Scot's arrest?" Deputy Harris waited to give the answer, so Emory demanded, "Answer me!"

Deputy Harris jumped. "After. But it couldn't have been him."

Wayne asked, "Did you see the delivery guy come through the front door?"

"How else could he…" the deputy started to answer before his voice trailed off.

Wayne followed up with, "What exactly did you see?"

Deputy Harris recounted, "I was taking a call, and I looked up and saw a delivery guy walking to the front door with a water bottle on his left shoulder. I didn't make out the face, but I wasn't paying attention to him."

Emory asked, "Besides the fact that he was carrying a water bottle, was there anything else about him that led you to believe he was, in fact, a water delivery guy? Uniform? Anything?"

"No," Deputy Harris mumbled. "It just seemed…normal."

Deputy Loggins gave the sheriff a look of vindication that said, "I told you it wasn't me."

Emory asked, "What time did you see him go?"

Deputy Harris responded, "Not long after you left. Maybe around five o'clock."

Wayne shook his head. "He's got a seventeen-hour head start on us. He could be anywhere."

"I'm so sorry about this," the sheriff said. "Now we know how he got out the front door, but I'd like to know how he got out of the holding room."

The men headed to the room, and halfway down the hall, the

sheriff stopped at the wall cabinet to get the key. Once the sheriff unlocked the holding room, Wayne investigated the open door for signs of damage while Emory and Jeff scanned everything else. The sheriff and his deputies loitered in the middle of the room watching the others.

"I already checked the door," said Deputy Harris. "It hasn't been tampered with."

Inspecting the bed, Emory told them, "Then he must've had a key."

"How on Earth could he have a key?" Deputy Harris asked.

Finishing his inspection of the door, Wayne stood up straight. "I don't know, but the lock wasn't picked, and he sure didn't walk through it."

The sheriff said, "Well, even if he did have a key somehow, we emptied his pockets, and we still have his personal effects."

"Did you search him?" Jeff asked.

"Standard procedure," the sheriff answered. "When you first brought him in, I processed him – fingerprints, mug shot and search. I made him undress, and I did a thorough search of his person and his clothes before we started questioning him. The only way he had a key on him was if he stuck it somewhere I wasn't about to search."

"No," Emory said. "He had no warning that he was about to be arrested, so he would've had no to time to hide a key...in himself." His mind clicked onto the answer. "The water."

The others looked at him like they were waiting for an explanation, but Jeff said, "Yes! He went to the water cooler before he was brought into this room."

Emory and Jeff hurried from the room, followed by the others. Once they reached the water cooler, the two began inspecting it for a possible hiding space. As Jeff checked the front, Emory looked at the side where the cup dispenser was attached. He noticed that the Algarotti logo to the left of the dispenser was inside a rectangular groove. He pushed on the logo, and a small drawer about the of a deck of cards popped out. "Found it!"

Sheriff Rome folded his arms. "I'll be. So he hid the key in there? I should've never let him get water alone."

"But how did he get the key in the first place?" Deputy Harris asked.

Emory responded, "He told me he came in regularly to service your cooler. My guess is he took the key from the cabinet when no one was looking, got a copy made and returned it to the cabinet."

The sheriff asked, "Why would he go to all that trouble?"

"He was arrested before in college," Wayne told them. "He wasn't convicted, but he did spend a couple days in jail. He probably wanted to make sure that never happened again, so he planned ahead once he started with his drug scheme. If the evidence against him was insurmountable, he'd escape."

Emory nodded. "You have his wallet, but I bet he has another ID and credit cards stored somewhere safe so he could get out of town, maybe out of the country."

"We'll never find him," Deputy Harris said.

"Speak for yourself," Wayne said. "He hasn't gone up against me yet. I'll find the son-of-a-bitch."

Emory told him, "While you do that, Jeff and I are going to chase the other lead we talked about."

"Fine." Wayne turned his attention from his partner to say, "Deputies, I'm going to need your help." He led them back into the deputy room, leaving Sheriff Rome, Emory and Jeff at the water cooler.

Emory told his father, "I have to ask you for another favor."

"First, are these yours?" Sheriff Rome pulled a pair of hand-cuffs from his pocket.

"Oh, you found them." Emory attached them to his belt.

"They were on the floor by the fireplace. How'd they end up there?"

Emory lied. "I'm not sure."

"So what's the favor?"

"I need you to talk Judge Harper into giving us two more search warrants. The one for Scot's place should be easy. It's the other one I'm concerned about."

"He should be on his way," the principal said after she paged Ian Algarotti on the overhead PA system. "I have to say, following your previous visit, I'm a bit leery of this whole affair."

Emory shifted in his seat, an unpadded, wooden chair facing the principal's austere oak desk. "I apologize for any...uneasiness on your part. I could always go to his class."

"No, no, no." The principal waved her forefinger as if she were admonishing a student. "We'll not have another brash race through my halls."

Seated next to Emory, Jeff spoke up for him, "A murder investigation is rarely a perfect process."

"I understand," the principal said. "It's your timing that's lamentable. School ends in eighty-seven minutes. Couldn't you come back then?"

Emory shook his head. "With serious crimes, once we have enough evidence for an arrest, I have an obligation to carry it out, regardless of convenience." He placed a hand on her desk. "I do promise you, we'll be as delicate as possible."

Jeff arose from his chair. "I'll stand by the door and block it once he comes in to make sure he doesn't run."

"Are you sure about this?" the principal asked. "Ian can be a little tightly wound, but to honestly believe..."

The principal had no time to finish her thought for, at that moment, Ian walked through her office door. He looked up at a cross-armed Jeff, who had his back against the wall beside the door. He turned his attention to Emory, who stood to face him. "Has something happened to Dad?"

"No," the principal told him. "Your father's fine, Ian."

Emory took over, explaining as he stepped toward the boy, "Ian, I'm placing you under arrest for the murder of Britt Algarotti, the murder of Rick Roberts and the attempted murder of Pristine Algarotti." Emory retrieved the handcuffs from his belt.

The principal jerked out of her chair, half-shouting, "Is that truly needed?"

With a nod from Jeff, Emory figured they could keep him under control, so he returned the cuffs to his belt. "You have the right to remain silent..." As Emory continued reciting the Miranda warning, tears streamed down the principal's anguished face.

"Do you understand each of these rights I have explained to you?" Ian answered with a single nod. "Having these rights in mind, do you wish to talk to us now?" The boy shook his head.

Emory escorted Ian out of the office, keeping a hand on his shoulder. The boy walked without emotion past the students and teachers, refusing eye contact, during the short distance from the principal's office to the nearest exit.

CHAPTER 40

A S SHERIFF ROME approached the water cooler in the sheriff's station, he gave little thought to grabbing a paper cup from the dispenser and placing it under the spigot. As the water flowed into the cup, however, his mind gave greater clarity to his actions.

The inverted five-gallon bottle on top was full. He wondered if the water could've been tampered with, and after a moment's contemplation, he opted not to take the risk. The sheriff threw the cup into the nearby wastebasket. "Loggins!" Sheriff Rome called to the deputy whose desk was nearest to him. "Get rid of this water. Cancel our account with Algarotti, and find us a new vendor."

Emory pushed open the door of the sheriff's station for Ian, who again said, "I didn't do it!"

Following them inside, Jeff told him, "Saying something a hundred times doesn't make it true,"

Sheriff Rome came out of his office and pointed to Deputy Loggins. "Could you process young Mr. Algarotti and take him to the interro…" Making eye contact with Ian, the sheriff softened his tone. "To the interview room."

Deputy Loggins gripped Ian's shoulder. "Come with me."

Wayne popped up from a chair beside Deputy Harris' desk and made a beeline for his partner. "Emory, we checked out Scot Trousdale's apartment. He went back there after he escaped. Looks like he packed in a hurry. We also found the sheriff's gun."

"So he was definitely the person who attacked him." Emory clenched his fists. "We need to find that son-of-a-bitch."

Deputy Harris approached and gave Emory a nod. "We're tracking down any activity on his accounts, and we've put an APB on him and his car."

Wayne pointed at the deputy. "Plus, Rudy here is trying to find out if his car has a tracking system."

Jeff tilted his head to the side. "Assuming he hasn't dumped it for another one."

Emory heard nothing after he learned the deputy's first name. *Rudy? They've certainly become chummy. Of course, they're hitting it off. Harris is a younger version of Wayne.*

Wayne didn't acknowledge Jeff or his words, keeping his eyes on Emory. "We'll reconnect with you when you're done with the kid." Walking back to the desk, he asked Deputy Harris, "Are there any car rental places in town?"

Hands on his hips, Sheriff Rome clicked his tongue. "I have to tell you, Son, I'm really dreading this."

Emory nodded. "Best just to get it over with. Where's the evidence from the house?"

"In my office. I'll go get it."

When the sheriff walked away, Emory noticed a sweet smile on Jeff's flawless face. "What is it?"

"It might've started a little bumpy, but working with you was not all that unpleasant." Jeff shook his hand.

"I feel the same."

Sheriff Rome returned with a ratty burlap bag. "Here's everything you gathered."

The sheriff and his son started walking in the same direction when Emory realized Jeff was too. He stopped the PI. "I can't let you in there while we're interrogating him."

Jeff reminded him, "You let me in for Scot's interrogation."

"And look how that turned out. I have to handle Ian carefully. I need a controlled environment."

Jeff leaned in to argue, but instead put up his hands in resignation. "That's fine. I'll just check in with Virginia and hang out until you're done." He took a seat on the bench by the door.

As the two resumed walking, Emory asked his father, "How are you feeling, physically?"

The sheriff waved off his concern. "Oh, I'm fine. I'm still sore but much better today."

When they entered the interrogation room, Ian wasn't yet there, so they sat at one end of the table and waited.

"How do you want to handle this?" Sheriff Rome asked.

"I just want to talk to him first. See if he'll open up. If not, I'll start bringing up the evidence."

"Sounds good. I called Victor. He should be here soon, and then we can begin."

"Dad, we're not waiting for Victor. Ian said he didn't want his dad present."

"He's a minor."

"It doesn't matter."

"A parent has to—"

"Ian has the right—"

Sheriff Rome slapped the table. "Victor will be present! That's the law."

Emory could no longer hide his irritation over his father's not-quite-right legal procedures. He slapped the table and told him, "No, Dad, actually it's not."

Sheriff Rome shoved his eyebrows together and shifted in his chair to face his son. "What are you talking about?"

"When a minor's arrested, we have to notify the parents, which you did, but it's up to the minor whether or not a parent is present during questioning. It's his right to be questioned alone."

The sheriff tapped the table three times with his pointing finger. "Listen here, Son. No minor's going to be questioned in my interrogation room without a parent present."

"Dad, this is so frustrating!" Emory clenched his fists on his lap. "For the record, we don't need a parent to be notified if we're just questioning a minor unless he's been arrested, at which point the minor decides if he wants a parent present. We also *can* take items into evidence from a crime scene without a warrant, and respect for the deceased does not supersede the mandate to fully document an undisturbed crime scene!" Emory gasped for air. "These rules of yours are made-up versions of the law, and they've been impeding my investigation!"

Sheriff Rome looked more hurt than angry, and he faced the table when he responded, "Lawmen don't have to be heartless fact-gatherers and jailors. We deal with people – real people with real feelings – and almost always at extremely stressful points in their lives." He again faced Emory, and his hands took on a life of their own as he gesticulated to stress his next words. "What's wrong with demonstrating some empathy and trying to help them through their difficulties? If asking a parent's permission to inter-view their child isn't written into the letter of the law, it's there in spirit – or it should be! Snapping pictures of a dead girl might be the right thing for us, but it's not for that girl's father. If that means it takes us a little longer to bring them justice, I can live with that."

Emory's face drooped, and he was about to apologize when he realized the door had swung open sometime during his scolding.

Deputy Loggins had a hand on Ian's shoulder, and they were standing in the doorway. "Should we come back?"

Sheriff Rome waved the deputy inside. "No, come in." The deputy led the boy to a chair on the opposite side of the table from the others. "Take those handcuffs off him." He looked at Emory and asked in a snide tone he had never used with his son, "Is that okay with you, Special Agent Rome?"

"Of course."

Deputy Loggins did as asked and left the room, closing the door behind him.

In a gentle voice, Sheriff Rome told Ian, "Son, I need to turn on the camera to record our conversation. Okay?" He walked over to a camera on a tripod at the adjacent end of the table. Once he turned it on, he nodded to Emory.

"Ian, could you tell me about your sister?" asked Emory, mimicking his father's tone.

The sheriff returned to his seat and clasped his hands together on the table.

Ian's head lifted, and he looked Emory square in the eyes. "What do you want to know?"

"What did you think of her? How did you see her?"

"I saw her as she was."

"What exactly was she?"

The boy responded with a question. "Do you have a brother or sister?"

Emory frowned at the redirection. "I was an only child."

Ian bowed his head. "How fortunate for you. Tell me, if you could've had a sibling, do you think you would've wanted one who was younger or older than you?"

Emory looked at his father, uncertain if he should stop the conversation's current path or continue humoring Ian. Sheriff Rome offered a quick nod, relating that he should do whatever it takes to keep the boy talking. "Older."

Ian's brows curled upward as he again faced Emory. "Not what I expected. Why older?"

Emory pursed his lips as he tried to think of the answer. "I guess I would've liked a protector when I was growing up."

"Protection from whom?" Ian looked at Sheriff Rome and again at Emory.

Does he know that's my father? "It's not important now."

"Could you have ever loved those who tormented you?"

"I know your sister didn't treat you well in front of others. Are you telling us that she was otherwise abusive toward you?"

"Were you protecting yourself?" Sheriff Rome asked. "Self-defense?"

"I didn't kill her!" Ian screamed. "I told you that! Why won't y'all listen to me?"

Sheriff Rome patted the table, and in his quiet church voice, he said, "Son, we just want to understand what happened to your sister. Don't you want that too?"

Emory displayed an admiring glance at the sheriff for his de-escalation skills – something he had learned from his father but rarely practiced.

"I don't know how I can help you." Ian stared at the empty space between Emory and the sheriff. "When Dad told me she was dead, he was so…heartbroken. I never even saw him cry when Mom died. What made Britt so special? I wanted to take that pain away, but there was nothing I could do."

Sheriff Rome asked, "Weren't you also upset about your sister's death?"

The boy looked at him with a blank face. "You want me to be honest?"

"Of course."

"Then if I'm being honest, I can't say that I'll miss her because I won't."

Emory lurched forward in his chair, and in his periphery, he saw his father do the same.

Ian explained, "I don't have to grieve to be innocent. I just really didn't like her. At all."

Emory reached down for the burlap bag and glanced at his father to let him know he was done with trying to coax a confession from Ian. He pulled out a hermetic glass storage jar about one-fifth full with a blackish powder and placed it on the table. "Do you know what this is?"

Ian examined it for a few seconds before answering, "It looks like calcium carbide."

"Excellent guess. While you were in school today, we searched your house."

"My dad let you do that?"

"He might not know yet." Emory tapped the jar. "Back to the evidence. Guess where we found it."

Ian shrugged. "I don't recognize the jar. I had some for a science project I was working on last year, but I got rid of it."

"Or maybe you just hid it. This jar was found in your room, behind the shoe rack in your closet."

Ian's face stretched into a look of surprise. "I did not have that jar in my room! Why are you even asking about calcium carbide anyway? It's not illegal to have."

"Your sister burned to death when this stuff ignited on the lake that she skated on. You sprinkled it all over the ice the night before she died, knowing exactly what would happen."

Ian popped up from his chair. "I did not! Stop saying that!" He held the table and gulped in several deep breaths. "I thought someone burned her and threw her in the lake. That's what the news said."

"Because that's what we told them," the sheriff said.

Ian returned to his seat. "So that's how she was killed? Did she suffer?" He waved off his question. "Never mind, I know."

He stared again at the empty space, his eyes almost gleaming. "She must've suffered. Everywhere she skated, the water under her blades leaving a trail for the flames to follow once her skates clipped. Fire spitting up all around her." The boy emitted a one-second laugh. "That's funny. She died in a real Lake of Fire. From a physical one to a spiritual one."

Emory shook his head to erase the stunned look from his face. He glanced at his father, whose lips were now a nickel's diameter apart.

The boy pointed to the jar. "Someone planted that in my room, if that's where you really found it. Someone's trying to set me up for my own sister's murder."

Emory leaned forward to rest his forearms on the table. "Okay. Let's talk about Rick Roberts."

"You think I killed Mr. Roberts too?"

Instead of answering, Emory delved back into the burlap bag and produced the framed photo from Rick's house, placing it on the table beside the jar. "He's the only teacher to ever give you less than an A on your report card. He humiliated you in front of everyone by calling you out for cheating—"

"I didn't cheat!" Ian slammed both fists on the table. "I was helping my lab partner by explaining the lab experiment to him, and I had to write it at the same time, or it wouldn't have been done before the end of class."

"I understand. I know you were trying to help someone, and it bit you on the butt."

"No good deed goes unpunished," the sheriff offered.

Emory continued, "Nevertheless, Mr. Roberts did call it cheating, and he did it in front of your whole class, and I'm sure word spread throughout the school. It had to be humiliating for you. On top of that humiliation and the frustration of not keeping your perfect record, you weren't allowed to compete in the science fair you were hoping to win. You had some good, valid reasons to want revenge. We heard from several people that you said repeatedly how much you wanted him dead."

Ian's pallid face patched with crimson, and his breathing became heavy as he once more looked at the empty space. "Like you said, I had good reason to hate him, and I did hate him. I still do. I'm glad he's dead, and I hope his death was painful – like all the pain he caused me."

Emory said, "So you killed him."

"I didn't kill him!" Ian pounded his fists again.

"Fine." Emory produced from the bag another hermetic glass storage jar – filled with dark granules.

"What's that?" Ian asked.

Emory gave him a like-you-don't-know glare. "Potassium permanganate. Can you guess where we found this?"

"Was that in my bedroom too?" When Emory nodded, Ian told him, "I've never even seen this stuff before. What is it?"

"You've never seen potassium permanganate before, yet it's used at your family's water factory."

"It is?"

"We also found the tea that you laced with potassium permanganate, poisoning Mr. Roberts."

"No, no, no! I didn't do it! I'm thirteen! I can't even drive yet. How did I get to his house to poison him?"

"You seem to get by pretty well on your bike. Mr. Roberts' house is 5.2 miles from yours. The snow had been plowed from all the roads leading there, so you could've easily biked there in thirty to forty minutes."

Ian pointed a skinny finger at Emory. "Wait a second. You said you found this picture in Mr. Roberts' house?"

"Yes. Why, where did you think I found it?"

"On his classroom wall. He has a picture from every science fair for the past twelve years on his wall. The event always takes a group shot of every team and gives it to the teacher. I never saw any of them in his house."

Sheriff Rome asked, "You admit being in his house?"

Ian huffed and opened his hands. "My sister used to drive me home from school. Sometimes she had to stop by Mr. Roberts' house on the way to pick up something or drop something off."

"Like what?" Emory asked.

"I don't know. Things for skating. Sometimes he had a new skating dress delivered for her, or she'd have new music for a routine. Things like that. I used to go into the house with her until I stopped speaking to him, and then I'd just wait out in the car. I never saw pictures from any of the other science fairs up in his house, just at school. Did you see any others?"

Emory shook his head. "This was the only one."

"You see? I'm being set up!"

Emory was silent for a moment as he thought about the dust that Jeff had noticed – or lack of it. This frame was the only one on the dresser without a layer of dust. *Maybe it was planted.*

"Can I see your phone?" Ian asked with his left hand held out. When Emory didn't move, the boy explained, "That deputy took mine. Please. It's important."

Without replying, Emory stood up and walked around the table to Ian. He pulled his phone from his pocket, unlocked it and handed it to the boy.

As Emory monitored him, Ian found the website for the local newspaper, the Barter Ridge Fountain, and searched for a specific date. Within a few seconds, he found an article about the science fair he was supposed to attend, and at the top of the article was the picture from the frame. Ian handed the phone back to Emory. "Anyone could've printed that picture and planted it at Mr. Roberts' house to throw suspicion on me."

Emory walked back to his seat and showed the picture to his

father. He was beginning to doubt Ian's guilt. "Let's move to the third crime scene."

"There's three?" Ian asked.

"Your house, where your stepmother was poisoned."

"Why would I want to hurt Pristine? She's my friend. When all that happened with Mr. Roberts, when he accused me of cheating, she was the only one I could talk to who was sympathetic. She'd listen to me go on and on about how embarrassing it was and how much I hated him. She understood." Ian let out a little laugh. "Most people sort of glaze over when I start talking about science, but not her. She let me explain every little detail of my experiment and how great my science project would've been if I had been allowed to go to the fair."

Emory told him, "Ian, we did find some evidence that points to you in your stepmother's attempted murder."

"Did you find strychnine in my room?" Ian asked, confident of the answer.

"How did you know about the strychnine?" the sheriff asked.

Ian huffed at the sheriff. "I was in Pristine's hospital room when the doctor told her that's what poisoned her."

"No, we didn't find any in your room." Emory placed a large plastic baggie containing shards of glass onto the table. "We did find the pieces of your stepmother's broken crystal glasses in the trash, and when we dusted them for fingerprints, we found three sets on some of the pieces – hers, the maid's and yours. My understanding is that only Pristine and the maid were allowed to touch her crystal, so how did your prints get there?"

CHAPTER 41

SEATED ON A bench in the deputy room of the sheriff's station, Jeff responded to a text from Virginia about a potential new client who wanted to meet him the next day. He texted that the Algarotti case was closing, so he would be able to make the meeting. Resting on his lap was a "Wanted" flyer of Scot Trousdale with his mug shots, a physical description and the number to call with information concerning his whereabouts. Each time Jeff sent a text, he would stare at the face on the flyer while he waited for Virginia's response.

He looked up from his phone and saw Wayne seated next to Deputy Harris with their eyes glued to the computer monitor. He grinned to himself. *Probably looking at porn.* He glanced over to Deputy Loggins, who was on a contentious phone call, presumably to his wife.

Jeff looked again at the flyer, at the mug shots of Scot Trousdale. *Hmm.* He got a pen from Deputy Loggins' desk, and when he sat down again, he began drawing on Scot's face. He drew a moustache and continued until he had a full beard. Once he was done, it struck him. "I do remember him!"

Jeff's words were drowned out by the front door slamming

open. Victor Algarotti stormed inside, and his eyes shot around the room like heat-seeking missiles. "Where's my son?"

Surprised to see him, Jeff threw himself into Victor's path to take the full impact of his wrath. "Victor, what are you doing here?"

"What am I doing here?" The man belted out an angry laugh. "Taking a break from all the damn phone calls I've been fielding since five this morning – nonstop calls from reporters and paranoid clients who keep asking me if their water has been drugged. No matter what I said, more than half of them canceled their service. Now on top of desperately trying to save my company, I get a phone call telling me my son's been arrested! Jesus, I had to ask my wife to take a taxi home from the hospital this afternoon because of all the shit I've been forced to slog through today! I swear if Scot weren't locked up, I'd kill that asshole for doing this to me!"

During Victor's tirade, Deputy Loggins had hung up his phone and joined Deputy Harris and Wayne in approaching the angry man.

"Speaking of Scot Trousdale," Deputy Harris began. "Mr. Algarotti, I need to inform you that he is no longer in our custody."

Victor appeared unfazed. "I don't care who has him – you or the TBI – as long as he never takes another breath of freedom for the rest of his miserable life."

"You don't understand," said Deputy Loggins, glancing at Deputy Harris like they were both in a race to put their spin on the story of why the accused was no longer in their custody. "Scot Trousdale escaped."

Victor's face lost all expression. "Didn't you have him locked up?"

Deputy Harris interjected before Deputy Loggins could explain, "We're still trying to figure out how he did it." He pointed to Wayne. "We're working with the TBI to find him."

Wayne assured him, "We have a solid lead we're following and should have him back in custody soon."

Victor threw both hands to his head. "This is unbelievable. You guys are idiots!"

Wayne came to Deputy Harris' defense. "With all due respect, they're not the ones who hired a Walter White wannabe. You are! And then you let him talk you into renovating your factory so he could build a secret drug lair."

Victor glared at Wayne and defended himself against part of his accusation. "The renovation wasn't Scot's idea. It was mine. Actually, Pristine's the one who realized we needed to modernize that area. I can't be blamed because Scot perverted the job I gave him to oversee. Now where is my son?"

Deputy Harris told him, "He's being questioned right now."

"For what?" asked Victor.

"You don't know?" asked Deputy Harris.

"The sheriff said he didn't want to go over it on the phone and to just get down here."

"I hate to tell you this, Victor," said Jeff. "I figured out – and the TBI agrees with me – that Ian is, in fact, responsible for your daughter's murder."

"What?"

"Rick Roberts' murder and the attempted murder of your wife."

"That's impossible! He's just a kid."

"Victor, I assure you I haven't made a mistake. All the evidence I've gathered…" Seeing a rising anger on Wayne's face, Jeff amended his train of thought. "With some help from the TBI, is irrefutable."

"That's insane. Where is he?" Victor stepped away from the others and looked around the room.

Wayne intercepted him. "You can't join them right now. I need you to stay out here and wait."

"Like hell!" Victor shouted, sidestepping him.

Jeff blocked him this time. "Victor, I need to talk to you in private."

"What could you possibly have to say to me after that ridiculous accusation?"

Jeff motioned toward the water cooler. "Please."

Victor relented and headed to the cooler, and Jeff waved the others off. "Victor, I realize it's not an outcome that any of us wanted, but we have reached the conclusion of this case."

"My son did not murder his sister!"

"I'm sorry, but you will need to come to terms with that. Speaking of terms, there's the matter of the reward."

Victor took a step back and sized him up. "Are you kidding me? You're just as responsible for my current troubles as Scot is – you and that TBI agent and that damn security guard. I don't believe for one second that Ian did what you say, and even if I did, I'm not giving you a reward. As a matter of fact, you're fired!"

"You can't do that! You promised a reward for finding your daughter's killer, and I delivered!"

Victor jabbed Jeff's chest with his index finger. "Sue me!"

Back in the interrogation room, Emory repeated the question, "Ian, how did your fingerprints get on the crystal?"

Ian hunched over the table as he sighed. "I took a glass and hid it in Margaret's house. I knew Pristine went through her stuff all the time."

Sheriff Rome asked, "Why would you frame her for stealing?"

"She saw something she wasn't supposed to, and I...couldn't look at her anymore."

"What did she see?" Sheriff Rome asked.

"Something private, and I'm not going to say what, so don't ask."

"That's okay." Emory reached inside the burlap bag. "I think I know."

Ian fidgeted in his chair, eyes dropping from Emory's face to what his hands were doing. "You don't…" His voice trailed off, and his face flushed when Emory presented at least two dozen photos he had printed from the boy's computer. He placed them on the table one by one so that all were visible at a single glance. Each photo showed a different angle of his nude, sleeping father in various stages of exposure.

Emory pointed at the table. "Do you recognize these pictures?"

Ian's mouth opened, but no sound came forth. The same reaction befell Sheriff Rome, who was seeing the photos for the first time.

"These pictures are from your computer."

Ian slapped his hands to the sides of his head, his fingers clutching at his hair. His eyes pierced the empty table space between his elbows. "I didn't put them there. Someone else must've done it. I swear it!"

Emory, however, was not done. He reached back into the burlap bag and pulled out three plastic baggies, placing them on the table so that they were above the photos from Ian's point of view. Each of the baggies contained one pair of used large men's underwear. "I found these in the footlocker in your bedroom."

Ian looked at Emory and then at Sheriff Rome, whose shock was still very much apparent. He whispered to Emory, "I'll tell you everything, but in private."

The sheriff scooted up from his chair so fast, he almost knocked it backwards. Without another glance at Ian, he told Emory, "That's okay. I'll wait outside for you to finish."

Even before the sheriff had reached the door, it flew open and Victor, red-faced with forehead veins on the verge of exploding,

barged in. "I demand to know what makes you think my son…"
His eyes moved from Ian to Emory and the sheriff and then to
the table – scrolling from the jar of calcium carbide to the framed
picture to the shards of glass and coming to rest on the unframed
photos and the baggies of underwear.

Sheriff Rome grabbed Victor's arm. "You shouldn't be in
here now."

Jeff bounded into the room. "I tried to keep him out."

"What is all this?" Victor pulled his arm free and stood behind
Ian's right shoulder.

Ian's breathing intensified, shaking his entire body. He kept
his tear-welled eyes focused on the empty space between his
elbows, afraid to look at his father.

Victor picked up a picture and looked at the men in the room,
his face a flurry of confusion. "Where did these come from? Who
took these pictures?"

Sheriff Rome again grabbed his arm, with greater force this
time, and he took the picture from him. "I need you to leave the
evidence alone, Victor."

"Evidence? That's not evidence. That's me!" He looked down
at Ian. "Why are you showing these to my son?!" He swept the
pictures away from the boy with his forearm.

Victor grabbed the back of Ian's chair and turned him around
to face him. He crouched to level his eyes with his son's. "Ian,
what's going on here?" He grabbed both of the boy's arms. "Ian!"

Ian kept his face down, tears dripping from his eyes.

Jeff hurried to Ian, and Sheriff Rome tried again to pull Victor
away. Hearing the commotion, Deputy Loggins ran into the room
and helped drag Victor from the room, leaving Jeff, Emory and
Ian alone.

Jeff asked Ian, "Are you okay?"

The boy lifted his head to face Jeff. His tears had stopped
flowing but not before leaving behind frosty dark eyes. He turned

to Emory and swore, "I'll never forgive you for this." He faced Jeff again. "Either of you!"

Jeff stumbled backed. He held up his index finger and told Ian, "Hold that thought." Nodding toward the door, he asked Emory, "Could I speak to you privately for a sec?" The two men exited the room, closing the door behind them. "Okay, before you start having to chant, 'The power of Christ compels you' in there, I need to ask you a favor."

"I'm kind of busy right now, and that's from The Exorcist, not The Omen."

"Whatever. Both were devil children. I need your car keys."

"Why?"

"Once Victor found out who we were charging with Britt's murder, he refused to pay me the reward. I'm going to see if I can wrangle it out of Pristine. Maybe she'll be grateful enough that we captured the person who tried to kill her."

"Fine." Emory handed him the keychain from his pocket. "Good luck."

"Do you want me to see if I can rustle up a crucifix before you go back in there?"

Emory patted him on the arm. "Go."

"Thanks." Jeff hurried off.

Emory clutched the doorknob but paused for a moment to think how he should approach Ian now that the interrogation approach he had planned had been slaughtered all to hell. *Empathy.* He returned to the interrogation room wearing his most empathetic face. He reclaimed his seat and clasped his hands on top of the table. Preceded by a sigh, he said, "I am so very sorry. I would've never allowed your father to see any of this. My only intention was to help you."

From the moment Emory returned, Ian had kept his eyes closed with his head bowed. In a whisper, the boy repeated Sheriff Rome's words from earlier. "No good deed goes unpunished."

Emory was taken off-guard by the remark, but he was quick to regain his composure. "Ian, I'm not judging you. I just think that your infatuation with your father has caused you to make some bad decisions. I think you were jealous of your sister's relationship with your father, particularly how close they became after your mother's death. Perhaps you felt shut out."

Ian glared at him. "I didn't kill my sister."

"I know it's difficult to come to terms with. You're scared. You need to realize that your motive is something that everyone on a jury would completely understand and empathize with. You don't even need to have a brother or sister to see why you might want to kill one. Sibling murder is as old as Cain and Abel."

Ian grabbed the front of his own shirt. "Am I here? Do you see me? Do you hear me? I did not kill my sister!"

"Ian, I want you to know that I understand you better than you think." He pointed at the boy's chair. "I've been right there where you are." Emory's face twisted with emotion as he found his next words difficult to say. "The first time you kill someone is always the most difficult. It oils the trigger to your impulses, making them easier to release."

Emory closed his eyes and hardened his face. "After Britt, the revenge you sought against Mr. Roberts evolved from something you wished to something you planned and executed."

"That's not true!"

"I think you also grew jealous of Pristine, and that jealousy ate away at your fondness for her until you decided she was a problem you could solve."

Ian sat back and crossed his arms. "I've humored you enough. I want a lawyer."

Emory stared at him for a moment. "As you wish." He gathered the evidence from the table and returned it to the burlap bag.

As he was finishing, his cell phone rang. Burlap bag in hand, he walked to the furthest corner of the room and answered. "Hi

Cathy. I'm sorry, but I'm right in the middle of something now. What do you have for me?" He glanced at Ian, whose eyes were now glued to him. Emory turned his back to the boy and tried to keep his voice down. "Seriously? Oh shit. Yes, I understand exactly what that means."

Emory hung up the phone and thought for a second about the news Cathy had given him. A worried look spread across his face. "Oh my god. Jeff!"

"Is something wrong?" Ian asked in a pleasant tone with a hint of mocking.

Although he found himself unnerved by the boy's creepy expression, Emory stared at him for three seconds before leaving the room. After shutting the door, he tried to call Jeff, but the call went to voicemail without a single ring. He tried again with the same result. He turned the key that was in the doorknob to lock Ian inside the room, and he hurried to the deputy room. The only person he saw was Deputy Loggins. "Where's my father?"

"In his office with Victor."

Emory handed the key to the deputy. "Keep Ian in there until I get back."

"Will do."

Emory sprinted across the room and looked through the glass door to his father's office. Victor was sitting with his head in his hands, while the sheriff leaned against the front of his desk. Not wanting to aggravate Victor again, Emory waved his arms to get his father's attention.

Sheriff Rome saw his son and nodded. He said some words to Victor before meeting Emory on the other side of the door. "What is it?"

Emory handed him the burlap bag. "Dad, you've got to let me borrow a car."

CHAPTER 42

JEFF WOODARD PULLED up to the Algarotti house and parked in front. As he exited Emory's car, he glanced up at the encroaching clouds concealing the disappearing sun. *I'd love to get out of here before the snow starts.*

Taking the steps two at a time to the porch, Jeff glanced at the sofa glider, where he'd had to wait earlier that day while Emory and two deputies opened the front door with a battering ram and searched inside. Walking up to the broken door, the heat from inside the house rushed past his face and bare hands as it escaped into the cold. The front door was propped against the jamb with just enough space on the right for him to squeeze through. He smirked. *How angry is Victor going to be when he sees that Emory broke a third door of his?*

Once he slipped through the doorway, Jeff knocked on the door. "Pristine? Pristine, are you here?"

He crept down the hall of the large house, a massive silence clenched within its walls. He looked at the grand staircase, but following a light, he turned left into the parlor. Two Tiffany lamps – one atop the bar, the other on top of the table by the fainting couch – exposed an emptiness in the room.

Zigzagging through a space left in polite disarray by the TBI's search earlier that day, Jeff walked to the covered portrait, realizing he had never seen what lies beneath the black cloth. Pulling up one corner, he peered at the portrait of Meredith Algarotti. Although the moment captured in the portrait had long since passed, the tortured eyes gazing from Meredith's smiling face seemed to foretell her family's fate.

"Help me," a voice pleaded.

Jeff jumped back, ripping the cloth from the frame. He turned around to see an anemic Pristine standing in the doorway, leaning against the jamb. He dropped the cloth and rushed to her aid. "Pristine! Are you okay?"

As Jeff wrapped an arm around her waist, Pristine rested her left hand on his shoulder and waved the other one in front of her face. "I'm fine. Just a little winded."

Jeff touched dampness as he pressed Pristine's turquoise cashmere sweater against the small of her back, and he looked down to see her glistening forehead. "You're sweating."

She pointed to the fainting couch. "The doctor warned me that I might experience episodes of weakness. I'll be fine in just a few minutes."

Jeff deposited her on the couch. "Where were you? I called for you."

"Did you see the front door?" Pristine looked around the room. "Someone broke in, and the place has been ransacked. I was upstairs seeing if they took any of my jewelry."

"About that…" Jeff removed his coat and threw it over the back of the settee, which he scooted so he could sit facing her. "The TBI came over here with a search warrant today, and no one was home."

Pristine's face contorted into an angry frown. "No one's home, so they just break in?"

Jeff offered a sympathetic tone, laying the groundwork to ask for the reward. "Unfortunately. I wish they had consulted me first.

I could've called Victor so he could meet them here. Would you like me to make you a drink?"

Pristine lost her frown but didn't quite smile. "That would be great. Thank you."

Jeff headed for the bar. "Are you still a dirty vodka martini?"

"You remembered. Make yourself something too."

"From your bar? No thanks."

Pristine laughed. "Victor bought all new bottles of liquor. They're still sealed, so you don't have to worry about any poison."

"In that case, I'll have a vodka cranberry. Uh, is the cranberry—"

"Brand new too."

Jeff mixed their drinks. "Aren't you curious about why the TBI searched your house?"

"Of course I am. I meant to ask, but my head drifted away. The doctor said that could be a lingering effect of being poisoned, but hopefully it'll go away. What were they looking for?"

Jeff handed Pristine a martini glass and sat down with his own drink. "I solved the murder of your stepdaughter."

"That's wonderful," Pristine said with a lilt in her voice. "Tell me."

"Your stepson has been arrested for the murders and your attempted murder." Jeff waited for a shocked reaction that never came. Instead, he received an expression of mild surprise with a simultaneous hand to the bosom but no immediate words. "The TBI was here looking for evidence to use against him."

"Oh my god," Pristine uttered at last. "Do you know if they found anything?"

"Ye…" Jeff tilted his head and squinted at her. "You don't seem all that surprised."

Pristine raised her eyebrows. "I don't?" She shook her head. "To tell the truth, I'm not surprised. Honestly, I believe that I always knew it. I just didn't want to admit it to myself. Ian hated both of them, and…Well, you've met him. There's something not right with him."

Jeff chuckled. "That's very true, but I thought you two were close."

"I feel sorry for him really. He doesn't have any real friends, so I've just tried to be there for him."

Jeff took a swig of his drink. "On the positive side, now you don't have to worry about being poisoned again."

"Thank god." Pristine sipped her drink and nodded to him. "No, thank you for putting an end to him." She raised her glass in a toast to Jeff and took another sip. "I knew you'd do it."

"Speaking of thankfulness, Victor promised a reward of one hundred thousand dollars if I brought Britt's killer to justice."

"Why don't you get it from him?"

Jeff put on his most concerned face. "He was too distraught by the news about Ian, and I really need to get back home tonight. I have another case waiting for me in the morning. It would be a big help if I could just settle up with you."

Pristine paused before smiling. "Sure. It's the least I could do for you. Let me get my purse."

As Pristine rose from the fainting couch, Jeff asked, "Do you want me to get it for you?"

"No." She held up her glass. "The drink is helping. I'm feeling much better now. Check?"

Jeff held up his phone. "I can take credit card."

Pristine went to her purse, which was behind the bar, while Jeff pulled his card reader from his pocket and attached it to his phone. He saw Emory calling, and he sent it to voicemail. *You're going have to wait.* As he brought up the app to accept the charge, he lost track of her location, so he was startled when she came up to him from behind the settee.

"I'm sorry." Pristine handed him her credit card. "I didn't mean to scare you."

"You didn't. I just got a shiver."

Pristine returned to the fainting couch. "Ooh, that means someone in the future is walking over your grave."

Jeff released a polite laugh at her reference to an old wives' tale. He handed her back her card and gave her his phone. "Just sign with your finger."

Pristine did as instructed and returned the phone to him. "Is that it?"

"That's it." Jeff sighed in relief at getting his big payday. "Thank you for your business. Now that the money matter is out of the way, I have something else I wanted to talk to you about." He pulled from his pocket the folded flyer he had drawn on while in the sheriff's station earlier. "Do you recognize this?" He handed the flyer to Pristine.

"It's Scot Trousdale. Someone drew a pretty lame-looking beard on him." Pristine got up and handed the flyer back to him. "I'm getting a refresher. Do you want another?"

Jeff handed her his glass. "Just cranberry juice this time. I have to drive."

"You got it, lightweight." Pristine carried their two glasses to the bar.

"That's something I've never been called before." Jeff turned his focus again to the flyer in his hand. "Getting back to my terrible artwork, I didn't realize until a little while ago that I had seen Scot before the first day I walked into the water factory. He looks different without the beard he was sporting the few times I noticed him in Knoxville, and I don't think he wore glasses then. You know, I like beards on some guys, but it wasn't doing him any favors. He was smart to lose it when he moved here." He again looked at Pristine, who was just putting ice in the mixing cup. He held the flyer up, facing her. "You still don't remember Scot looking like this?"

"Should I?"

"He was the manager at If Tomorrow Comes at the same time you worked there as a waitress. He had to be your boss."

Pristine threw her hands up. "Fine. You got me there. Scot called me after he got fired from the club, and he asked if I could give him a job. Of course, I have no say over who Victor hires, but I helped him the same way you helped me get hired."

Jeff realized that last bit was to remind him she was no worse than he was.

Pristine began shaking the mixing cup, and the rattling ice paused the conversation. Once she was done, Jeff asked, "Were you surprised when you heard Scot was arrested and learned what he had been doing at your husband's company?"

"Naturally, I was shocked." Pristine drained the mixing cup into her glass.

"I'll tell you what bothered me about it, apart from all of the obvious. The hidden room. We didn't take time to find the way in. We just knocked down the wall, but there had to be one. Scot's clever – the scheme he devised, the formulation of the drug and planning ahead in case he ever got caught. I know the hidden door is not an original idea, but how many have you seen in the real world?"

Pristine poured cranberry juice into his glass. "You have one in your office."

"Exactly!" Jeff exclaimed. "But I've loved mystery novels all my life, including the gothic ones with secret doorways and rooms. I've wanted a hidden passage in my home since I was a kid. I just don't think the idea would pop into most people's heads unless they had seen one in action or perhaps heard about it."

"What are you saying?" Pristine brought his glass to him.

"You and Scot have a shared history that I have a feeling involves more than his past two jobs. He's never been to my office, but you have."

"Here's your drink."

"Thank you." Jeff realized that he didn't see another glass, or her other hand for that matter. "Where's yours?"

Pristine swung her other hand around toward Jeff. Something popped against the nape of his neck like a snapped rubber band.

He heard a loud yelp and realized it came from him. He could no longer control his body as his muscles convulsed, sending him scooting to the floor. He looked up, unable to move, and only then saw the object in Pristine's other hand.

She told him, "We also share an affinity for stun guns."

CHAPTER 43

PRISTINE LEFT JEFF'S line of sight for a moment and came back with a roll of duct tape. She rolled him onto his stomach and tried to get his hands together behind his back, but the paralysis was wearing off, and he was able keep his hands at his side. She hit his neck again with the stun gun. Now immobilized, Jeff couldn't keep her from restraining his hands by wrapping the tape around his wrists several times. Next, she taped his ankles together just before he was able to start kicking.

Once he was bound, Pristine picked up the stun gun and held it to Jeff's neck for several seconds. He screamed and writhed in agony, as every muscle seemed to cramp at once. He was in so much pain, he wished he could pass out. When she stopped, he didn't have the strength to even open his eyes. As he lay there, immobilized and in agony, he heard her leave the room.

Jeff forced his eyelids up and found himself staring at the floor. He tried to will his body into motion, but all of his muscles were numb and aching. Drool dripping from the corner of his mouth, he grunted as he tried to move his hands so he could get the phone from his pocket, but they wouldn't reach past his hip. *You've got to get up!* He attempted to pull his knees up to his stomach so he could stand until he heard something above his head. *Please let it be Emory.* It wasn't.

Pristine had returned, and she was pushing a wheelbarrow. She stopped beside him and put the wheelbarrow on its side with the top toward Jeff. She hit him again with the stun gun before crouching beside him and pushing him into the wheelbarrow. With all her might, she pushed against the side rim until it was once again upright with Jeff lying inside.

Pristine hurried over to the covered portrait of Meredith Algarotti, and she pulled on one side of the frame, revealing a safe hidden behind it. She punched in a code and opened the door to retrieve a glass jar half-filled with black powder. "I'm glad I had to come back for this," said Pristine. "I might have missed you."

Calcium carbide! Jeff struggled to pull his hands free.

Pristine hit him again with the stun gun. The rapid muscle contractions caused his head to smack the metal rim of the wheelbarrow until at last, he blacked out.

When he opened his eyes again, he was still in the wheelbarrow but outside in the falling snow with the jar of calcium carbide nestled at his side. He could see Pristine straining as she pushed him – to where, he didn't know. He couldn't move his head, but he saw a structure in their path. It looked familiar, but he couldn't quite place it. *The maid's house!*

A few moments later, Pristine stopped the wheelbarrow in front of Margaret's former living quarters. She opened the door and heaved the wheelbarrow inside.

As she maneuvered it through the small living room, Jeff saw several candles burning within his field of vision. He could feel the mobility return to his neck, so he tried to turn his head to the left. He succeeded, although he wished he hadn't. Propped against the back of the couch was Scot Trousdale with a clear, plastic bag tied over his head! His dead eyes seemed to follow Jeff as the wheelbarrow rolled past. With renewed urgency, Jeff struggled as hard as he could to force his muscles into action.

Pristine released the handles of the wheelbarrow and retrieved the stun gun from her coat pocket. She rammed it against his neck once again and shocked him into submission.

Jeff's eye's rolled back as his head banged against the metal.

Pristine pushed the wheelbarrow forward a little further. "He came here to hide out after he broke out of jail. He had the nerve to ask me for help." She looked down at him as she came to a stop in the kitchen. "Son-of-a-bitch wanted to screw me out of half of the drug profits." She grabbed the jar and placed it on the counter. She tilted the wheelbarrow, sending Jeff dropping to the linoleum floor.

Jeff sat himself up with his back against a cabinet door. Through blurred vision he watched the flickering flames of at least a dozen candles burning on the kitchen countertops. Pristine came at him again with the stun gun. He lifted his heavy legs and tried to kick her away.

She dodged his feet and jabbed the gun to his throat. When his head hung limp at the neck, she placed the gun on the counter by the jar. She crouched down at his side and began mimicking Scot. "He told me, 'I didn't poison you. Why would I do that? I need you.' What an asshole."

Pristine ran her fingers through Jeff's hair. "I am sorry about this. I really am. I always liked you. I wish you had left well enough alone – taken your reward and gone back to Knoxville. I guess I didn't realize how good you were at your job. On the other hand, I am kind of glad you're here. I put so much work into everything, it was killing me not to share it with someone." She pointed over her shoulder. "I didn't tell Scot about the murders. I couldn't trust him not to blackmail me."

Jeff slurred, "You?"

Pristine grinned and gave him a bashful glance. "Yeah, Ian

didn't do that either." She stood and looked through a nearby drawer, returning with a gallon-size baggie.

Once he saw it, Jeff started fidgeting and trying to get up. "Pris...tine...don't—"

Pristine zapped him again with the stun gun, and as soon as she stopped, she dropped the baggie over his head. The mouth of the baggie now rested around the nape of his neck, allowing in precious little air for him to breathe.

"When you think about it, this is all your fault." She unbuckled his belt and slipped it from his pants. Wrapping it over the mouth of the baggie, she tightened it around his neck. "You promised me a rich man, but you didn't quite deliver on that promise. His kids had all the money. That left me no choice. I had to kill Britt and frame Ian so the entire estate would belong solely to Victor and me."

"Of course, no matter how much Ian disliked his sister, he truly hated Rick Roberts much, much more, and everyone knew it. I couldn't frame him for the premeditated murder of his sister without the number-one person on his hit list dying too."

Jeff gasped for air as the baggie began to fog. He tried to get his legs to work, but utter exhaustion kept them still.

Pristine arose again and continued talking as she worked. "My plan had a couple of variables that were not completely within my control." She plugged the kitchen sink and turned on the faucet. "I could plant evidence pointing to Ian but it had to be subtle enough not to be an obvious setup while still being blatant enough to be noticed. Fine line."

Pristine opened the jar of calcium carbide and held it up. "This is amazing stuff, by the way. I'm so glad Ian turned me on to it. It creates a fire that burns extremely hot, destroying all the evidence, even itself."

Almost unconscious, Jeff could feel himself slipping away.

CHAPTER 44

PRISTINE SPRINKLED THE calcium carbide all over the floor and onto Jeff's legs. "The good thing is that you're going to die a hero. You came to see me, to see how I was doing before you left town. You spotted smoke coming from behind the house. Thinking I was in trouble, you rushed into the maid's house to save me. Instead you found Scot, who had already succumbed to the fire he accidentally started. You tried to get back out, but you became trapped."

Pristine put the empty jar by the stun gun and crouched once more beside Jeff. She took a credit card from her pocket and shoved it into Jeff's. "Just in case someone spots that last transaction. I'll say that you must've come inside the main house first, while I was sleeping upstairs, recovering from being poisoned. You saw my purse in the parlor and took my credit card to claim your precious reward. Knowing you, I don't believe for a second that you didn't ask Victor for the money, and he must've turned you down. Anyway, while you charged my card, you smelled smoke, which brings us back to the beginning of this little tale of your last minutes on Earth."

Seeing his eyes close, she loosened the belt around his neck. "No, not yet. We still have a couple of minutes, and I really want to finish my story." She pulled the bag off his head and let him gasp in a few breaths.

As she lowered the bag over his head again, Jeff pleaded, "Don't...please—"

Pristine tightened the belt. "The second variable was Victor. I can feel him drifting away from me with each extra minute he spends at work every passing day. I signed an airtight pre-nup. I couldn't take a chance that he would leave me once his kids were out of the picture, and I certainly wouldn't be able to arrange an accident for him without putting suspicion squarely on me – at least not anytime soon.

"When Scot came to me with his idea to start a mini drug empire, it sounded like the perfect Plan B. We developed a five-million-dollar business plan over the next two years. There's so much money to be made in drugs."

Jeff's eyes drooped shut.

"That's all shot now. Thank you very much. Now I have to ensure Victor stays in love with me at least for a couple more years, until I can safely execute an accident for him. I was thinking I'd play up the poison's impact on me. Play a victim for a year or so, like his first wife. He seems to be attracted to that."

As Jeff's eyes closed for a final time, he saw a strange figure appear, but he couldn't be sure if it were real or imagined.

Emory stepped into the kitchen. As soon as he saw Jeff, he ran and rammed Pristine, sending her flying to the floor.

He fiddled with the belt around Jeff's neck, but frustrated, he grabbed the bag and ripped it in half.

"Jeff!" Emory slapped his face again and again.

Out of the corner of his eye, he saw Pristine coming at him.

She picked up the stun gun and was about to aim it at Emory when he grabbed her wrist. He banged her hand against the corner of the counter. She dropped the gun into the sink, which was two inches from being full of water. He flung her to the ground and ordered, "Stay down!"

Jeff gasped and opened his eyes, wild with anguish.

Emory ran to his side and crouched beside him to hold his face. "Are you okay?"

Jeff half-nodded but didn't speak. Emory unwrapped the duct tape from around his wrists, unaware that Pristine had gone looking for a weapon in the kitchen drawers.

Instead of a knife, she found a claw hammer. She held it high and lunged for Emory.

"Behind you!" Jeff croaked.

Emory turned around and was about to stand when he saw Pristine swinging the hammer around toward the side of his head. He ducked. The hammer slammed the faucet instead, sending the handle bouncing off the backsplash tile before clinking to the floor. Emory wrestled the hammer out of her hand.

He twisted her arms behind her, drew his handcuffs from his belt and slapped them onto her wrists.

Jeff began unwrapping the tape around his ankles. "Emory!" He nodded to the powder on the floor. "Calcium carbide."

While Pristine ran for the door, Emory looked at the water filling the sink almost to the rim. He tried to turn it off but couldn't. "She broke the damn faucet handle!"

"I don't think I can walk yet," Jeff told him. "Help me get out of here!"

Emory saw the water had now reached the rim. "We can't let this place burn." He began blowing out the candles. "I don't have time to get you and Scot both out."

Jeff scowled at him. "He's dead!"

"He's evidence." Emory retorted as he blew out the final candle in the kitchen.

Jeff freed his legs. "There are more in the living room."

Emory ran into the other room to blow out the remaining candles. By the time he returned to the kitchen, Jeff had made it to his feet and was walking out. "We need to go! The water's overflowing onto the floor."

Emory returned to his side. "We're fine. There's no flame to ignite the acetylene gas."

Jeff threw his right arm over Emory's shoulder, and the two walked from the house. Once they were about fifty feet from the maid's house, Jeff pointed at the main house. "Look."

Pristine was trying her best to open the back door to the house but finding it very difficult with her hands cuffed behind her back.

"I better get her," Emory said. "Are you okay?"

"I'm fine." Jeff looked down and saw smoke rising from his pant legs. "Emory!"

Emory realized the snow was melting on Jeff's pants and mixing with the calcium carbide powder stuck to them.

"Oh my god!" Jeff screamed. "I'm going to catch fire!" His fingers fumbled as he hurried to unbuttoned his pants.

Emory laughed and told him, "You're fine. Seriously. The gas isn't going to ignite as long as you don't get near an open flame."

BOOM!

An explosion caused them both to duck and cover their heads. The maid's house erupted into a fireball, raining flaming shrapnel all around them.

Emory looked at Jeff and yelled, "Take off your clothes!"

Jeff pulled off his shirt and kicked off his shoes with as much force as he could. He pushed his pants down and tried to get them from around his ankles, but he lost his balance. He fell backwards onto Emory, whose back hit the snowy ground.

"I forgot the pilot light," Emory muttered.

Jeff turned his body around to straddle Emory, planting a hand on the ground beside each of his shoulders. "You forgot?! You were in no hurry to get out that house. You could've killed us both!"

As Jeff yelled in his face, Emory smiled.

"Don't smile. I'm mad at you."

"Look up. It's snowing."

"That's ash." Still on top of Emory, Jeff craned his neck toward the dark sky, now peppered with falling snow. "You're right."

Emory raised his hands to the sides of Jeff's cold and goose-bumpy torso. As the PI faced him again, Emory's gaze traveled from his blue boxer shorts up to his six-pack and striated chest before locking on his green eyes. "You are just stunning."

Jeff dropped his chest onto Emory's. "Compliments? Is that how you wiggle out of an argument?"

Emory shrugged. "It's a new tactic I'm trying."

Jeff smiled, his lips now an inch from Emory's. "I think it's working."

Emory locked his arms across Jeff's bare back and kissed him. A moment later, when their lips smacked apart, he felt Jeff shiver. "You're freezing. Take my jacket."

Jeff pushed off him and stood, his pants still at his ankles.

Before Emory could make it to his feet, he saw someone approaching. Wayne walked toward them with his hand vised around Pristine's arm and Deputy Harris at his side.

CHAPTER 45

THE SHERIFF'S STATION on Monday evening was livelier than it had been in eight years, as enthusiastic debriefs and verbal backslapping filled the coffee-scented air. While Deputy Loggins booked Pristine, the nightshift deputies had arrived, and they joined the sheriff, Deputy Harris, Wayne and Victor in listening to Emory and Jeff relate in feverish detail the events of the evening and all unanswered questions involving the murder of three Barter Ridge residents, as well as the attempted murder of the PI. Wayne didn't look at either of them, and he had grunted maybe two words to Emory after catching him kissing Jeff. Ian, now released and no longer a suspect in any of the crimes, sat on the bench by the front door, listening with his eyes on the floor.

Jeff rubbed his aching neck, bright red and welted from the numerous electric shocks he had endured. Now barefoot, he wore an old deputy uniform shirt and pants that Sheriff Rome found in a cabinet, but the clothes were, of course, too small for him. Emory had also given him his jacket to wear, telling him, "Try not to stretch out the shoulders."

Jeff explained how he figured out that Pristine was involved in the drug scheme, and he told them about her confessing to the killings and her attempt on his life.

Victor seemed to have regressed into an emotional numbness that kept his face stuck in desolation. Every once in a while, he shook his head and moved his lips for lamentations like, "I can't believe I married that woman," and, "She destroyed my life."

Jeff told Emory, "I still don't know how you found out about Pristine."

Emory pointed to his dad. "It was the snake handlers. Dad told me about the controversy that surrounded their arrival here a year ago."

"Got that right," said Deputy Harris. "Those freaks should've never come to this town."

"Stop being a bigot, Deputy," ordered Sheriff Rome. "They have a right to their religion, same as you."

Emory continued, "I imagine the news stories about them included some of their rituals." The sheriff nodded. "They drink strychnine during their services, but they don't just pick it up one day and take a swig, hoping it doesn't kill them. They build up a tolerance by ingesting a little at a time over months or years."

Victor said, "Pristine's not a snake handler."

"No, but I think that's what gave her the idea to fake her own poisoning with strychnine."

Victor asked, "Why would she poison herself?"

"To throw suspicion off her by making us think that whoever killed Britt and Rick was after her too."

Jeff shook his head. "I was there when she took the strychnine. Her reaction looked real to me."

Emory said, "I think she ingested more than she anticipated. Regardless, the amount of strychnine she ingested would've killed someone who hadn't built up a tolerance to it. I took some of Pristine's hair from her hairbrush when she was in the hospital, and I gave it to the lab for testing. I got the call from Cathy when I was interviewing Ian, and she told me that Pristine had been taking strychnine for at least eleven months."

Jeff said, "So that's how you knew I was in trouble."

Emory nodded before asking Wayne and Deputy Harris, "How did you end up at Victor's house?"

Deputy Harris responded, "We thought Scot might've rented a car so we checked the only rental place in town. He used a fake credit card and ID, but the clerk recognized his picture when we showed it to him. The car he rented had a tracking system, and we found it parked in the woods, just off the road near the driveway to the Algarotti house. We thought he might've gone there to get revenge on Victor. When we got to the house, we heard the explosion."

The next second, all eyes turned to the same face. Deputy Loggins had returned to the room with Pristine.

"Victor!" Pristine called with her cuffed hands reaching out for him.

To Emory's surprise, Victor advanced toward her. With each step he took, the emotions that he appeared to have dammed up inside him seeped through expanding cracks until the wall crumbled as he stood before her.

"Pristine, why?" he asked. "I loved you. Why would you do this to Britt? To my son? To me?"

"Victor." Pristine grabbed his hands before Deputy Loggins pushed her forearms back down. "I love you. This is a mistake. None of it's true. I would never hurt you."

Victor told her, "That's how you did it, isn't it?"

"What are you talking about?"

"You lie with such conviction. I couldn't see it before."

With that, Pristine's sadness evaporated, leaving behind a salty indignation. "You know nothing about me! You just wanted someone to plug the hole left by your precious Meredith."

Victor turned from her, and Sheriff Rome told Deputy Loggins, "Take her to the interrogation room."

Jeff smirked at Pristine. "What's your plan B for this?"

She glared at him while asking, "Victor, did Jeff tell you how you and I met?"

Victor turned back around. "What do you mean?"

Emory approached her in an attempt to get her out of the room. "If you have a statement to make, save it for us."

"We didn't meet by chance." Pristine smiled at the growing nervousness in Jeff. "He set it up."

"That's enough!" proclaimed Emory. He placed a hand on Deputy Loggins' shoulder urging him to move her out.

Victor turned to Jeff. "What's she talking about?"

Jeff sighed and gritted his teeth. "Pristine hired me to find her a rich man to marry…" He trailed off when he saw Victor drawing back his right fist.

Emory sprung to Jeff's defense, pushing him out of the way. Victor's punch landed on Emory's left jaw, and the special agent fell to the floor on top of Jeff.

"You brought this plague on my house!" Victor shouted, looking at Jeff but pointing at Pristine. "This is all on you!"

The sheriff and Deputy Harris rushed to restrain Victor, while Wayne only watched. "Lock him up for assault!" ordered Sheriff Rome.

"No!" Emory countered as he climbed back to his feet and helped up Jeff. He tilted his head toward Ian. "He shouldn't be alone right now."

The sheriff frowned at his son's decision. He pointed an angry finger in Victor's face. "Control yourself, or I will lock you up. Don't test me!"

Victor nodded, and Deputy Harris released him. Sheriff Rome told Deputy Loggins, "Get her out of here. Victor, take your son and go home. You both have been through too much."

Victor walked to the front door without looking at Ian. "Let's go." The boy hopped from the bench and followed his dad, closing the door behind them.

Sheriff Rome put a hand on Emory's shoulder. "Are you all right?"

"I'm fine."

The sheriff inspected the bruising skin just below his eye. "I'll get you something for that eye." He hurried to his office, past Wayne, who was now sitting on the edge of Deputy Harris' desk with his arms crossed and eyes down.

Emory asked Jeff, "How are you?"

Jeff checked out the damage to Emory's face. "You shouldn't have done that. I deserved that punch."

"And you should've gone to the hospital like the paramedics suggested. I guess we're both good at ignoring what's best for us."

Sheriff Rome returned with an emergency ice pack. "Here you go, Son."

Emory took it and placed it against his cheek. "Well, I think we've done enough damage here. We'll be heading out."

The sheriff smiled at him and gave him a hug. "Thank you for everything, Son. There's no way I would've seen this outcome. Don't tell your mother about the shiner. She'd blame me for not keeping you safe."

"I won't. Dad..." Emory stopped, as he searched for the right words to say.

"What is it, Son?"

"I'm sorry about losing my temper earlier."

His father waved off the need for any apology. "It's forgotten. This case was tough on us, and we both needed to blow off some steam."

Emory started to get choked up. "You're a wonderful lawman, and you know you're the reason I wanted to be one too."

"I know." The sheriff flashed a smile that let Emory know it was good to hear. "Now don't be such a stranger."

Emory nodded. "Wayne, are you ready to go?"

Wayne glanced up but not enough to make eye contact. He pointed to the man at his side. "I'm catching a ride with Deputy Harris."

"You are?"

Deputy Harris explained, "I'm driving Pristine Algarotti up to Knox County tonight. I'm not risking another escape."

Instead of arguing with Wayne, Emory felt it best to leave him alone. He escorted the still-weak PI from the sheriff's station.

Once buckled into the car, Jeff reclined in his seat. "Do you mind if I rest my eyes a bit? I'm exhausted."

"Of course not." Emory drove the car from the parking lot and onto the main road out of town.

His eyes closed, Jeff smiled. "You took a punch for me."

"Only because you're too out of it right now to defend your-self." Emory grinned and added, "Otherwise, I would've let you take it."

When Jeff didn't reply, Emory glanced over at him and saw his eyes were closed and mouth open. Jeff didn't stir again until they got back to Knoxville and pulled up to his place. Emory stared at the office building for Mourning Dove Investigations for a moment before whispering, "We're here."

As Jeff opened his eyes and stretched, Emory hopped out of the car and ran to the other side to open his door and help him out. He grabbed the PI's right arm and placed it over his shoulders, and he helped him walk to the front door. "Do you need me to stay with you?"

Jeff leaned his back against the office door. "I'll be fine. I'm going to fall into bed and hibernate until spring."

"Do you need anything?"

"Just to thank you for saving my life."

"It's a life worth saving." Emory walked away, turning back just to say, "Call me when spring comes."

CHAPTER 46

WHEN EMORY ENTERED the TBI office the next morning, he was wearing his usual suit and tie under his field jacket with his satchel strapped over his shoulder. He was also sporting the shiner from Victor's punch the night before.

As he walked past the rows of desks in the large room, he could sense tension in the air. The other special agents who noticed him either gave him an apprehensive stare or couldn't look away fast enough – as if they all knew a secret to which he was not yet privy.

He glanced at Eve Bachman's office at the back of the room when he saw Wayne leaving it. He could tell that Wayne saw him, but he still refused to look at him as he made his way to his desk. Emory wondered how his partner would treat him today. No matter what, he was determined that they would talk about Wayne's apparent uneasiness concerning his long-held secret and that this day would see some sort of resolution to the matter. Either Wayne would need to get a grip, or Emory would be forced to request a new partner.

He was about to place his satchel on his chair when he saw Fran Havel working at her desk with a worried look on her face.

Curious, Emory walked up to her. "Good morning, Fran. Is everything okay?"

"Emory…" Fran began before stopping herself. "Bachman wants to see you."

"Okay. Is something wrong?"

"She really wants to see you."

Wayne told Bachman about the kiss! Apprehensive about her reaction to the news, Emory tapped two tepid knocks on the nearby door to his boss' office and creaked it open when she invited him in. The first thing he noticed when he entered wasn't Bachman's shrieking red hair. It was something hanging from the wall behind her that he had always tried to ignore before. It was the stone-painted wood in the shape of two Bronze-Age tablets with the Ten Commandments etched in the charred handwriting of god.

"Sit down," Bachman ordered, and he complied. Her eyes darted up to him and then back down to a small stack of papers on her desk. "I've reviewed the injury report you submitted regarding your 'accidental' drugging with an ecstasy-like substance."

"Yes?" Emory asked, wondering about her curious enunciation of the adjective.

"Your statement suggests that the drug was inside a bottle of water you were given by a private investigator named Jeff Woodard."

"It doesn't suggest," Emory told her. "It clearly states that's what happened. He picked it up from Scot Trousdale's desk—"

"Enough." Bachman looked at him with the eyes of an executioner, separating herself from the thing she was obligated to destroy. "And this is the same man you were seen kissing at the scene of one of the crimes?"

Emory froze for a moment as he tried to think of how to respond. "He was hired by the father of the victim to help with the case."

"I know from experience, as do you, that the clientele for these types of drugs are very often…people like yourself."

"People like me?" asked Emory.

"You were at the factory where the drug was being infused into bottled water."

"Yes." *Where is she going with this?*

"Of all the times you could've come into contact with the drugged water, how do you expect me to believe that it just happened to occur on a Friday night in Knoxville – nearly sixty miles from the factory – when you were in the company of a man who you were obviously…well, doing what you do?"

Emory popped up to his feet. "I did not take that drug by choice!"

Bachman didn't flinch. "I need your badge and your gun."

Emory hesitated before muttering, "Wha—"

"Your badge and your gun!"

Emory plopped both onto her desk. She transferred the items to one of her desk drawers and turned her attention to her computer. "I need you to take your personal belongings and leave. Do not sign into your computer. Do not talk to anyone on your way out."

"You know damn well I didn't do this. You're just looking for an excuse to get rid of me."

Bachman glanced at him once more. "You know, I've had a feeling about you from the beginning. Leviticus 18:22. Do yourself a favor, and read it."

"You can't fire me for this."

Bachman let out a stilted laugh. "The Bureau puts away deviants. We don't employ them."

In desperation, Emory told her, "I'll sue to keep my job."

"State law doesn't afford you any special privileges. You'd be wasting your time."

There was no use arguing with her. Emory left her office

to find two special agents waiting for him. He could hear Fran crying as he walked with his escorts to his desk, where he found an empty box waiting for him. Wayne was now missing from his desk. *Convenient.*

No one said a word as he collected his belongings and left the building for the last time.

Emory's escorts abandoned him to trek to his car alone, in a state of shock. He opened the driver-side door and slipped behind the wheel with the box on his lap. He stared at the building through his windshield but didn't see it. When at last he moved, he put the box on the passenger seat and grabbed the wheel. Tears began dripping down his face.

CHAPTER 47

S TILL WEARING HIS suit and field jacket, Emory Rome
sat on the couch in his apartment staring at the only two
objects on his coffee table – a bottle of pills and a glass
of water. Light from a candle on the kitchen bar and the amber
desk lamp strained to reach him, stopping just shy of the bottle's
label. Small ceramic cherubs hanging outside the window kept the
silence at bay with gentle taps on the glass.

Emory took a pill from the bottle and swallowed it, chasing it
with a swig of water. He tipped the bottle over a second time and
emptied its contents into the palm of his hand. *This would do it.*
He stared at the fifty-something powdery white pills.

He heard a faint swoosh and looked toward the front door to
see that an envelope had been pushed through the crack underneath. Annoyed yet intrigued, he spilled the pills onto the coffee
table and walked to the door. He grabbed the unsealed envelope
and pulled from it a postcard with a picture of his thirteen-year-
old self at Crescent Lake – before it had disappeared and before
the Romes had adopted him. The other side of the card was black
with silver writing that read, "Who bears the iniquity of the son?"

"What the hell?"

He opened the door and saw no one there, so he shut it again.

He hurried to the window with the hanging cherubs and saw a man in a white ski mask opening the door to a blue sedan parked across the street from his apartment. As if sensing Emory's gaze, the man looked up at his window, revealing the grotesque red smile stitched onto his mask. Emory ran to the door to try catching the man before he could drive away, but when he swung his apartment door open again, he found Jeff Woodard standing on the other side.

"Is my cologne that strong?" Jeff asked.

"Jeff. What are you doing here?"

The PI was dressed in his usual attire but with a thick woolen scarf coiled around his neck. "I heard what happened to you at the TBI."

Emory shoved the postcard and envelope into his back pocket. "Can we talk about this later?"

"I'll be quick."

Emory held up a finger. "Hang on one second." Closing the door, he ran to the window, and his shoulders dropped when he saw that the blue sedan was now gone. *The pills!* He removed his jacket and placed it over the pills before returning to the front door.

Jeff smiled when he noticed that Emory was no longer wearing his jacket. "I see you've made yourself more comfortable."

"What do you want?"

"An invitation inside to begin with."

"Come in." Emory waved his hand toward the living room. "How did you know where I live?"

"Jeff Woodard, private investigator. Perhaps you've heard of me." He walked in as he inspected the surroundings. "You have a nice nihilistic Chi going on here. I like it."

"I'm really busy right now."

Jeff plopped down on the couch and patted the cushion beside him.

"How are you doing, by the way?" Emory asked as he joined him on the couch.

"My whole body is sore. I slept until noon today. Even then, I could barely get out of bed." He unwrapped his scarf to reveal the black welts covering his neck. "Oh, and I've got like ten dates' worth of hickeys from Pristine's damn stun gun."

"They'll go away," Emory assured him.

"I hope so. I don't think they make turtleneck tank tops." He touched Emory's bruised face. "Does it hurt?"

"Not bad."

"So listen. I have a proposal for you, and before you get excited, it's not that kind of proposal."

Emory tried not to, but he ended up laughing. "I appreciate your coming over to check on me, but I'm in no mood to be cheered up right now."

"Then it's good that's not the purpose of my visit. I've talked it over with Virginia, and we want to offer you a partnership in the agency."

"What do you mean?"

"I've convinced Virginia that you would be an asset to the company. I think you're a good investigator, and under my tutelage, you could be a great one."

"You think so, huh?"

Jeff's tone grew serious. "The truth is I...we need you. I've had some judgment issues with clients, as you're aware, and we could use you and your pesky ethics."

"Look, you can't hold yourself responsible for what Pristine did. Should you have turned away a gold-digger client looking for a rich husband?" Emory shrugged. "Honestly, yeah. But what she wanted and what you did was not a crime. Even with the best judgment, you can't know with absolute certainty what your clients' ultimate motives are."

"That's the level-headedness I'm talking about it. We already know what we can accomplish when we work together. So what do you say? Will you join our team?"

Emory didn't know how to respond. He had never imagined himself as anything but a government law enforcement agent. He stared at his jacket on the coffee table, thinking about what lay beneath it.

He jumped up with his back to Jeff. "I don't think that's a good idea."

"Why not?" Jeff darted in front of him. "You need a job, and I'm offering you one that you'll love. Plus, you'll be working with me. There's no downside."

Emory walked past him and opened the door. "I'll think about it."

Jeff approached him with a mock scowl. "This isn't an open-ended invitation."

"I'll talk to you tomorrow," Emory insisted with a smile.

Jeff threw his hands up. "Fine. Call me first thing in the morning. First thing."

"Good night." Emory closed the door with Jeff on the other side. He returned to the couch and transferred his jacket from the coffee table to the cushion beside him. He stared at the pills for a moment before scooping them up and returning them to the bottle.

CHAPTER 48

IAN OPENED A door in the Algarotti house, holding an empty garbage bag in one hand. Flicking the light switch on, he descended the stairs to the basement and walked to a section of the brick wall behind the furnace. As he pulled a small patch of loose bricks from the wall near the floor, his mind drifted to thoughts of his sister, eliciting an unintentional smile.

When their mother died, the loss only seemed to bring Britt and his father closer together. Ian tried to compete – waiting on his father hand and foot, doing special things for him, like shining his shoes – but nothing garnered more than a muttered, "Thanks."

Britt had a special connection with their dad that Ian just couldn't break. She knew it too. She made a sport out of berating Ian whenever her father was in the room, and just to prove she had him on her side, she would give Ian grief until their father could no longer contain his laughter. To his father's credit, he would look away so Ian couldn't see his face, but Ian could still see his shoulders bouncing up and down.

In spite of his father's laughter, Ian worshipped him. During the days before Pristine came into the picture, he would sometimes slip into his father's bedroom at night and hide under the bed, waiting for him to come in and fall asleep. He would slip out from under the bed as soon as the deep breathing started. His father preferred not to be confined by blankets, so he would always toss those aside and sleep only under a single thin sheet. Ian would pull the sheet up – a little at a time – from his feet and legs and higher and then fold it over to the side. If his father didn't stir, Ian would pull down his own pajama bottoms, kneel on the floor and satisfy himself while staring at the sleeping man.

Back in the basement, Ian sighed as he removed the last brick. He reached into the wall and pulled out a jar. As he did, he pictured Pristine's pretty face.

When his dad married that woman, Ian lost yet another piece of him. Nevertheless, Ian hadn't viewed his new stepmother as an obstacle. Rather, she was an essential means to a Britt-free end.

He was listening outside the parlor when his father told Pristine about the family's financial situation – after the marriage, of course – and although she acted like it wasn't important that her husband didn't have full control of the fortune, Ian watched her twisted emotions and heard her mutter her grave disappointment to the news as soon as his father left the room. The boy knew what she wanted, and he was betting she was ruthless enough to do whatever it took to secure her future.

Thereafter, Ian befriended her, and Pristine played along, whether or not she had any true affection for her new stepson. People seemed to think she was stupid, perhaps because of her looks or the way she mispronounced the occasional word. Perhaps it was her tantrums, but Ian knew she wasn't stupid. She was, however, pliable – a trait he exploited.

When Ian came up with an experiment for the science fair, he told his stepmother he was nervous about his presentation and asked her to help him with it. He showed her his experiments with calcium carbide numerous times, and each time he explained in great detail its properties and often joked how it would make the perfect murder weapon. He would "let slip" the supposed selfish plans Britt had for her half of the family money once she turned eighteen – a birthday that was fast approaching. Not wanting to be too obvious, he left it up to Pristine to see how Britt's death would benefit her, leaving only one other heir, who wouldn't gain control of the money for several years more.

In the basement, Ian placed the jar into the garbage bag and returned the bricks to the wall.

He recalled how enraged he was when Mr. Roberts accused him of cheating and kicked him off the team for the science fair. He almost killed the man himself after that, but he controlled his rage long enough to realize he might be able to convince Pristine to do it for him. He had already laid the groundwork for her to murder Britt, and even though she hadn't yet acted, he knew in his heart that she would when she worked up her nerve. How could he convince her to kill someone else when it would not profit her in the least?

Of course, one of the most important factors in planning any crime is having a legitimate candidate to blame it on other than the actual perpetrator. He knew in spite of their close relationship, Pristine wouldn't hesitate to throw him under the bus to get what she wanted, so he played on that character weakness and the fact that he had the most to gain from the two murders – ridding himself of a teacher he hated and blamed for a blemished school record, as well as the sister who would take half his fortune and more than half of his father's love.

He told everyone how much he wanted Mr. Roberts dead and cried to Pristine on numerous occasions. Ian knew it would make no sense for him to plan a methodical murder for a sister people believed he loved, regardless of how she treated him, instead of the teacher who everyone knew he wanted dead. He hoped that Pristine would realize that too and off them both. He even helped her out by telling her about his plans for the next science fair, an experiment involving potassium permanganate that he had taken from the water factory.

Ian ascended the basement stairs and turned out the light as he walked through the door. He carried the garbage bag to the nearest bathroom and locked the door behind him. Pulling out the jar of strychnine, he poured it down the toilet. He needed a silver bullet that would destroy Pristine's plans to nail him for the murders. He had read about the snake handlers and their penchant for drinking poison, and that gave him the idea to build up Pristine's tolerance. He had been dispersing a precise amount in her protein powder ever since. Once he knew all signs for the two murders were pointing to him, he upped the dosage in her powder to ensure she overdosed enough to have to go to the hospital. Of course, he had no way of knowing she would happen to use more protein powder than usual that day – a miscalculation that almost killed her, not to mention Ian's chances at freedom. He flashed to the memory of packing Pristine's overnight bag for the hospital and leaving the brush out so he could make sure Emory saw it.

Ian heard a noise overhead. *Dad must be awake. It's unfortunate he found out about my urgings, but I'll be the perfect son, and over time, he'll push those memories away. He's going to need me. After all, there's no one else for him to turn to now.*

As he flushed the toilet and returned the empty jar to the garbage bag, he reflected on his new enemies, Emory Rome and Jeff Woodard. They had embarrassed him in front of his father, and they would have to pay for that – not now, but someday soon. He walked to the door and looked back at the toilet.

It was so easy. Imagine what I can accomplish when I turn eighteen and have a fortune at my fingertips.

EPILOGUE

Curled up on his couch with Bobbie nestled beside him, Jeff finished typing his case report into his laptop. When he was done, he closed the file and looked at the name of the document, which as usual, he left as a sequential case number until it was finished. He right-clicked on the file and changed the name to "Murder on the Lake of Fire" before moving it to the folder named…

Case Closed

70497318R10184